Apprentice to the Flower Poet Z.

"Witty and generous . . . The world of poetry may be rarefied, but Debra Weinstein now gives it something usually associated with magazines and movies: a tell-all novel in the roman à clef, ingrate-assistant genre. . . . Weinstein has fun with her material. But her book also takes its heroine and her ambitions seriously."
—*The New York Times*

"[A] brilliant send-up of the world of poets, workshops and literary ambition . . . *Apprentice to the Flower Poet Z.* is as acid a parody of academia as anything from David Lodge or Kingsley Amis, and yet it never loses its disarming sweetness. And, like any great work of poetry, it can be read in countless ways, as the title suggests, from A to Z."
—*Los Angeles Times Book Review*

"Deliciously nasty . . . Weinstein has buoyant fun with the pettiness and pretension of New York's literati. It's *All About Eve* for the sonnet set. . . . Weinstein captures the great poet's majestic self-regard."
—*The New York Times Book Review*

"Hugely entertaining…Written in spare, lucid prose, full of deadpan wit and entertaining characters . . . [and a] genuine love of poetry."
—*The Washington Post Book World*

"Keenly observed . . . [Weinstein] adroitly lampoons the petty peculiarities of academia. . . . Like Lauren Weisberger's popular *The Devil Wears Prada*, *Apprentice* bears the markings of a delicious roman à clef, but it is leaner and smarter."
—*The Miami Herald*

"[A] comic gem . . . Weinstein conveys an overall authenticity that is a perfect, hilariously on-target cameo of the world of New York arts and letters. . . . Peppered with poetry, some deliberately and hilariously awful, some quite good, *Apprentice to the Flower Poet Z.* is an auspicious debut."
—*St. Petersburg Times*

"Weinstein captures the essence of the low-paying, insular world of poetry and carefully crafts a pedagogic nemesis who wears slinky dresses rather than tattered tweed. . . . [*Apprentice* will] have appeal for anyone who has suffered from the indignities of a boss from hell."
—*San Francisco Chronicle*

"Sharp and funny . . . [*Apprentice*] had me spitting out my coffee while reading it. . . . A wickedly good start." —*Detroit Free Press*

"Ferociously witty . . . [*Apprentice*] exacts revenge on behalf of all the poor sods who ever mistook an internship for anything other than an education in toner, Excel, and carryout food. . . . [Weinstein accomplishes] in single lines what a wordier novelist would take reams to describe." —*The Onion*

"Brilliantly satirical." —*O, The Oprah Magazine*

"Hilarious . . . [Weinstein] has crafted a send-up of pretension that lightly grazes such themes as betrayal, family dysfunction, lust, sexuality, and plagiarism. . . . *Apprentice* is a delightful read." —*Library Journal*

"Weinstein captures perfectly the reality of research assistants who labor long hours for little reward. . . . The novel evokes much laughter. It's brain candy for aspiring poets everywhere." —*The Rocky Mountain News*

"[A] brilliant elegy to the abuse of subordinates . . . Weinstein, a published poet herself, knows where all the bodies are buried." —*The Christian Science Monitor*

"Thought the fashion-mag world was vicious? Meet Manhattan poet Z." —*New York*

"A pitch-perfect take on the self-obsessed artist." —*The Village Voice*

"Viciously funny . . . Weinstein's brilliant sketches of debauchery, pretense and pettiness take a page from *The Nanny Diaries*." —*Time Out New York*

"Anyone who appreciates poetry and has a sense of humor will very much enjoy reading Debra Weinstein's entertaining first novel." —Azar Nafisi, author of *Reading Lolita in Tehran*

"Extremely funny and touching . . . Debra Weinstein has plenty to say about protégés and mentors, and art and ambition. I thoroughly enjoyed this book." —Meg Wolitzer

Apprentice to the Flower Poet Z.

APPRENTICE TO THE FLOWER POET Z.

A NOVEL

Debra Weinstein

BALLANTINE BOOKS / NEW YORK

2005 Ballantine Books Trade Paperback Edition

Published in the United States by Ballantine Books, an imprint of The Random House Publishing Group, a division of Random House, Inc., New York.

Ballantine and colophon are trademarks of Random House, Inc.
Ballantine Reader's Circle and colophon are trademarks of Random House, Inc.

Originally published in hardcover in the United States by Random House, an imprint of The Random House Publishing Group, a division of Random House, Inc., in 2004.

Library of Congress Cataloging-in-Publication Data
Weinstein, Debra.
Apprentice to the flower poet Z. : a novel / Debra Weinstein.
p.   cm.
ISBN 0-8129-7094-2
1. Poets—Fiction.   2. Mentoring—Fiction.   3. Young women—Fiction.
4. New York (N.Y.)—Fiction.   I. Title.
PS3573.E39648A66 2004
813'.54—dc21   2003047064

Printed in the United States of America

Ballantine Books website address: www.ballantinebooks.com

246897531

Book design by Casey Hampton

FOR DEBORAH, GABRIELLE, AND ZACHARY

Immature poets imitate; mature poets steal.

—T. S. ELIOT

Apprentice to the Flower Poet Z.

What Is Poetry?

═══

This is the story of how I came to momentary prominence in the world of poetry and, through a series of misunderstandings, destroyed my good name and became a nobody.

It was fall, my junior year.

Because I was eager and on scholarship, I was the student chosen to type the poems of the visiting professors. Because I was young, and maybe too hungry, they loved me the way my parents loved me.

What is poetry, I would ask myself, over and over, typing,

the sudden, half-chirped, pecked-hem of morning
or
my arthritic half-moon, far-reaching thought (?), spine (?)

And then in the margin, this note to me from the visiting professor, asking for advice on his poem: "Annabelle, which sounds better?" And I would think to myself, hmm, "far-reaching thought" or "far-reaching spine"? Hard to know.

I want to say that my own poetry suffered from being exposed to so much bad writing, but my own poetry was free of chirping, hems, thoughts, and spines. It would be more accurate to say that *I* suffered. I felt like the lowest member of the poetry food chain, the one who sits at the foot of the goddess simply because it's the natural order of things.

When the visiting professors left, I got another assignment. I became the assistant to Professor Z. Professor Z.! Her book *Flowers of Fate* had just come out to critical acclaim—and made history as the first poetry book ever to land on a national bestseller list.

In the poetry world, Z. was part of an elite subculture—the celebrity poet. Conversations stopped when she entered a room. Z. was the face in a crowd that people looked for at the department's weekly wine and cheese soirees. She held an endowed chair in creative writing.

And it was my destiny to be her undergraduate assistant.

I was in love with Z.'s astonishing poetry about nature. In her poems, beautiful, intelligent flowers ruled the world. Z. was a master of the turn of phrase, the startling association. She could transform a garden into a flower bed, a flower bed into a wedding bed. Flowers violated other flowers, and you actually believed it.

There was so much I wanted to learn from Z.

In a rare, quiet moment, I would be sitting in her office and, closing my steno pad, I would say, "I want to ask you a question about 'unnatural world, whorled, begotten, petaled.' Why did you choose those adjectives: 'whorled, begotten, petaled'?" and Z. would lean forward, pause for a moment to absorb the question, and answer in a voice that told me how much my interest mattered to her.

At those times, I would learn something about how poems are made.

"In the poem 'Unnatural World,' I was thinking about prostitution, and knew I had to disguise that thought! When I said, 'unnatural world, whorled, begotten, petaled,' I was really thinking, 'Unnatural world—whores begotten, peddled.' Anyway, that was the idea that inspired that poem," and then, without missing a beat, she smiled and added, "Annabelle, I need black ink for my fountain pen. I want the blackest ink you can find. *Jet* black, not midnight black, not shoeshine black. And don't forget to get a handwritten receipt."

That afternoon, in the stationery store, watching the clerk write out the receipt for Z.'s fountain pen ink, I began to understand that the life of poetry was not only about choosing words; it was also about shopping.

There were things I did for Z. which were actually favors for other people. I handled her correspondence, and if she adored people, she would send them poems, but these were often obscure poems, poems you could find only in small magazines.

I would think of this activity as the Great Poetry Hunt, and every time I got a note sending me on one, my heart would sink a little.

Annabelle,
I am looking for a poem by Yvonne Miller (?) in a journal that had a very short publication life, perhaps *Poesis? Poet-Speak?* I recall this line: "the lark singing twer-will, twer-will . . ."

Then I would be lost for hours in the library, among the towering stacks, with my sad slip of paper, trying to match a long sequence of letters and numbers to one of the nondescript blue bindings that made up the reference section of bound poetry journals. What is literature anyway, I wondered, looking at the students squeezed into their little cubicles. I will end up here too someday, unread, dust-coated; another lost document. And that's only if I'm successful.

Dear Henry,
Thank you so much for your letter. Your new poems are breathless! Especially "Truck Driving South"—bold, punchy, acerbic. A trip to the microfiche room to scrutinize *The Journal of Poetry Concordance* led me to that poem by Yvonne Miller "The

Lark." Do you know it? Miller's approach is similar to yours. Both of you have an uncanny ability to accentuate the stillness . . .

And then this handwritten note to me,

Annabelle,

For this letter to Henry Mann, please dry some rose petals and put them in the envelope, mail letter in padded envelope, mark HAND CANCEL PLEASE.

I wrote back,

Done! But I wonder about "*accentuate* the stillness." Perhaps *articulate* is a better word?

I was lucky to have her, but she was also lucky to have me. Then another note:

Annabelle,

Please call Mrs. Van Elder and see if there is anything you can do for her.

"Mrs. Van Elder, my name is Annabelle, and I am Professor Z.'s assistant."

"Oh, yes, dear, how lovely of you to phone."

"She wanted to know if there was anything you needed—"

"Oh, yes, dear, Z. mentioned that you might call . . ."

Then I would be taking down Mrs. Van Elder's list.

Prescription cat food
Black sealing wax
Someone to read "The Circus Animals' Desertion"

I, of course, was that someone. She liked the W. B. Yeats poem read in a whisper. "Please, dear," she would say, "softer, softer." And eventually I learned these lines by heart:

Now that my ladder's gone,
I must lie down where all the ladders start,
In the foul rag-and-bone shop of the heart.

Who was Mrs. Van Elder to Z.? The flower poet didn't offer, but I knew the name. Mrs. Van Elder was a renowned reviewer of poetry books, reputed to be the meanest literary critic alive. In her younger days, she could bring a poet to prominence or ruin with a single adjective.

But to me Mrs. Van Elder was a short gray-haired woman in a yellow housedress; a frail woman like my grandmother, happy to have company on a lonely afternoon.

Z. had told me to be useful during my visits, to ask Mrs. Van Elder if there was anything she might need help with.

Mrs. Van Elder said she would like a cup of tea, but she had lost all her spoons. Would I go into the kitchen and find her a spoon? Being so young and so smart, I could probably see things that she couldn't.

"Mrs. Van Elder," I said, "I'll bet your spoons are hidden underneath all these dishes." I pointed to her sink, where dirty plates and bowls and mugs were piled high.

I said, "Would you like me to do your dishes?"

Mrs. Van Elder held her hand over her heart. She was so overcome with gratitude that she could barely speak. And would I mind also polishing her teakettle? It was tarnished to a sticky bronze. Then she told me to remember that, when boiling water, I must never let the kettle shriek. She had a cat with a nervous condition.

And so it became my Tuesday afternoon ritual, tea and poetry with Mrs. Van Elder once the dishes were out of the way.

It was a dark, airless apartment that smelled like decaying apples.

She had an ancient Remington Noiseless typewriter on her dining room table. I imagined Mrs. Van Elder in her prime composing one of her famous reviews; the torrent of metal keys that would come to signify the death of another writer.

But these days, rheumatoid arthritis made typing a simple thank-you note an ordeal. Rubbing her gnarled fingers, she said it would probably take her all afternoon to type one letter because she had forgotten to take her pills.

When I said, "Mrs. Van Elder, I can type the letter for you," she told me that I was a dream come true.

To Mr. Michael Leeds
Administrator of the Hortense Berg First Book Prize

Dear Mr. Leeds,

Though I am honored to have been asked to judge the Hortense Berg First Book Prize for Lyric Poetry, I write to say I find no manuscript worthy of this honor. Having known Hortense as a colleague and friend, I believe it would be an insult to her fine memory to award any of the five shameless manuscripts you sent me this distinction. Each one is worse than the next, and ignorant of the fine musical tradition that is poetry.

Sincerely,
Miriam Van Elder

I took my weekly visits to Mrs. Van Elder in stride, believing that if I proved myself dependable—if I did all my assignments well and without complaint—Z. might give me something really interesting to do.

Then came the prize. I was asked to go to New York City's public gardens to catalog flowers. Now I was Z.'s research assistant on my knees examining a flower, writing a brief description, and sketching the flower in a notebook. Z. gave me a box of one hundred colored pencils so I could be exact in the shade of my renderings.

"Annabelle," she had asked, "have you ever read Virginia Woolf's essay 'Professions for Women'?"

"No," I said. "I've only read *A Room of One's Own*."

"Well, it's 1931 and Woolf is speaking to a group of women at a college, and she's telling them how it is she came to be a writer . . . about the absolute joy of discovering that she could earn money from moving her pen back and forth across the page.

"Woolf learned that if she wrote a book review, she could earn enough money to buy a Persian cat. And then she learned that if she wrote a novel, she could buy a car."

"A reward for all that hard work," I said.

"Of course, for most people there's nothing to be made from writing poetry," Z. said. "Writing poetry is its own reward."

She was thinking.

"Annabelle, Virginia Woolf had that moment of exaltation when she got money for her writing, and I think that's something every young writer should experience.

"A defining feeling of self-respect, dignity. Imagine a woman with her own wallet, spending her own money; money that she has earned with her own writing! She knows her writing is of value because it gives her power in the marketplace. Annabelle, I'm going to offer you something rare. I'm going to give you an opportunity to earn money for *your* writing. I want to pay you for your words, and not only that, I want to pay you for your *poetry*."

"It sounds too good to be true," I said.

"Well, in truth, you would be helping me. I haven't the time anymore to do this kind of research. I want to pay you to sit in the garden and describe flowers: two dollars a description. It will be our contract. It would be a great way to develop your writing skills. And you could learn a lot about the process of revision. I will show you the strengths, the weaknesses in your own words as I transform them into my own vernacular."

"Really," I said. "You wouldn't have to pay me extra. I have the scholarship. I'm supposed to work twenty hours."

Z. said, "I would insist. This is creative work; it is separate from your work-study responsibilities."

I was thinking about the money. It was autumn, and I wanted to look like everyone else in New York City. I wanted a brown leather bomber jacket. I had seen one in the window of Charivari. It cost almost five hundred dollars. With this extra money from Z., it was suddenly a possibility.

Z. said, "And I will pay for your travel time, for your admission to the gardens, and your transportation costs—public transportation, of course."

"If it's close enough, I can walk," I said. "I like to walk."

"And, Annabelle, I want you to go a little over the top in your descriptions. I want you to abandon yourself to this work, to feel free to write anything you want."

"But you want me to accurately describe the flower—"

"Yes. You should evoke the flower to the best of your ability. . . . I think this will be a good exercise for you. Writing is like a muscle—the more you use it, the stronger it becomes. And the more *you* write, the stronger your own writing will become."

So, because a leather jacket cost roughly 250 flowers; because sitting in a garden with a notebook would mean I wouldn't be spending that time whispering "The Circus Animals' Desertion" to Mrs. Van Elder; because writing poetry was like running a marathon—you have to be in training to win the race—I agreed.

FLOWERING ASTERS: *each like a star, the glint in an eye, a tubular flower, yellow, pointed.*

MAIDEN PINKS: *a simple flower, like a button, braided through a young girl's hair.*

WISTERIA: *like hysteria, only it clings to a building, a bunch of purple flowers hiding a sturdy vine.*

Writing these flower briefs, I began, once again, to start questioning "What is poetry?" I thought of Keats's "wealth of globed peonies" and knew that I would never write a line that beautiful.

But I was writing, and though it wasn't my finest hour, I had work to show for my labor. I carried *The Garden Guide to New York City* in my backpack and tried to visit a different garden every time I set out on my assignment. One day I visited the Lotus Garden, a rooftop affair on the Upper West Side, and saw my first serviceberry and my first fringe tree.

My fringe tree description came back with this written across the top margin:

Annabelle, irony is fine, but less "lunatic fringe" please.

In the Channel Gardens in Rockefeller Center, I found myself in the center of a cacti display, looking for a new way to say *needle*.

I loved New York City's gardens. I loved the idea that something so lush could be tucked away behind granite; and that under all that asphalt and concrete there was only dirt. I would have written my own poem about it, had I not been writing for Z.

Annabelle,
  Please take this flower press to the public gardens and surreptitiously press me any flower from the lobelia family.

Z.

How not to attract attention when you have come to a place with the intention to vandalize? I must have looked so earnest leaning down to examine the *Lobelia inflata* with my magnifying glass, lifting the tiny blue-violet petals. Then I swiftly broke the smooth, inflated calyx in which they were seated, stuck my hand into my large canvas bag (as if feeling absentmindedly for a notebook and pencil), and placed the flower in a plastic bag. Later on the subway, between stops, I opened the wing nuts of the flower press, placed my lobelia in the wax paper, screwed the wing nuts back on, and tightened them with all my might.

A week later, when my spiked lobelia was sufficiently dry, I removed it from the flower press and carefully placed it inside a note I left in Z.'s mailbox.

Professor Z.,

Here is the spiked lobelia. I traveled to the Brooklyn Botanic Garden to find this flower (two subway tokens, 40 minutes underground, $1.00 admission). I learned that the brightly colored *Lobelia cardinalis* is rightly classed as among our most beautiful wildflowers. A pretty flower in its prime, but not ideal for pressing. (Its leaves vary greatly from lance-shaped to oblong, making them difficult to lay flat.) Please find my effort in the attached envelope.

Sincerely,

Annabelle

My note came back with a big slash mark through it and this written across the top:

Annabelle,

What is this? If a flower—not recognizable!

Remember: tenacity is a poet's most important quality!

Please work to make future pressings more flowerlike.

Also, please find me a photo and artist's rendering—

19th century or earlier—of this flower.

Z.

Spiked Lobelia

———

In the beginning I was simply Z.'s reader. A young woman alone in her bedroom absorbing every word of *The Amazing Journey of the Singular Flower*. How startling and original those poems were.

I wrote my first poem when I was four years old. My mother has a copy in my baby album.

I learned to read poetry my senior year of high school, the year my parents' marriage fell apart. I turned to literature for comfort; I found the Flower Poet Z.

I would read Z.'s poems over and over, savoring the nuanced language. Sometimes I would type a poem on my typewriter just to get a deeper sense of Z.'s rhythm.

I was learning about flowers, music, the seasons of the heart.

In my mind, she was the finest poet writing in the English language.

Later, when Z. became my teacher, and still later, when she became my employer and mentor, I would have a hard time reconciling the person with the poems. The voice in the poems was so lyrical and unassuming. And in the classroom Z. was known to be a patient teacher

who nodded when you spoke and then presented you with an insight-
ful reading of your poem's strengths and weaknesses. But at home the
poet yelled from one end of her apartment to the other: "Annabelle, can
you *please* refill my water pitcher? And this time lots of ice! Lots and
lots of ice! Small pieces of ice from the small ice tray!"

I remember when I first saw her:

It was October 1983. I was walking aimlessly in the Village when
suddenly the skies opened up, and I stepped inside a small bookstore to
wait out the rain. I was wearing a yellow slicker.

Everyone looked up when I walked in and then returned to the
matter at hand: a poetry reading.

I remember her long, slender hands, her straight black hair falling
into her eyes, that whisper worthy of Mrs. Van Elder,

> . . . *unnatural world, whorled, begotten, petaled—*
> *I see you and forget desire . . .*

There was the shock of recognition: This was the poet Z.

She was dark, thin, and elegant, like the flowers she wrote about.
She wore shiny black glasses, rectangular, which made her look the
height of literary fashion.

I introduced myself as Annabelle, and told her that I had all of her
books.

Then Z. signed a hardcover first edition of *The Flower Daughter
Poems*.

I don't remember why I had come to the city that night or what I
had been doing in the Village. If I had been there to meet friends, I
can't recall who they were. I remember only the thrill of connecting the
voice in my head to a living one.

The fall I stumbled into the reading, I was a sophomore at Long Island
Community College, enrolled in my first poetry workshop. My teacher
was Arthur Feld, the author of a little-known book of poems called
The Uncompromising Vision of Arthur Feld. Arthur was a bearlike man

with a big, hearty laugh, a fine poet who time—and many award committees—had passed over.

In class he told us that, to be poets, we "must first be lovers."

"Take life by its reins and embrace it," Arthur said, only he didn't use the word *embrace*. In our weekly conferences he would turn from my poems—always deeply troubling to Arthur, for, after all, why shouldn't a young woman born to middle-class upbringing and Jewish parents be happy?—and shake his head.

"There is life," Arthur would say, "and there is poetry. Your poems need to find life as much as you need to find poetry."

He was my poetry father.

It was a bittersweet day in May when I left Arthur Feld's classroom to become a scholarship student at a world-famous private university in New York City. Arthur knew the director of the writing program and had encouraged me to apply. I still remember the excitement of ripping open that envelope:

> Congratulations! Because of your fine academic record, we are delighted to offer you the prestigious Edgar Allan Poe Fellowship. Named for Greenwich Village's legendary writer, this fellowship offers full tuition and a work-study stipend to an undergraduate poet of promise.

Saying good-bye, Arthur opened his arms to hug me. "You have been blessed with a great talent. Use it well. Listen closely, take good notes, and make friends, Annabelle."

That fall, when I began my fellowship, Z. was reveling in the success of *In the Garden of the Golden Flowers,* a book that, with its endorsement from Louise Crankshaw, president of London's distinguished Christina Georgina Rossetti Society, had made her famous around the world.

Here is a poet of heroic stature—a lone, accomplished, classical voice singing in an ocean of marginality.

She must have meant the ocean that I was drowning in. It all began each day at seven: my mother at the breakfast table drinking her second cup of coffee, bitterly recounting her marriage to my father. Sometimes I would tell her some of the things I was thinking: Was there anything new a writer could say about flowers? Could a woman really support herself writing poetry? And why didn't New Yorkers own dishwashers? Then suddenly, from nowhere, my mother would ask a question like "Annabelle, whatever happened to that nice young man you were dating in high school?"

After breakfast, I would race to the train station for the 9:04 into Manhattan. (I saved almost fifteen dollars a week traveling at an off-peak hour.) At 10:15, I would be taking the subway stairs two at a time so I wouldn't be late for my 10:40 class, Readings in the Psychological Novel, with the famous literary critic Walter Peterson.

They were hectic days, running errands all over the city, and I welcomed the rare Tuesday when I could stand in place at the Xerox machine in the English Department copying poems for Z. to hand out to her graduate writing class.

Here is one of the poems I copied:

CLOCK
Oh clock, how do I measure your failures?
You go round and round and round and round . . .
            —Jason Spence, "The Failed, Miserable Life"

Annabelle,
    Please meet me at the Metropolitan Café at 4:30 p.m.
Type attached, Spiked Lobelia poem, and leave a copy on my desk.
Bring the original draft with you.

                                    Z.

This is what I typed:

SPIKED LOBELIA

Oh, brightly colored cardinalis,
I want to press you,
but your flowers keep breaking.
I would travel underground
to reach you in your garden.
Brooklyn is a garden,
thorny in memory.
The memory of knees.
The memory of palms.

Did I hear the echo of my own voice in these words? I rummaged in my backpack for the note I had written Z. about my spiked lobelia pressing but couldn't find it. Then I gathered my belongings and walked up to the Metropolitan Café.

When you grow up on Long Island, you see New York as a mythical city where rich people sit in restaurants at shiny black tables, holding important conversations. For my high school graduation, I wanted to go to a beautiful restaurant, but my parents insisted on dinner at the Big Top, a steakhouse with a popcorn machine at the center of its dining room.

So here was Z. with a smart-looking man in a tweed jacket in the window of the Metropolitan Café. She had taken off her trademark black glasses and was cleaning them with a small chamois cloth. He was leaning in to tell her something, and she cocked her head at an angle that said she was really listening.

"Oh, Annabelle, you're here!" Z. said. "Do join us! Annabelle, this is Jason Spence. Mr. Spence has just been appointed executive director of the Society for the Preservation of American Poetry." She smiled over at him, then added, "Jason, this is my assistant, Annabelle Goldsmith, poetry's brave and vibrant future."

"Hello, Annabelle." Spence put out his hand to greet me and held it for a moment. He motioned to the waiter for a chair.

"Professor Z., here's your poem," I said, settling in.

"Oh, wonderful," Z. said as she took the envelope. "What can we get you? Can I offer you a drink, or are you too young? What *is* the drinking age now, Annabelle? Oh, never mind, get her a Coke, will you, Jason?"

This was Z. after hours: casual, sexy, adult. At her elbow was a glass of white wine. She had a cigarette burning in an ashtray. I had never, in my wildest dreams, imagined myself at the center of such a scene. Spence held up a finger.

"A Coca-Cola for the young lady."

"Jason, will you take a look at my new poem? Annabelle helped with the research. For this poem, she actually brought me a pressed spiked lobelia."

"It was lovely in its prime," I mumbled, but both of them must have heard me, for together they recited this line from Robert Herrick's "To the Virgins, to Make Much of Time":

For having lost but once your prime, you may for ever tarry!

"Ha! Ha! Ha!"

Spence took out a green fountain pen. His fingers were large and ink-stained. His jacket was the kind you might wear if you suddenly found yourself cast in the role of college professor, threadbare with worn-out elbow pads.

"Give it here."

Z. put the poem in front of him, and he put on his reading glasses. Then she picked up her cigarette—it was smeared with lipstick—and mashed it out. She was trying to cut down on her smoking, she said.

His head bounced while he read. When he was through, he looked up and said, "I see a woman holding flowers, but I cannot see the poet's body."

Z. laughed.

"I see the 'brightly colored cardinalis,' but I want the world turned flesh. Show me her nipples upright in their sweet, pink blossoms."

Suddenly the poets were staring deep into each other's eyes. Outside, trash was blowing down Park Avenue.

Then the soda arrived and the waiter was asking questions: Did I want to see a menu? Would I be staying for dinner?

Z. hesitated. "Annabelle, would you like something to eat?"

Spence said, "Do have something."

Z. said, "The chef is famous for his vertical appetizers. If you're very bold, you'll try his pan-Asian stack—"

"Thank you," I said, "but I can't."

"They have a superb foie gras," Spence said, "if you prefer horizontal fare."

I was too nervous to eat. I shook my head just enough so that they knew I was serious.

Spence rapped his pen against her poem. "Z., are you familiar with Auden's 'Tonight at Seven Thirty'?"

Z. said, "Remind me."

Spence said, " 'The life of plants is one continuous solitary meal . . .' " Then he spoke the line again slowly, with great drama.

He was writing something on Z.'s poem. "I think it's something you should think about. . . . 'One continuous solitary meal,' " he said.

"Yes," Z. whispered. "Yes."

He pushed the paper over to her. "Do you see what I mean?"

Z. said, looking down at her poem, "Jason, your reading is as incisive as ever."

Now there was a glint in Spence's eye. I could see what she saw in him: an angular jawline, a hidden machismo. For how many men in the world loved poetry?

Everything I knew about Jason Spence I had learned while photocopying Z.'s files; the rest I gleaned from her phone conversations as I sat in her office waiting to take dictation.

Spence was the author of a first book called *Homeless,* which was hailed "a masterpiece" by the reigning British poet laureate. It was the story of James, who lived in the London tubes.

He published two more books of poetry, *James* and *The James Chronicles,* before publishing a novel, *James and Friends*. That book was dismembered by the *London Telegraph*'s most renowned poet-novelist, who asked in his review that simple, stinging question: "Who cares?"

Then Spence turned to sheep, raising them in the Scottish Highlands.

His last book was a thin volume called *The Failed, Miserable Life,* and the British critics used the title to deride him.

Now he was in New York City, where none of that mattered. The fact that he had a British accent made him somehow more literary. That he quoted Auden further enhanced his mystique.

You had to wonder why an Englishman would be chosen as executive director of a society whose mission was to preserve American poetry.

Z. had ordered twelve copies of *The Failed, Miserable Life* for her class and twenty more to give away to her colleagues.

I had been typing up little slips for her to attach to each book:

To Chairman Marks:

Dear David,

I thought you might be interested in *The Failed, Miserable Life.* The author—who had chosen the Scottish countryside over the rather incestuous U.K. poetry scene—has finally decided to give up farming for arts administration. He has just been named Executive Director of the Society, and is working to expand university outreach programs. He's a passionate scholar of Auden, and eager to teach (Workshop I?).

Let me know what you think.

Z.

To Dean Bellingham:

Dear Margaret,

I so enjoyed lunch. I am attaching the information about the spa I told you about. The facial cream can only be purchased by overnight guests, but it is well worth the two-night minimum.

On the subject of poetry: I don't know if you've heard of Jason Spence. He was recruited from the U.K. by the Society after a prolonged search. This is his latest book and I think it's a good one. I wonder if there might be some opportunities for collaboration.

I am returning Jeremy's poems as promised. (If he's bored with his anthology, then perhaps he's ready to read one poet in depth. I recommend Auden. There is a handsome cloth edition of his selected poems available, and I think Jeremy might enjoy his subtle brand of humor.) And certainly he can use my name on his college application.

Fondly,
Z.

Spence lifted his glass, looked at me, and said, "I'm so glad we have you here for this historic moment, Annabelle. Let us toast our distinguished friend, Z., who has this very day been named chancellor of the Society for the Preservation of American Poetry!"

We clinked glasses. I thought of Arthur's advice: make friends, take good notes. I had so much to tell him.

". . . The highest honor a poet can achieve . . . the governing body for American poetry . . . the organization which sponsors Annual Poetry Week and gives the esteemed Fowler Grant, the only hundred-thousand-dollar poetry prize in the land."

I wanted a Fowler Grant someday.

According to Spence, Z. was the first woman in the Society's seventy-year history to be appointed chancellor, and they were drinking La Grande Dame champagne to celebrate.

I said that Z. was an inspiration, and Spence patted her arm in agreement. Then I asked her if she had any plans for her chancellorship.

She said that in fact she had. She had decided that the Society should publish a series of books about women poets. She was hoping to bring out one book a year.

Then Spence told Z. that as wonderful and as burdensome as her new position might be, she must continue to write her poems; that she should not get caught up in the *politics* of poetry.

For the world was in love with Z.'s poetry. And the loss of even a single flower poem would be tragic.

Then he reached for her hand across the table, and with the other hand he lifted her chin.

Spence said, looking into her eyes, "My mission is to have the Society give birth to a poetry renaissance. I want the world to think poetry, the way it thinks television. Can I count on your support?"

"I give you my word," Z. said.

Spence said, "My aim is to send poetry to the farthest corners of the world. Would you lead a poetry delegation to Tibet?"

"I will follow poetry to the ends of the earth," Z. said with a laugh.

Then Spence said, "I picture you on the mountaintop in your army-issue parka; you're wearing those big, hairy dog boots with bells."

He took both of her hands.

"But seriously . . . I envision a world where everyone will learn to appreciate poetry. A world where writing workshops will be free and available to every aspiring poet! A world of young, inspired missionaries going out to teach poetry. . . . Wherever there is hope or triumph, poetry. Wherever there is poverty and despair, poetry. Wherever people gather under the night sky in search of a single star, poetry."

I imagined it must have been very lonely for Spence raising sheep.

"Poetry on buses, in subways, in supermarkets. . . . We must all become missionaries of the sacred word . . ."

It was the word *supermarket* that propelled me back to reality. I had promised my mother I would make us dinner, and if I didn't leave right away, I would miss the 5:35 to Huntington. I waited for Spence to finish his speech, took one last sip of my Coke, and excused myself. I said I was sorry to be leaving.

Mouth Sounds

—————

"Annabelle, come into my office," Z. said, motioning me off my chair in the lobby of the English Department, where I sat among students holding five-pound books on their laps.

She stood behind her immense oak desk, which took up most of her office. It was a sunny day, and she had drawn the blind on the window behind her.

"Annabelle, some wonderful news. Dr. Marks, our chairman, has agreed to let you work as my personal assistant. As you can imagine, this is very much a step up.

"Would you like to work in my home? It would mean answering the mail, the phone, typing letters, running errands. Does that appeal to you?"

I was flattered by the offer, and so I said, "Yes, I would love to be your personal assistant, Professor Z.," and then, to let her know that I was quite the go-getter, I said, "When do I start?"

Then I was adding twenty minutes to my daily commute to get to Z.'s East Side apartment.

Z.'s building was on a dead-end street that gave out on the East River. The street was made up of diminutive apartment buildings. Quiet and stately, it was far from the hustle and bustle of city life. I had come from my mother's house, a split-level which was in a state of disrepair since my father left. A leak in the upstairs bathroom had resulted in a crack in the ceiling that you saw the moment you walked through the front door.

That morning at breakfast, I had told my mother I was getting a promotion.

"From assistant to personal assistant to the Flower Poet Z.," I said. My mother, who worked in a large department store, told me that once she had worked as a secretary, too.

But I wasn't going to be a secretary, I told my mother. Then I tried to explain the world of poetry, and how this was really a giant leap forward.

A white-gloved doorman greeted me outside Z.'s building. I was standing there for a while eyeing the cornices, holding the slip of paper where she had written down her address. The lobby of 424 was marble yet intimate, with warm lighting and a red Persian rug in the center of the room. A large painting called *Under the Flemish Sky* graced one wall. When I told the doorman who I was and who I would be visiting, he said, "Yes, Annabelle, she is expecting you," and he pointed to the elevator and said, "The penthouse," and I stood up a little taller.

Z. was beautiful in a New York City sort of way—black hair, black clothes, silver accessories, and a splash of red lipstick. She was a woman of a certain age.

"Annabelle," she said, "come in, come in," and I was invited into a huge living room that looked straight out on the river. In the distance you could see two metal barges floating downstream. The river and the barges would survive long after the death of every living poet. Suddenly, even Z. seemed truly mortal.

"How beautiful," I said.

"Yes," Z. said. "But the light can be blinding."

On the walls hung ancient botanical prints. There was a large green-and-white-striped couch positioned to maximize fully the river view. Even from a distance I could tell it was silk.

"But how are you today, Annabelle? Can I get you some water?"

"No, thank you," I said, and Z. gave me a tight smile and motioned me down the hallway.

Z. said, "Annabelle, thank you for coming. I'm so glad you'll be working here with me." When we reached the end of the corridor, she opened a door and switched on a light. "This will be your office," she said.

It was a grim little room with space enough for a tiny desk. The floor was covered with linoleum, and a window showed the dingy white brick of the next building. Then again, I had never had an office before.

I didn't know what to say, so I said, "It's very nice."

"I'm so pleased you like it," Z. said. "Let me show you the files."

I put my poetry book, *His Mistress,* down on the desk.

Z. opened the closet door to reveal two white metal cabinets. I nodded. She opened and closed the drawers, which were jammed with papers. Then she pointed to my book.

"Braun Brown," she said. "She's teaching a workshop for us this semester."

"I heard that . . . Actually, I like the book a lot. Have you read it?"

"No, I'm afraid I have far too much serious reading to do."

At that time, Braun Brown's book was in the window of nearly every bookstore in the city, and her poems were appearing regularly in *The New York Literary Review*. Braun was even on the newsstands— on the cover of the newspaper *Poet & Poem*—the subject of a special supplement (fourteen new poems, a critical assessment, and an interview). *Book News* had just given *His Mistress* a rave.

I recited,

Halfhearted, and away from home
with a bible, her mouth sounds mimic the fall of snow
and outside, at the Holiday Inn, the businessmen arrive
for the pharmaceutical convention.
This is my life. I am his mistress.
My breasts, pink, luscious globes.
He calls them "my fruit."
My legs are a lady's, long and smooth.

I said, "It's that word *pharmaceutical* that I find so arresting."

Z. shook her head and muttered, "Mouth sounds."

I said, "I wonder why she chose that phrase. . . . I wish I could audit Braun Brown's workshop. I would ask her."

Z. said, "I'm afraid that class is only open to students in the Graduate Creative Writing Program. But tell me, what makes you want to take her class?"

"To hear what she has to say about her craft, how to be a poet in the world, that sort of thing."

"Annabelle, please don't take this the wrong way, but to my mind Braun Brown represents the *death* of American letters. She is the *enemy* of poetry—"

"She's a career poet." Then she said softly, "And a poetry careerist . . ."

"You mean, that award she got—"

Braun had recently been given a large grant from the National Arts Foundation. It may have been the reason she had been invited to teach at the university.

"Big money doesn't come to minor poets, Annabelle. Braun Brown is obviously a woman with friends in high places . . . but enough shoptalk."

Z. opened another door. There was a desk, a chair, and a blue chaise longue.

"This is my office, Annabelle." She closed the door behind her. "Whenever you're walking down this hall, glance over and make sure my door is closed. I consider it a sacred space."

"I am very respectful of that," I said.

She pointed to the bathroom.

"I keep a stack of hand towels next to the sink for my guests. As my assistant, your job will be to monitor the stack and buy more hand towels as necessary."

"At the university," I said, "I monitor the typewriter in the student lounge and change the ribbon before it runs out."

"A keen eye is essential in a poet," Z. said, walking me back into the living room. "I like deep, rich colors for my hand towels—blues, burgundies, and purples. I like the paper to be thick and textured."

"And soft," I added.

"Yes," Z. said. "Absolutely. The feel should be more cotton than paper. Now, Annabelle, I want to be very clear about what I require.

"There will be domestic errands. I have a weekly gathering which requires a bit of advance preparation—"

"I can arrange my schedule to accommodate your gathering," I said.

"Throughout the week you can count on having a steady supply of clerical work. Aside from my letters, I occasionally take on complicated editing projects . . ."

"I'm good at proofreading," I said, "and I really do enjoy typing."

"Good." Then Z. added in a very serious voice, "I don't want there ever to be any misunderstanding about your duties."

I nodded my head.

"But I need to say, first of all, as my assistant your job will be to protect my privacy. I will need you to be discreet."

"Of course," I said. "At school, I never mention my work for you. I even conceal what I'm copying at the Xerox machine."

"That's why you're in this position of responsibility," Z. said. "For your impeccable judgment. Now, with respect to my family, I will, at times, need you to run interference for me."

"Your family?"

"Yes, right now my husband and daughter are abroad. When they return . . . When I write, I must disappear. I need you to serve as my emissary, to stand guard over my time so that I can work."

I said I understood, but this was the first I'd heard of a family. I had assumed that Z. was a divorced woman or a widow, with the "flower daughter" she wrote about in her book away at school. I had imagined that with Jason Spence she had suddenly, inexplicably—after a long period of being alone—fallen in love, as if for the first time in her life.

"You may think my writing habits are unconventional, and they are. I rarely sit at my desk. I do all my writing in my head, and I sometimes scribble notes on random pages you might find about the apartment. It will be your job to gather those pages and keep them in a file for me on your desk. As my assistant, you will need to be quiet in my presence, so I can think. I get a sense that this is something that will come easily to you. . . . I know I can trust you to be the guardian of my psychic space."

"Yes, " I said. Why say more and risk invading the force field?

"There are times when I write for days and don't leave my office. My family calls this my 'white heat.' During a white heat, I will need you to be extremely flexible about your responsibilities. I may need to call on you to come early to my apartment and bring groceries or make trips to the post office or the library."

"Easy," I said.

"You have already proved yourself to be a competent research assistant. I know I can also rely on you to be versatile and selfless.

"By *selfless,* I mean this is your moment to step back and let other people shine. The experience will put you in good stead later in life. Of course, some people are not able to defer to anyone. I once had an assistant who . . ." Her voice trailed off. "It's not important."

"That has never been a problem of mine."

"Annabelle, I need an assistant who will be—and I don't mean to insult you, but I'll be blunt—wallpaper."

I thought about the wallpaper in my mother's kitchen. It had a pattern of huge yellow and orange flowers that seemed to scream out when you entered the room.

"Annabelle, to be plain, I need someone who will tend the castle garden. Like the gardener at Versailles, someone who keeps my life pruned, shaped . . ."

"Who will make your life her own creative project?"

"Yes," she said. "That's right. Someone who will dedicate herself to me the way that Véra Nabokov devoted her life to her husband's literary career."

I repeated, "Someone who is happy to make your life her own creative project."

Z. nodded in acknowledgment, then said, very seriously, "You see, Annabelle, I've entered a terribly busy phase in my life. Each day is a balancing act, with obligations pulling me in every direction."

"And now, being named chancellor," I said. "You'll have even more to do."

"Yes, and I can hardly find a minute to think, let alone do my own work."

I said, "You need some quiet time for reflection."

"I need someone to help me put my life in order, so I don't have to think so much about it," Z. said.

"Professor Z.," I said, "I am that person."

"Annabelle, I think we're on the same wavelength here. I feel as if you truly understand me. . . . But are you sure you're comfortable with this arrangement?"

I wanted to say something large and poetic, but instead I said, "It sounds great," and took a seat on the couch.

"And what about your own ambition, Annabelle?"

But before I could answer, Z. said she felt chilled and disappeared into the kitchen. A few moments later, she returned with a silver tea service.

"I'd like to finish my degree. That's my first ambition," I pressed on.

Passing me a napkin, she touched my hand. It was a small, accidental gesture, but to me it was filled with the meaning of our connection.

"Do you take milk and sugar?"

"Just sugar," I said, and Z. poured a stream of amber tea.

"Tell me, where do you see yourself in five years?"

"In five years," I said, "I'd like to have published a book of poetry and traveled around the world."

By that time I would be twenty-six.

Then Z. told me how excited she was about our collaboration.

"I'll be honest," Z. said. "I've hired a few assistants in my day, but there's something different about you. . . . You seem to be *apprentice* material. It's your passion for poetry that sets you apart."

Z. shifted her weight on the couch and brought her legs up under her. "Tell me, Annabelle, what do you know of literary apprenticeships?"

I remembered how Emily Dickinson corresponded with Thomas Wentworth Higginson, an eminent man of letters, for almost her entire life. And then I asked, "Was that an apprenticeship?"

"Did they write to each other about poetry?" Z. asked.

"Yes," I said.

"Then it was an apprenticeship."

I mentioned an article I'd read by Elizabeth Bishop about how she visited the home of Marianne Moore, and even wrote a poem about the time they spent together.

"Yes!" Z. said. "You're very well read, Annabelle. It's a terribly important matter for an apprentice of mine to be well read." Then she leaned in and said, "The world will know you as my assistant, but *I* will know you as my *apprentice*."

It was the word *my* that made me shiver.

Then Z. told me about her current writing projects; how there might be occasion to travel. She had a house in Sag Harbor, where she went during intersession and school breaks.

I said it would be easy for me to get to Sag Harbor, since I already lived on Long Island.

I told her that I had to leave early on Mondays because I had therapy.

She told me I should remind her on Mondays because she had a very short memory. And then she smiled uncomfortably, which made me wonder if she had once been in therapy herself or she simply disapproved of the variation in schedule.

Then Z. said, "Now, about the work. Annabelle, have you ever attended the readings at the Society?"

"Yes," I said. "I went with my writing class last year. Arthur Feld took us to see An Evening of Tribal Poetry. . . . Do you know Arthur Feld?"

"Is he a poet?"

"Yes," I said, and I felt a stab of pain for my poetry father. That room, with its elegant tea service, botanical prints, and ever-changing river light, would be a place where Arthur would be named but not recognized.

While Z. went in search of a flyer, I took in the room, the view, examined the teacups. They were pink floral, bone china, not at all like the old brown mugs in my mother's cabinet.

"You can keep this," Z. said, handing me the brochure. At a glance, I could see that she would be having a retrospective in the spring.

"Celebrate the Celebrated Poet Z.," the copy read.

The occasion was the publication of her selected poems.

I said, "I should get a ticket before they sell out."

Z. said, "Don't worry. I have a private stash."

And Braun Brown was reading a few weeks later! I looked from Z. to Braun's photo. Braun had angular features, full lips, and long, wild hair. This was not the photo of a writer at her desk with a typewriter and ashtray full of cigarette butts but rather a portrait of the hip young artist as glamorous woman.

"One of the first things I would like you to do is distribute that brochure," Z. said. "The university has a label service, and they can print out the names and addresses of faculty in my division. There are also some fledgling organizations that provide services to young writers in the city. I would like you to call them and get their mailing lists, too."

I opened my backpack and ripped a piece of paper from my day planner: August 31, 1984. I tried to remember who I was a month ago, before I was apprentice to the Flower Poet Z., but the question seemed irrelevant. This was my new life. I resolved to be organized. I made this note:

GET MAILING LABELS

Then I asked Z. if she could tell me the names of some of the small organizations. She said she could not, and smiled apologetically.

Then Z. said, "Annabelle, I want to remind you that the issue of confidentiality is paramount for me. I may need you to keep certain information private. You must be able to make a distinction between privacy and secrecy, and be sure never to convey the latter. I know I can count on you to keep a secret."

"Professor Z., when I send your mail out in the department, I put tape across the back and stamp it confidential."

"Working in my house, doing my correspondence, you will know things about me. I suspect you already do. But I trust you, Annabelle, more fully than I have any of your predecessors."

"Yes," I said. I felt myself blushing.

"There will be poems, drafts, questions. Questions will arise."

At the center of her poem "Flower Soliloquy" was the purple flower with its long, throbbing stigma.

O buried ovary in the body of the flower . . . O buried flower!

"No," I said. "I would never ask intrusive questions."

"Good," Z. said. "Now I have a question for you: Can you cook?"

Lord, I Am Naked

Standing in Z.'s kitchen, refilling her filtered water pitcher, I sometimes thought, What is poetry?

From her kitchen sink, you got a spectacular view of the East River, and I kept a pad in my pocket in case I got an idea. The pad was slightly waterlogged, and the lines, even some of my words, were smeared.

I liked cracking the ice cube trays, the crunch of eighteen little pieces of ice breaking free from their blue plastic shell.

My journal from that time records the swirl of detail that was my daily life in New York City:

> a rind, a peel, cherry tomatoes, chèvre and chives,
> a taxi, the Times, a discarded coffee lid

I wanted to be like Keats: intelligent, lively, writing with gusto about a world overwrought with beauty.

But I didn't see beauty. I was too busy typing Z.'s letters, straightening her living room, and preparing food for her weekly salon—

cocktails and hors d'oeuvres on Wednesday afternoons for some of the most prominent voices in contemporary poetry.

For working ten extra hours in Z.'s home, I got a hundred dollars a week above my stipend (and flower research fee), and a status unlike anything I'd ever experienced in my life. I was appointed assistant editor of *Torch!,* the English Department's undergraduate literary magazine. I was granted permission to audit Braun Brown's exclusive graduate writing workshop. And suddenly I was the celebrity assistant. Everyone, it seemed, wanted to talk to me.

There was Harry Banks, a graduate student, always at the copy machine, asking questions about my job: Did I get to see Z.'s original manuscripts? Who actually attended Z.'s weekly salon? What did her apartment look like?

And did she really eat her assistants?

Harry winked at me, and I looked away.

I wanted to tell him that I was different from the others. It was my love of poetry that set me apart; Z. wouldn't be making a meal of me.

Of course, confidentiality being paramount, I revealed very little.

"When I worked for Marshall Greene, I walked his dog," Harry said.

"Z. doesn't have any pets," I said.

"When I worked for Marshall Greene, I sometimes took Thomas Wyatt for the weekend."

Now Marshall Greene was dead, and the dog, Thomas Wyatt, roamed the English Department, a ghost of its former owner. Greene had been killed racing his MG across train tracks in Kingston, New York, and the department secretary, Maurita Collins, had taken the dog in the accident's aftermath.

" 'They flee from me that sometime did me seek,' " Harry said, a reference to his loss and to Thomas Wyatt the sixteenth-century poet.

I said, "You write fiction, right?"

" 'Whoso list to hunt, I know where is an hind. . . . But as for me, alas, I may no more . . .' "

The poor, sad story of Harry Banks: He had given up a job teaching English in a private school to work with Greene, the author of those fictional Bible rewrites, the most famous being *Adam and Eve*. ("Lord, I am naked," the Marshall Greene detractors would later say of him in mockery.) Greene had just finished the first draft of a three-thousand-page manuscript, *Job*—said to be his masterpiece—when he was killed.

Now there was a great controversy over who should put *Job* together for the publishers. Harry Banks wanted to but was quickly put out of the running because—though he had worked with Greene and even typed much of the manuscript—he was a thirty-year-old unpublished writer.

Since his teacher was dead, and no one seemed to know what to do with him, Harry was assigned to help the department secretary. These days Maurita Collins was helping Greene's estate settle his tax record—which was what accounted for Harry's spending so much time at the copy machine.

"Receipt for a dinner you never attended," Harry said wistfully as he lay what looked to be a restaurant stub on the glass.

I would gladly have let Harry go ahead of me—he only ever had one or two items to copy—but he always insisted on waiting his turn.

"The wine digested; the dinner, a memory . . ."

One day Harry said, "Tell me about yourself, Annabelle."

How could I tell him how happy I was to be working for a poet I admired, how excited I was about my own writing—I had recently submitted a poem I'd written about Emily Dickinson to a new literary magazine called *A! Muse*—when his own life was so pathetic?

So I told Harry Banks that I lived with my mother on Long Island and that every night I made sure I got home early so I could make her dinner—steak, potatoes, and a frozen vegetable.

"Long Island," Harry said. "You've got a lot of malls out there."

I said that I grew up in the town where Walt Whitman had once made his home and that I had actually attended Walt Whitman High School.

He told me that my literary connection to Walt Whitman was original.

I told him the suburbs weren't entirely devoid of culture like everyone believed. In my town, we had a bookstore called Oscars, where an entire room was devoted to poetry.

I told him that my parents didn't understand poetry.

Then Harry said, "Let me tell you something about parents," and he motioned for me to come closer. He cupped his hands around my ear—as if to tell me a secret—and I leaned in to listen. He ran his tongue around my earlobe, dipping once or twice into my ear.

Harry Banks: blue eyes, curly black hair, rimless glasses, a love of poetry.

He may once have basked in the glory of a world-famous novelist, but when your writer is dead, you are no one.

"I know a place off campus where we can drink red wine and recite poetry to each other," Harry said.

"I wish I could," I said. "But I have to run some errands for Z."

Those words, "a place off campus where we can drink red wine and recite poetry," played themselves over and over in my head for weeks. At night, alone in my childhood bed . . . What would have happened, I asked myself, if, for a few hours, I had strayed from my prescribed path?

I saw myself in a coffee shop trading war stories with Harry Banks.

Myself on the edge of a bed in the Washington Square Motel. Harry's open palms grazing my nipples, *upright in their sweet, pink blossoms* . . .

Myself, naked and on my stomach, on my lavender bedspread. The jangling of Harry's belt unbuckling . . .

Harry naked from the waist down and on top of me on the green-and-white-striped couch in Z.'s living room. The sound of Z.'s key turning in the lock . . .

A Cat Named Virginia

At a writing program in a small midwestern college, Z. studied with Clark Anderson and Samuel Owens—poets you've never heard of, whose books you would pass up at a yard sale. She learned from them lyric precision, attention to detail, and a kind of formal, buttoned-up poetry that, at its best, sounded like W. H. Auden.

This is a couplet from Z.'s poem "Pie Maker," which recently appeared in a special issue of *Writers and Their Early Work:*

Sky blue, the heron flies—
A woman at the oven, baking pies.

This was Z. in the fifties, writing groundbreaking feminist poetry no one would ever read. For anyone interested in her oeuvre, that first book, *Household Rhyme*—which she chose never to publish—is a sometimes wry, sometimes terse, formal record of her domestic life. It was, she would say, her "certificate of apprenticeship."

"Those poems grew out of the famous Clark Anderson workshop called Employing Wit, where I studied Donne ('Love's Alchemy') and read lots of Shakespeare. What I learned," Z. said, "was that I could be funny, but it came at a great cost to my poetry."

In the sixties she raised a daughter and wrote more household rhymes.

> *In the garden, a swarm of red ants,*
> *Remember to buy diapers and training pants.*

"But it wasn't until the Women's Poetry Revolution of the nineteen seventies that I became totally free of that nonsense," Z. said.

We were sitting in her office at the university. She had just gotten off the phone with Mrs. Van Elder and had a new list of supplies.

"The late sixties/early seventies: That was a time of explosive activity in women's poetry," Z. said. "Everywhere, everyone was writing about the body. We had Anne Sexton writing in celebration of her uterus. We had Muriel Rukeyser reminding us not to despise our clitorises. In those years, we were breaking all the rules, and I felt permission to give up my strict end-rhymes."

Clitoris! I thought. There was a word I would never have thought to use in a poem. I said, "You stopped writing in form?"

"Yes," Z. said. "And I never looked back."

"And your poems, were they 'revolutionary'?"

Z. laughed. "Not in so many words, but these poets gave me the courage to strip down to my essential element. I gave up all my adjectives and wrote 'Peony Poem,' which was quite a departure for me."

Then I said, " 'Peony Poem,' " cleared my throat, and recited,

PEONY POEM
Divide in fall,
Bloom mid-May,
Live 100 years.

Z. tilted her head to one side and smiled.

I said, "The poem is complex, but also so simple. It reminds me of Emily Dickinson. Professor Z., do you like Emily Dickinson?"

"Do I like Dickinson? Why do you ask?"

I said, "Do you think all young girls love Emily Dickinson? Actually, I've just written a poem about Emily Dickinson."

Z. said, "Lovely . . . Do all girls love Emily Dickinson? We could write a book around that question."

I said, "How can a woman poet not feel a deep affinity for Emily Dickinson?" But I was thinking, How can a woman poet not be curious to read her apprentice's poem about Emily Dickinson?

Z. said, "Well, Dickinson is hard to master . . . and she was a bit of a weirdo . . . those long white dresses, shutting herself in that sterile room . . . I don't know how she did it. There are days when I can't bear my office for two seconds—"

I said, "And yet it is a sacred space."

"My shrine," Z. said.

"Sometimes, reading Dickinson, I'm reminded of your poems. Emily wrote a lot about the natural world. She was a gardener."

"A gardener of the imagination perhaps—"

"You know, bees, flies, birds . . . hope being a thing with feathers."

Z. said, "I'll tell you a secret, Annabelle, and this is strictly between us: I don't know as much about Emily Dickinson as I might. She was out of fashion when I was at Vassar, and I've never really spent time getting to know her."

"You wouldn't regret it," I said.

Z. said, "Those short, 'feminine,' singsongy poems. Well, who cared? We were students of the long line, the long poem . . . Tennyson . . ." Her voice trailed off, then she said to the middle distance, "A book that looks at the legacy of Emily Dickinson; women writers being that legacy . . ."

I said, "My own poem uses Emily Dickinson as a mystery, a riddle."

Z. said, "Emily as sphinx! Annabelle, I see a very interesting project here."

I said, "What about a book for the Society called *We Play at Paste*? I always thought that poem was the seminal Dickinson. A poem about the childlike joy of making poems . . . about the poet's relationship to her own creativity."

Z. said, "Let's never use the word *seminal* when discussing poetry, Annabelle. I hear *seminal* and I think *vesicle*."

"You could call the book *Emily Dickinson at One Hundred and Fifty,*" I said. "It could be an anthology, a collection of poems, letters, essays, photos, and interviews looking at her today. A tribute to Emily Dickinson."

Z. said, "A poet's work is solitary, but collaboration is the key to creation."

I got the feeling she was quite pleased with me.

"Annabelle, have you ever interviewed anyone?"

"Maybe once for my high school paper—"

Z. said, "Then this project will be your apprenticeship in journalism. Why don't you work up a list of ten questions to ask our poets about Emily Dickinson? And when you go to the library, take a look at what has been written on her legacy."

I wanted to talk about my own poem. I wanted to recite it. I wanted to ask her how she was going to put a book about Emily Dickinson together if she'd never even read her poems.

Z. said, "When you see Mrs. Van Elder this afternoon, why don't you ask her about Emily Dickinson? Try out a few questions on her. . . . Annabelle, how is Mrs. Van Elder doing these days?"

"She seems to be in good spirits."

"Annabelle, what I am asking is: How is her mind?"

I paused for a moment, then said, "She can write a sharp letter, but she can't seem to find her utensils."

Z. shook her head and said, "The curse of age."

"Professor Z.," I said, "who *is* Mrs. Van Elder?"

Z. said, "Simply put, she is the woman who wrote the review that launched my career. One day, you may know that pleasure—"

I was dying to read Z. my Emily Dickinson poem.

"And then the world of letters seemed to open up for me. She arranged a reading for me at the Royal Botanic Gardens in London . . . and there I came to know the deep, rich smell of flowers. After everyone had left, I sat with my notebook, and like a painter, I began to sketch the world around me—"

"Your apprenticeship in the garden," I said.

"Yes," Z. said. "And it was there I wrote *A Field of Flowers*."

I said, "I actually know 'A Field of Flowers' by heart."

Z. was smiling. "Annabelle," she said. "You flatter me."

"And 'The Wind Sings to the Field of Flowers,' I can recite that one, too."

Z. shook her head. Then she said, "Now, about Mrs. Van Elder . . . I would visit her myself, but I'm terribly allergic to cats. I get asthma just thinking about it."

"Well, I typed a letter for her, and it was a good one. She said that no writer was worthy of the Hortense Berg Prize. . . . But, on the whole, she does seem to be a little out to lunch."

"Then you wouldn't recommend her as a panelist for the Society's Coffee with the Critics series?"

I shook my head. "It would be risky."

"Well, that's that, then," she said, handing me a list. "She told me she's looking forward to your visit today."

On the way to Mrs. Van Elder's, I picked up:

prescription cat food (10 cans—wide variety, no seafood!)
black carbon paper
Windex
a graham cracker piecrust

It was hard to find a piecrust that wasn't broken. When I finally found the perfect one, I had to work to keep it from banging against the bag of cat food I was carrying. I grabbed the carbon paper off a stack at the stationery store but obviously wasn't paying that much attention, because I discovered on the subway that I had picked up blue rather than black.

Mrs. Van Elder lived in a building on the Upper West Side called the Patriot. The walls of the lobby were a red, white, and blue mosaic of an American flag. The hallway leading to Mrs. Van Elder's apartment was newly carpeted, the walls freshly painted. When Mrs. Van Elder opened her door, you saw brown sheets draped across the furniture, a broken candelabra, and boxes of laundry detergent.

Today she was wearing a pale green housedress. She peered out through the safety lock.

"Come in, Annabelle. Come in, please." She closed the door, locked us back in, then led me to the kitchen.

Mrs. Van Elder had written the review that launched Z.'s career, but who was she really?

She started unpacking the bag.

I heard a few cans hit the floor and start to roll. Then the cat scurried out of the kitchen and dove under the couch.

"Seafood! You brought seafood!"

It was true. I had seen the words *variety* and *seafood* on Z.'s note and had picked up four cans: salmon, tuna, mackerel, and Captain's Delight.

Mrs. Van Elder said, "This is unacceptable."

I picked the cans off the floor and put them back in the bag. Then I took the kettle off the stove, filled it with water, and put it up to boil. I said, "I'm very sorry, Mrs. Van Elder. It was my mistake. I'll exchange them. "

"I told Z. no seafood!" She shook her head in a gesture of disgust, then got down on her hands and knees and whispered, "Ginny. Ginny." Eventually the animal came out from her hiding place.

She was a Siamese cat who had been named Virginia Woolf in what Mrs. Van Elder called her "great moment of presumption."

I said, "So, the great writers are not dead; they live among us as our animals."

She shot me a dirty look. No doubt I had added insult to injury.

Mrs. Van Elder held Virginia Woolf in her lap and petted her. She was a hairy creature with a mean little face. I like Virginia Woolf, but I do not like cats.

Which made me think of Marshall Greene's dog, Thomas Wyatt, and the odd little note Harry Banks had left that morning in my mailbox.

Dear Annabelle,

I am a student of creative writing, but I find it hard to write a simple letter. I want to tell you that you are the most interesting person I've met in a long time. I know we've hardly spoken, but I like your take on the world. And you have beautiful eyes. They are deep and piercing and mysterious; sepia. I like how you see, and would like to get to know you better. I'm wild at heart and I think you are, too. I would like to write you shameless letters, the kind that Joyce wrote to his beloved, Nora. (He said he wanted to see the brown stain that came on her girlish white drawers! I'd like to see yours!) Will you be my Nora Joyce? Can you write me a letter (or poem) madder and dirtier than this one?

                                                        Harry

"Mrs. Van Elder," I said, "what do you think of Emily Dickinson?" She was stroking the cat lightly with her fingertips. "Too many poems."

I said, "Well, her business was circumference," but the allusion was lost on her. Perhaps Mrs. Van Elder, like Z., had never read Dickinson. Then I looked up at the bookcase, and suddenly noticed that her books were organized by color. In the pink row was *Forms of Intercourse and Address*. I looked away.

"Do you like James Joyce?"

Mrs. Van Elder sighed. She nodded at the well-worn copy of Yeats on the end table, and I leaned over to retrieve it. At the same moment, the teakettle shrieked and Virginia Woolf leapt out of Mrs. Van Elder's arms, ripping the sleeve of her cotton housedress. Then Mrs. Van Elder was yelling, "Didn't I tell you when you last visited, never let the teakettle shriek?"

I jumped up and ran to the kitchen to turn off the flame. I was saying, "I don't know how that happened. I'm so sorry. And, here, let me help you." As the blood drained out of her face, I offered her aspirin, peroxide. I offered to whisper "The Circus Animals' Desertion."

"Some ice might take away the sting."

Now Mrs. Van Elder was moaning in pain.

It was a truly terrible moment, for which I could not take responsibility. It was brought on by Virginia Woolf, and made worse by Virginia Woolf, who was in the kitchen howling like a stray cat in heat. A line of blood was beginning to form on Mrs. Van Elder's scaly forearm. Desperate, I said, "Mrs. Van Elder, I have your piecrust, I can make you a pie if you wish."

She shook her head.

"Shall I get you ice?"

"No," she said. "No!"

"I have your carbon paper," I said, and I added, "I hope you don't mind, but it's blue."

"Blue?" she said, startled, and I was sure she meant: *How dare you, you impostor, you shall never . . .*

"Please go," she said.

Walking to the elevator, I heard the symphony of locks and chains and the whining of a far-off cat. I was on a bus heading downtown when I realized that I'd left behind the four cans of prescription cat food I had promised to exchange for Mrs. Van Elder.

Salad Days

The highlight of my fifteenth year was being Sylvia Plath in English class during an oral presentation of *The Bell Jar*. What fun I had doing a decompensating Esther Greenwood to the confused looks of the young men and women I so painfully wanted to impress.

"Daddy, you bastard, I'm through," I said, throwing my index cards on the floor.

It was this behavior that landed me in the Great Neck, Long Island, office of Dr. Helene Sanger.

My father drove me to my first appointment. On the way, he asked if he had done something to make me angry.

It was a Saturday morning, and we arrived early. Dr. Sanger came to the door chewing something. I always thought—and still think—that she was chewing a piece of chicken, though I couldn't have known that.

We sat in the waiting room. I heard the rumble of a dryer somewhere—a sound like a big sneaker going up the side of the machine, then falling with a thud. My father found a magazine and settled in comfortably. The walls were covered in brown faux cork wallpaper, and an orange tapestry of the Three Graces hung on one wall.

Dr. Sanger was a stout woman in her late thirties, comfortable in her body. She wore her hair as Farrah Fawcett did, cut at an angle, with the sides curled back, cascading loosely around her face.

I told Dr. Sanger that I wanted to be a poet. I told her that I loved Sylvia Plath.

"Now tell me," Dr. Sanger said, "what comes to mind when you think of Sylvia Plath?"

I told her about the crawl space, the "sticky pearls," the near-rape at the party.

I said, "I think the guy threw mud in her face, but I can't remember." Then I recited, "Dying is an art, like everything else. I do it exceptionally well."

And, of course, Dr. Sanger asked me if I thought about suicide. And then she told me that I wasn't ever to think about suicide.

Then I quoted some more lines from "Lady Lazarus," and Dr. Sanger wondered if I sometimes used poetry as a way of avoiding my feelings.

Did I have a boyfriend? Dr. Sanger asked. Did I think a lot about boys?

I couldn't look at her face, so I looked at her shoe, a big leather clog that she had a habit of dangling so that it always came dangerously close to falling off the edge of her foot.

"I think so," I said.

"What you need to do is go home and masturbate," Dr. Sanger said. Or perhaps I am remembering incorrectly.

That's what I was thinking on the 9:04 into Manhattan the next morning. So many evenings learning to sublimate desire with Dr. Sanger in that Great Neck office, only to find myself attracted to a wild man.

I had played Sylvia Plath in English class, but did I really want to play Nora Joyce? It was one thing to adopt the persona of a famous literary neurotic, quite another to be showing someone your underwear. I had never written a mad and dirty letter, and I didn't want to start writing dirty poems. I had learned from my teacher, Arthur Feld, that the details of daily life might not necessarily be the details you want in your poetry.

I owed Arthur a letter. I took out my notebook and wrote:

Dear Arthur,

How are you? Life at the university is very exciting. Thank you for all your help getting me here. At your suggestion, I have taken life by the reins, and am now working as Z.'s assistant, which is actually an amazing apprenticeship—at school and in her home. Every Wednesday morning I prepare food for her salon. (It sounds like drudgery, but it is actually fun. I've had the opportunity to observe some important writers just standing in her kitchen.) I have written a poem about Emily Dickinson, which I've just submitted for publication. (I'm hoping it gets accepted.) I have included it. Please tell me what you think.

Annabelle

P.S. I would love to meet you for coffee.

MASK OF THE POET
Stripped of meter, who can I be?
The dress, the sandal, the elegant hose,
the basket she lets down with string?
The museum dress stands
by the four-poster bed.
I wore the mask of the poet,
now I am dead.

Reading over my poem, I wondered about the last line (should she be "dead" or "read"?) and was afraid that no one would catch the allusion to *A Masque of Poets,* an 1878 anthology that had published Dickinson's "Success is counted sweetest," without her name. It was the only poem she would ever see published in a book in her lifetime.

These were the salad days of my apprenticeship: I arrived early each morning and stayed well beyond my appointed time. I spent hours painstakingly typing Z.'s letters. She was particular about her correspondence, unable to tolerate even a single typo. For signing, she wanted her letters presented to her in a certain order, and she might return them for "reorganization" if they seemed out of sequence.

This was the sequence:

First Z. signed correspondence related to the publication of her poetry; next regarding invitations to read her work (acceptances only); letters of a personal nature, including bills—I typed out checks for her to sign—came next. Then came letters related to her academic life at the university and rejection letters of all sorts. (Thank you for your kind invitation, but I am sorry to say my reading schedule is full for the next two years.) And, finally, if you were a student for whom Z. was writing a letter of recommendation, you would be at the end of the signing queue. This was because Z. needed to read these letters closely, I told myself, but actually, she read everything closely. She even saw the shadows left by correction tape.

Z. signed all letters in jet-black ink with a gold-nibbed Mont Blanc fountain pen. When it came to nibs, there was no comparison between fourteen karat and the other metals, Z. had told me.

Through trial and error (and practice in my spare time), I learned how to convert Z.'s handwritten draft into a perfectly centered and left-justified document, so that each letter I typed was a miniature work of art.

Once, during the ritual letter signing, Z. said, "The text of this letter seems to float like a lily pad on the clear lake of my stationery. Your typing is beautiful, Annabelle."

In those early weeks, it was my goal to organize the overstuffed file cabinet in my office. (Could a recalcitrant former assistant—sorely lacking in discipline and character—have just shoved all those papers in there?) Going through the stack of documents, I wondered about her fate. She left behind discarded envelopes, check stubs, and a stack of reviews where Z.'s name was circled in red. I would distinguish myself from her by being more than the poet's file clerk. After all, I was the poet's apprentice. I would create a filing system so methodical and precise that even Z. would be able to use it. When I was done, I brought her into my office.

Z. said, running a finger across the color-coded files, "Annabelle, you really are quite enterprising!"

I said, "And look at this." I took a three-ring binder off the shelf. Inside the notebook was every letter I had sent out for Z. since I had started as her personal assistant.

"This is your Chrono File," I said. "Every letter you've signed filed chronologically, by date."

She shook her head. "Brilliant," she said. "You are an organizational wonder."

It was on one of those afternoons that Z. came out of her study absentmindedly flapping a sheaf of papers.

"Annabelle," she said. "Brainstorm with me, if you would."

I was sitting cross-legged on the living room floor, alphabetizing the books on Z.'s bottom shelf. I put down my feather duster.

Only months ago the Flower Poet Z. was an iconic voice in my head. Now she was a flesh-and-blood woman who was seeking my advice.

I imagined a day in the future, holding a book with this inscription:

FOR ANNABELLE, MY APPRENTICE IN LIFE AND ART —

MAY YOU FLOWER

Z.

I turned from the shelf and rubbed my dusty hands together. Then I stood, ready to take part in literary history.

"I'm drafting an address to the Society on the state of American poetry. I'm trying to praise them for striving to incorporate the voices of women and minorities into their agenda, but it all sounds so . . . limp."

She began tearing the papers in her hand into ribbons.

All of Z.'s behavior seemed noteworthy.

"The essay is a form I have never mastered," Z. said.

"Then think of it as a prose poem instead."

"A prose poem?"

I thought I heard a trace of indignation in her voice.

"Annabelle, remember I'm a purist. It's either prose or it's poetry. One or the other. I don't take coffee in my tea."

I said, "Maybe in your address you could talk about how poetry has become integrated into the fabric of our culture. There's a new movement called the Spoken Word, and you can actually go to a café where everybody is talking poetry."

"Annabelle, there's nothing new about 'talking poetry.' It's simply a return to the oral tradition, which is the source of all poetry as it exists today. The idea of poetry for the populace might sound good in theory, but do we really want poetry written by the illiterate?"

"You know," I said, "every day I ask myself one question."

"Tell me."

"What is poetry?"

"What is poetry?"

"Well, yes. I know what it is, sort of. But does anyone know *precisely* what it is?"

Z. said, "Tell me, 'what is poetry' as you know it?"

"Well, these days I think of it as *fire* and *air,* as passionate words soaring high into the atmosphere."

Z. opened the desk drawer and took out a legal pad.

"Every once in a while, a poet must remind herself what it is she loves about poetry."

"Yes," I said. "I love its redemptive power. The concept of the garden in your poems can be very life-affirming."

Her poems had given me hope at a time when I had no friend but my therapist and my future looked bleak.

With her pad, taking notes, Z. seemed a vision of the early Dr. Sanger.

"Do you believe that poetry can save the world, Annabelle?"

I had to think quickly.

"Yes," I said.

Z. said, "I want to believe this too. But I see a future where poetry is lost to bad writing. Where bad writing has become the status quo and beauty has fallen by the wayside."

"As civilization advances, poetry declines," I said. "I learned this in my lit class this week."

Z. said, "But it's such a bleak vision to present to the Society."

She started pacing.

"Maybe the speech is about how we must resist change. How poetry should stay the way it is, under the bell jar; out of reach to those who would poison it—"

Z. said, "If only there was a way to say that without offending anyone."

She handed me the legal pad. "Annabelle, write this down. Let's call this version 'Keeping Poetry Alive in the Age of Ugliness.' Though I'm not sure about the word *ugliness*. It may be a little too obvious. Put a check mark above it, and a question mark in the margin."

Then Z. dictated:

Poetry is in crisis. We are living in an era of the common word, an age of coarse vernacular, a time when poetry is written by everyone and no one, a poetry created without inspiration, without imagination . . . a tone-deaf poetry which marches to the beat of a drummer who has no musical training. . . . What is poetry? we ask, and the answer is everything and nothing.

She spoke fast and I wrote quickly, not wanting to let one precious word slip by. What is poetry? Z. had asked, turning my words into a question of her own hand and vernacular, so that I was now a part of a discourse on poetry. She had paid me tribute; I felt honored.

A Fiction of the Self

Z. was Braun Brown's favorite living poet. Her favorite dead poet was Robert Frost. For our first creative writing workshop, she asked us to learn a Robert Frost poem by heart and recite it. I memorized "The Oven Bird."

" 'There is a singer everyone has heard— Loud, a mid-summer and a mid-wood bird . . . ,' " I began, then lost my way, quickly forgetting the poem I had memorized on my daily train ride to and from New York City.

Nearly everyone else recited "The Road Not Taken" except for a scrappy-faced boy named Ben. Ben recited "To Earthward," a poem that began

> *Love at the lip was touch*
> *As sweet as I could bear . . .*

Braun's class was entrée into the university's exclusive Graduate Creative Writing Program. Every year, hundreds of poets applied; only ten were accepted.

Z. had gone out of her way to get me into this class, and I wanted her to know how much the chance to study with Braun meant to me.

The morning before our first meeting, I popped my head into Z.'s office. She was sitting at her desk, a stack of papers spread out before her.

I said, "Today is my first poetry workshop, and I just want to thank you again, Professor Z., for getting me admitted. I had no idea such a thing would be possible."

Z. said, "It's fine, Annabelle. I just thought it important for you to see firsthand how *not* to study poetry."

Z.'s view having been plainly stated, I approached Braun Brown's class with a sense of caution and reserve. Mainly, I was afraid of liking her too much.

I got there early and watched the students arrive, each carrying a cup of coffee or a soda. Then Braun arrived in a black leather miniskirt holding a potted plant.

The plant was a gift from a friend, she said, who wanted to wish her well on her first day of class. Braun told us that this was her first workshop in New York City.

During recitation, Braun listened with rapt delight. After it was over, she said, "I have asked you to memorize Robert Frost because I think that Frost is the quintessential American poet, and also—he's easy to memorize. Learning Frost by heart *is* having American poetry in your heart. The heart is the heart and soul of poetry."

Then we went around the room and introduced ourselves.

There was Meg Cross, the editor of a magazine, who loved Braun Brown's work.

Meg was a pale woman, older than the other students, though I couldn't say how much older. Something in her face—a frown line or a wrinkle—gave her an appearance of permanent distress.

There was Benjamin Adams, who had not recited "The Road Not Taken." He was also the editor of a magazine: a downtown, self-published periodical, he explained. He had long, unruly hair, and he smiled a lot. He was the only man in the class.

There was Penny Jones, a self-proclaimed minimalist who was interested in perfecting the two-word line. She was small with black hair and red glasses.

When it was my turn, I said I was a junior who had been given permission to audit this workshop.

Braun said, "And, as I understand, you have a very special job at the university. . . . Annabelle is the assistant to Professor Z."

Now people were really looking at me. I thought that Ben smiled at me in a compassionate way. But there were other looks: looks that acknowledged the reflected glory, looks that took you in and dismissed you, looks that questioned your right to be there, dirty looks.

"Let's start with a poem," Braun said. "Does anyone have a poem for our first meeting?"

Meg Cross said that she did. Meg Cross had made copies for everyone.

This is what she read:

CROSS
On mountainsides, in graveyards
The grave family symbol I've come to know and love.
Mexican crosses, Celtic crosses—
The crosses in churches are religious.
The patriarchal cross has two lines.
The papal cross has three.
When my father comes to the table
He is bejeweled in the anger of the Cross family.
When I close my eyes, I see Jesus.

The intersection of arrogance and betrayal
Drove nails into the crucifix.
I make a cruciform sign to invoke the blessing.
I touch my forehead, breasts, and shoulders
In the way a lover might transverse
The body to bless the erogenous zones.

Christ brought me to my name.
And love brings me back to the cross
And to my father. My father
Was a fighter who threw a boxer's cross.

You can uncross a cross,
But you cannot criss a cross
or Christ.

Meg's reading was emotional and direct. She enunciated every syllable in every word so that the whole poem galloped to its illogical conclusion. She read like a television journalist at the scene of a fire, reporting a few dull facts with a sense of emergency. You had to keep reminding yourself that this was only a poem about crosses, not a fire. Then Braun said she would like to hear it again. Could one of us read it? And Ben read it quickly, which hardly gave us enough time to appreciate the richness of Meg's language, Braun said. Ben seemed embarrassed. Then Braun read Meg's poem as Braun said she thought it should be read, speaking the word *cross* each time in a whisper.

Braun had a rich, full-bodied voice. I remembered that she, too, was reading at the Society for the Preservation of American Poetry, and I thought of Z. and Braun as a study in contrast. Z.'s voice had an edge, an urgency, an intensity. Braun, on the other hand, sounded like someone you would want holding your hand, counting backward with you from twenty-five, as you waited for the anesthesia to take effect.

And Z. was always tastefully dressed. When you looked at Z., you saw the woman; but when you looked at Braun, you saw the dress. That day, under her very conservative black suit jacket, Braun wore a black bra, nothing else. You could see the bra when she leaned forward.

It was said that Z. was gentle in the classroom but a tyrant in her private tutorials. There she would seize on a terrible piece of writing and explain, with brutal honesty, why it should never have been written.

Studying with Z., you either became a better writer or you gave up writing completely.

But a student had nothing to fear from Braun Brown. At that first meeting, she told us that every poem was a gift and it was her job (and ours) to be its "good parent," to love it completely, flaws and all.

After Braun read Meg's poem, there was silence. Lots of it.

"So, let's talk about this poem," Braun said.

Penny Jones said that she admired Meg's ability to write long lines, the expansiveness of Meg's vernacular. How she wished she could write a longer line! Perhaps Meg would like to meet her some evening for coffee.

Then Ben said, "I like all the *c* sounds. They all sound good together."

Braun said, "Yes, there is powerful repetition and alliteration at work here. Give us some examples, Ben."

"Well, *crosses, churches, crucifix.* And I like when she talks about her father. Was your father really a boxer, Meg?"

Meg said nothing. Braun said, "Let's talk about Ben's question. I think it helps us see that we need some ground rules for discussing poetry. So let's talk about how to talk about a poem."

I opened my notebook.

"The speaker in the poem is an imaginary person who speaks the words of the poem. Are we in agreement on this?"

Yes, we were.

"It is a mistake to assume that the speaker is the poet himself. The speaker is often different from the poet. The speaker in Meg's poem has a personality, but we cannot assume that it is Meg's personality."

Because Meg has no personality, I thought.

"Never assume that any poem is the lived experience of the author. Intimate, introspective verse is not necessarily 'confessional' *or* the true-life experience of the author. Do we understand?"

I wrote in my notebook:

WHAT IS POETRY?

Ben said, "I'm sorry. I just thought because she was writing about her father and her grandfather that it was true. If it were my poem, I would make it true."

Braun said, "As I understand it, the reader should never assume that a poem is true. We approach each poem as a fiction of the self."

There were confused looks.

"So when we discuss a poem we never say, 'It's about your father.' We say, 'It's about the speaker's father.' "

I said, "Yes, but what about the reader? Won't the reader assume that it's about your father?"

Braun said, "Annabelle, a good point. . . . The reader can assume whatever she wants. But I do think the question of the reader is an outdated construct—especially in these postconfessional times."

Discussing Meg's poem, we came to these conclusions: It was good; it was inventive. Things people liked: graveyards, cruciform, erogenous zones. We questioned the repetition of the word *crosses*. Were there too many? Had Meg earned her metaphor? "And didn't *x* also equal *cross?*" somebody asked. Braun said that "Cross" was a wonderful poem about the birth of the poet and could be the first poem in a book someday.

Then Meg Cross told us that indeed it was the first poem in her book, *Double Crossed,* soon to be issued by the Apple Tree Press.

Then I said, "Well, I like it very much, but I think the line 'The crosses in churches are religious' is redundant."

Braun said, "How do you mean?"

I said, "Redundant because, obviously, when we think of a cross in a church our association is religious." Then, because there was silence and people were listening, I added, "I thought the introduction of the father in the seventh line was a weak moment, but I loved the phrase 'bejeweled in the anger of the Cross family.' Perhaps the poem is complete this way," and I read from my own copy where I had crossed out lines, drawn arrows, and circled words.

CROSS

~~On mountainsides, in graveyards~~
The grave family symbol, I've come to know and love.
Mexican crosses, Celtic crosses--
The crosses in churches are religious.
The patriarchal cross has two lines.
The papal cross has three.
~~When my father comes to the table~~
~~He is~~ bejeweled in the anger of the Cross family.
~~When I close my eyes, I see Jesus.~~

→ The intersection of arrogance and betrayal
Drove nails into the crucifix.
I make a cruciform sign to invoke the blessing, *and invoke*
~~I touch my forehead, breasts, and shoulders~~
~~In the way a lover might transverse~~
~~The body to bless the erogenous zones.~~

~~Christ brought me to my name.~~
~~And love brings me back to the cross~~
~~And to my father.~~ My father,
~~Was a fighter who threw~~ a boxer's ~~cross.~~

~~You can uncross a cross,~~
~~But you cannot criss a cross~~
~~or Christ.~~

                                        --Meg Cross

This is what I read:

CROSS
The intersection of arrogance and betrayal
drove nails into the crucifix.
I make a cruciform sign to invoke the blessing,
and invoke my father,
a boxer,
bejeweled in the anger of the Cross family.

My heart was beating as I read, and just as I was finishing, I saw Braun sit up tall in her seat. She was looking over at Meg, who was staring off into the distance, looking very cross.

Paste

═══

Probably it was wrong to have rewritten Meg's poem after she let us know that it was the first poem in her new book, *Double Crossed*. That's what I was thinking as I sat in Z.'s office at the university, sewing a gold button on her navy blue blazer.

One of the buttons had come off.

I loved Z.'s jacket. I loved the sound the buttons made when she moved. They banged against each other in a cacophony of jangling.

Z. was at her desk. Behind her was the Washington Square Arch, the great symbol of Greenwich Village. It connected you with all the poets and writers who passed through lower Manhattan: Walt Whitman, Henry James, Edith Wharton, Hart Crane, and Edgar Allan Poe, my patron saint.

I was sewing while the important people in the English Department walked past her office. I had one button to go.

Z. had said, "Annabelle, maybe you should reinforce all of them while you're at it."

I didn't want Maurita Collins to see me sewing on Z.'s buttons. I liked to think that in the departmental hierarchy, I was a little higher than the department secretary, though she was the executor of the Marshall Greene estate.

In truth, even if I had been recruited by the university for reasons of academic record and promise, I could never compete with Maurita Collins, who held a master's degree in higher education administration. To the faculty of the English Department, Maurita's degree meant a daily deliverance from the worldly matters of filing a petty cash form or ordering your own office supplies.

Maurita had a very dated look; long black hair held in place with a big leather barrette. Part of Maurita's job was to supervise students who worked in the department. She was the one who matched fellowship students to faculty members. So I had Maurita to thank for my assistantship with Z., and Harry had her to thank for his life sentence at the Xerox machine.

As I was sewing the buttons, my mind went to Harry Banks. The courtship which began on line at the copy machine was heating up, and I still didn't know how I felt about him. That morning I had found this note in my mailbox:

> To Annabelle,
>   Won't you be Nora to my James?
>   Harry

At 2:00 P.M., after Braun's class ended, I made a mad dash for Z.'s office. I didn't want to run into Harry Banks until I was sure of my answer.

Z. was in conference with a graduate student.

"Come in, Annabelle. Sit down," she said. "Annabelle, this is my doctoral student, Jane Fisher."

Jane nodded.

Z. pointed to a chair in the back of the room. There was a suit jacket draped across it, and when I went to remove it, Z. said, "Annabelle, there's a sewing kit in the pocket. Would you mind sewing on a button for me?"

"No problem," I said. "I'm a very skilled seamstress."

Jane smiled. She was wearing a business suit with flat black buttons, and I wondered if she had taken off from a full-time job for this conference with Z. I wondered if she was the assistant to a CEO at a very large company and knew the indignity of being asked to sew on a button.

Z. said, "Jane, really, it is a fine poem, and yet it seems—apt."

"Apt?"

"Yes, apt. A poem ladled out of the great soup bowl of poetry that feeds our quarterlies."

"Jane, you are a gifted poet; a woman writing in the tradition of Marvell, of Keats. But neither one of them could ever be called apt."

Jane looked over at me, and I smiled. Instead of smiling back, she picked up her chair and moved it closer to Z.'s desk.

"Engage your passion," Z. said. She shuffled some papers on her desk, then read, "Wind sock on the cottage calling the sailors home— come home blue and white sailors . . ."

Then Z. said, " 'Come home blue and white sailors.' Who in the world speaks like that?"

"Well," Jane said, "I was writing from the point of view of a woman whose fiancé is at sea."

"Well," Z. said. "Try writing like a whore who is pining for her john."

What followed was nervous laughter, but who can say?

Z. said, with the slightest edge of sarcasm in her voice, "Come home, Johnny. Come home."

"Yes," Jane said, "I see what you mean. But I *wanted* to use the word *sailor*."

"Well, I could see why the word *sailor* would be important here. But think about this poor woman—she's worrying; she's pining; she's obsessed with this man. There's danger at sea. Will he come back alive? Right now—and I don't mean to insult you—it's limp. It reads like a poem sung to a wind sock. And what about *wind sock*? Is that really what you mean? Frankly, Jane, I hear *wind sock* and I think laundry flapping in the breeze. I don't hear a loud sound calling anybody home. If I were you, I'd toss the whole thing to the wind and start again."

There was silence, then Z., leaning forward on her desk, said: "Jane, is poetry your vocation or your avocation?

"Have you given your heart and soul to poetry—the way the speaker gives herself to the sailor, the whore to her john?"

The silence that follows certain rhetorical questions.

"Jane? Annabelle?"

"Yes," I said, looking up from my sewing. "I have given myself to poetry the way a prostitute gives herself to sex."

"Well," Z. said, "that's a metaphor you'll need to work on, Annabelle."

Jane was looking at me, and then she turned again to her teacher.

She said, "I don't know if I can live as a poet in the world. . . . I mean . . . I want . . ." And here she fell silent. ". . . things. I want *things*."

"What kinds of things?" Z. asked.

Jane said, "I like earrings."

And here I took in Jane's earrings: two stars surrounded by tiny pearls and diamonds.

Z. said, "How interesting, Jane," and started to organize the papers on her desk. "Then don't write like a sailor's wife. Write like a madam who loves garish jewelry. . . . And don't be afraid to show me another revision."

Z. handed Jane her poem, and Jane leaned over and picked up her shoulder bag. There was a feeling of expectation in the air. Jane should have been getting up to leave, but she didn't.

She looked over at me. I got the feeling that if I were not in the room she might spill her heart and try to explain what made her poetry "apt."

Then Z. said, "Something occurs to me. You like antique jewelry. What do you know about paste?"

"Oh, paste, yes, I know about paste."

"Annabelle," Z. said. "Please, take notes."

I set aside the jacket and my needle and took out my pen.

Jane said, "*Paste* was a term used to describe fake diamonds—often used in accompaniment with other jewels in Victorian settings."

"Like rhinestones?"

"No, something completely different."

I wrote in my notebook:

NOT LIKE RHINESTONES.

"What about that poem by Dickinson?" Z. said. "Annabelle, recite for Jane that paste line."

I said, "We play at paste— Till qualified, for Pearl."

"Yes," Z. said. "Jane, do you know that one?"

Jane nodded yes.

"Would you say that in that poem Dickinson is talking about jewelry?"

Jane sat upright in her chair. "Yes, yes, it could be."

"And what kind of jewelry would Emily Dickinson have worn? Have you ever thought about that?"

"I think she scorns paste in that poem, though I could be wrong," Jane said.

"Yes," Z. said. "I think she scorns costume jewelry."

I said, "In many poems we find Dickinson casting off her jewels, as if to cast off her femininity." But nobody responded.

"Jane," Z. said, "I'm embarking on a writing project about Emily Dickinson. Why don't you try writing me a paper? In my experience, grand ambition is what every writer needs to get her juices flowing. Let my anthology be your grand ambition."

"But what would I write about?"

"Paste. Give Dickinson's poem some cultural context. Let us know the style of jewelry worn in her day. Did other members of the Dickinson household wear jewelry? You might need to take a trip to that museum in Amherst. Perhaps you could use that phrase, 'we play at paste,' as a metaphor for the creative artist, a way of describing what poets do."

This was my metaphor. She had chosen me as her apprentice because I was intelligent and well read.

Z. said, "Jane, do you think you could undertake such a research project?"

Jane said, "I think, Professor Z., it would be a lot of work, but quite interesting work."

"And it might help you with your own poems, to get a clearer sense of how a poem works—words making friction against other words—the world of meaning . . ."

Then Z. said, "Annabelle here knows a lot about Dickinson. You may call on her for her assistance, anytime. Isn't that right, Annabelle?"

Leaning against the door after Jane leaves, Z. says, "God, this is work."

I say, "You seem tired."

"A little . . . Now, what can I do for you, Annabelle?"

"I've come for the shopping list."

"I haven't had a minute to think, let alone compose a list . . . I've been so busy." Z. takes a breath. "Do you think you could come in early tomorrow and shop?"

"I guess I could come in early," I say with the needle in my mouth. I'm holding the thread between my fingers, just about to finish sewing on the last button.

I hand the jacket back to Z. and say, "I learned to sew in eighth-grade home economics."

"I can't stand these buttons, making noise every time I move," Z. says.

"Cats learn to outwalk their bells," I say.

Z. looks at me squarely. "Annabelle, how would you feel about going to a notions store and finding me different buttons? I'm not sure I can live with the constant jangling."

"That's fine," I say. The truth is that if I had any feelings about it, I would never reveal them to Z. I am, after all, the guardian of her psychic space.

Then, apropos of nothing, she says, "Annabelle, there aren't many famous poets named Jane, are there?"

"I can't think of one," I say.

"Why don't you go to the library this afternoon and research the Janes of poetry. I'd like to see some names before I go home."

His Mistress

In the history of poetry, there are many Anns, Marys, and Elizabeths. In the seventeenth and eighteenth centuries, there were also famous Janes.

There was the witty Jane Brereton, writing under her nom de guerre, Melissa, for the *Gentleman's Magazine*:

I scorn this mean fallacious art
By which you'd steal, not win, my heart . . .

There was Lady Jane Cavendish, writing poems with her sister Lady Elizabeth Brackley:

You owne yourselfe to bee a wife
And yet you practice not that life.

There was Jane Barker, author of "A Virgin Life," and "Fidelia arguing with her self on the difficulty of finding her true Religion."

"I find the fact that she uses the persona Fidelia quite compelling," I tell Z.

"Yes," Z. says. "Melissa, Fidelia—Jane trying to be more than just Jane. Such a hideous name, Fidelia."

"And finally, there is Miss Jane Elliot, author of 'A Lament for Flodden.' "

I take out a piece of paper and read:

I've heard them lilting at our ewe-milking,
Lasses a'lilting before the dawn o' day;
But now they are moaning on ilka green loaning—
The Flowers of the Forest are a wede away.

Z. repeats, " 'A weed away.' I like that."

I say, "Do you think it's harder to endure as a poet if you have a common name like Jane?"

Z. tilts her head to one side, a gesture that seems to say she is thinking.

"No, Annabelle, not at all. It's easier; it's been done before."

"Though there's a kind of music to an uncommon name—like Maurita or Braun . . ."

Z. says, "It's such a strange, unsettling world. Who is Braun Brown and where did she come from? Who launched this literary debut of hers?"

"Her publisher?"

"No," Z. says. "Publishers don't put poets on the cover of *Vogue*. . . . And the idea of glorifying infidelity—"

She shakes her head.

"If I wrote a book called *His Mistress,* the world would call me backward. . . . So tell me, Annabelle, why is this book so popular?"

"Because Braun is popular?"

"And why is a signed copy of this book in the window of every bookstore in Manhattan? Tell me."

"Because Braun went into each store and signed them?"

Z. says, "Someone is marketing Braun Brown. That's it. She must have hired a publicist."

She crosses her arms. "That's what this is about: commerce."

I am thinking of Braun reciting Frost in the dingy, windowless seminar room. Why would anyone with an interest in making money choose to eke out her afternoons in such a depressing place?

"I struggled day after day to learn my craft. I worked at it sleep-deprived, while I walked the streets of New York, pushing a baby carriage. I sent poem after poem to one indifferent editor after another. I faced my rejections head-on. . . . I climbed my own ladder," Z. says.

Maybe you should have hired a publicist, I want to say, but think better of it. The art of being with Z. is knowing when to say nothing.

"Annabelle, recite for me those lines from Dylan Thomas's 'In My Craft or Sullen Art.' Remind me why we write poetry."

I tell Z. I don't know that poem. But I promise to look it up when I get home and commit it to memory. Then I ask her if there are any other poems she thinks I should memorize.

Scanning her shelves, Z. says, "The poet says something like this: I don't write for ambition or money, not for fame or the great white way, but for the lovers asleep in their beds, holding each other and the grief of the ages."

I think of Spence.

Then I say, clearing my throat: "I wrote a poem about Emily Dickinson because I love Emily Dickinson."

Z. says, "Then you understand the thrust of the poet's declaration."

"Yes," and then, quite nervously, I add, "I sent it to a magazine, and just yesterday it came back with a rejection note. . . . When you were starting out, did you just send your poems out anywhere?"

Z. says, "I went to libraries and bookshops and found the magazines that my poems might be suitable for."

"How long was it before you got published?"

"I was very methodical. I sent my poems out all the time."

I want to show Z. my poem. I want to recite it. I say, "I wonder if you have any ideas about where I might send my poems."

Z. says, "This is my current thinking: Delay publication, Annabelle."

She must see I am crestfallen, because she adds this caveat: "Annabelle, we write poetry as an act of love. As the poet says, we do not write it for fame or publication. It's a gift to the lovers, to our fellow man."

"I just thought they might eventually want to read it in a magazine," I say.

"Annabelle," Z. says. "You must master your grandiosity. Accept the fact that it's too soon for you to be published, and this will make your life much easier. No hopes, no expectation, and you are free to write great poetry."

I say I understand. Clearly, Z. isn't going to help me. Or maybe this *is* help: She is challenging me to write better, to be the best I can be before I publish, to climb my own ladder.

It is something that I'm also learning at home. My mother has decided that since I'm now employed, I should give her money for room and board. My father has decided that since I'm of college age, I should pay for my own therapy. Though my parents are no longer on speaking terms, they've somehow managed to reach the same conclusion: that I am my own responsibility. From this, I'm expected to learn a great lesson: how precious are the things I achieve on my own.

So far I'm learning how precious money is when you don't have it. I've worked out a payment schedule with Dr. Sanger that should keep me in debt until the millennium.

Then I'm taking down the shopping list:

Celery
Olives
Carrots
French Onion Dip Mix or Sour Cream and Onion Soup
Eggs, spinach, small muffin tins (for miniature quiches)
Chablis, Vodka (call Sutton Wines and Spirits for delivery)

These items are for Z.'s salon, which will occur tomorrow afternoon, which I'll be preparing for tomorrow morning. But while I'm writing down the list, I feel distracted by Jane, Meg, and the Elizabeths.

I start to wonder: *What if Emily Dickinson wrote like a whore?*

Then Z. calls me back to the world: "Annabelle, do you enjoy shopping for men?"

"Yes," I say. "I have once or twice, in a record store."

She laughs. "No, I mean in a fine department store. . . . I love the Men's Department. I love to let my hands, my cheek, brush against the silks, the ties. . . . Annabelle, I have a very important assignment for you."

I sit up straight in my chair.

"Tomorrow during the three hours my salon is in progress, I will need you to shop for a a friend's birthday gift. I need a black turtleneck and a pair of boxer shorts. His size is somewhere between medium and large. I need it for the weekend."

Z. opens her wallet. "It's for someone very dear, so I want to be generous. If you can't decide what boxers to buy, bring back more than one selection. . . . Try to be tasteful."

"Tasteful?"

"Yes. Silk boxers, a tasteful pattern, and a cashmere turtleneck. And please, don't forget to pick up hand towels. As I'm sure you've noticed, we're running out."

So it sounds like I won't be staying for Z.'s salon tomorrow afternoon. In fact, each week since I've worked for her, I've been sent off on some kind of mission the minute the drinks were poured.

Salonnarde

At home, I sat in the pink room at the top of the stairs and tried to write poetry. It was a quiet time. I would have to accept the fact that this might not be the year of my startling debut.

Which was fine with me, because it was harder and harder to figure out what I wanted to write about.

I turned to my book collection for inspiration. But the only writer on the shelf who inspired me besides Emily Dickinson was Z. I pulled out an old copy of *Poet & Poem*. That was Z.'s issue: She was the subject of a special center section, six poems and an interview. I'd read it a million times before, but that night I picked it up to see if I might learn something new. More and more our conversations strayed from the subject of poetry, but here, on my bookshelf, Z. was always available.

ON BUDDING SEXUALITY: A LOOK INSIDE Z.'S MIGHTY FLOWER

O, MIGHTY FLOWER
Dolorous, the flower head
bobbing in the garden.

The weight of the single blossom,
inflorescent in design.

We cultivate, we sublimate.
The flower bud produces only a flower.
The stigma sways.

O teeth, o tongue, o touch,
bend down and lift the head
of the almighty flower.

Lift your dress, your skirt—

O, mighty flower!
You are the mouth, the lips, the song,
singing in the eternal garden.

This is an excerpt from the interview that followed:

INTERVIEWER: Let's talk about "O, Mighty Flowers." I'm especially interested in the word *dolorous,* which opens the poem.
An important moment, because the reader expects a poem
about mourning but, instead, gets a poem about longing.

z.: I've always thought *dolorous* was a little hole in that poem.

INTERVIEWER: Hole?

z.: I yearn for each poem to be whole and perfect. . . . The word
dolorous strikes me as conveying the right sound, but it does
not convey my exact meaning, my desire for a very particular
meaning.

INTERVIEWER: What is the desire of poetry?

z.: Poetry's desire, hmm. . . . As a poet, I know what I want in
a poem. I know what I want as a reader. . . . But a *poem's* desire . . . ?

INTERVIEWER: Getting back to those flowers. I remember a
poem called "Wild Ginger," in which the reader is invited to

dance with a flower. In "Astilbes," the reader actually lies down in the garden and fondles the flower in her hand. Or is it *his* hand? I must tell you, honestly, sometimes I can't tell who is doing what to whom. What do we make of this moment in your poem "Flower Power"?

> *The she-flower touches her.*
> *She touches the she-flower,*
> *as once I touched the maiden pink.*

z.: I was hoping to convey a sense of eroticism, the loveliness of touching flowers in the garden. But if poetry is an indictment, well, then, indict me.

It was such a bold statement, one that filled me with a sense of excitement about my own future. Indict me! I thought, going back to Z.'s apartment the next morning with my bag of groceries.

But indict me for what?

For a life not yet lived?

I wanted to be like Z. I wanted to fall deeply and passionately in love. I wanted to have an affair that would change my life, one that would inspire me to plumb the depths of my soul. I wanted to have emotions so strong that no metaphor could contain them.

The night before, I had found yet another note in my mailbox:

To Annabelle—

Make up your body for me. Come to me in beauty and happiness and desire. Be loving and provocative and full of cravings when we meet. . . . When I look at your body, I think musical, strange, and perfumed. Will you be my Nora Joyce?

Harry

My own body "musical, strange, and perfumed"? It was hard to imagine. And it was hard to imagine anyone wanting me so much. (I am petite, waiflike, not feminine in the conventional sense of the word.) I was reveling in the idea of being desired, warming to the idea of Harry Banks desiring me, when I stepped inside Z.'s apartment and found this note on her counter:

Annabelle,
    I will return shortly before salon.
    PLEASE have food ready . . .
    Check that wineglasses don't have spots;
    Wipe silver with cotton cloth—
    Tidy living room—vacuum, dust—
    Use tablecloth with blue cross-stitch flowers;
    Matching napkins in linen closet.
    IRON with starch. Careful!
    Remember to put out hand towels!
    Family returning this evening—
    Please arrive before end of salon,
    quickly put apartment back in order.
    Re: *Emily Dickinson at 150*—
    Your list of questions!
    Add Meg Cross to list of poets to be interviewed.

And then, as Virginia Woolf had written, "the shackles of the day were upon me."

I read Z.'s note over a few times, deciding finally that what was written between the lines was some deep-rooted anxiety: a family returning.

But, in truth, we *were* running low on hand towels, so I had put only a few out. Then, carefully ironing the beautiful cross-stitch napkins in my tiny office with its sooty white-brick view, I thought about the soon-to-be-published Meg Cross and how—with this inclusion in Z.'s anthology—she would immediately be lifted into the world of Dickinson scholars and renown, and I couldn't even publish my poem about Dickinson.

I saw myself standing in Z.'s living room in the dusky glow of the

East River, in a black dress and white apron, holding out a glass of champagne to Meg Cross on the occasion of the publication of *Emily Dickinson at One Hundred and Fifty*.

No, I thought, I would never let that happen.

Clearly, Z. wasn't going to invite me to write an essay for her book, but perhaps she would at least publish my poem about Dickinson?

And then I cheered up. I would throw myself into the Emily Dickinson project. I would make myself so invaluable that Z. would be only too happy to publish me. I would proudly show her my poem.

Z. arrived just minutes before the other poets. She brought roses and put them out in a huge vase on the coffee table.

The poets came off the elevator en masse. They were led by Jason Spence, who immediately found a place on Z.'s green-and-white silk couch. They were a demanding group, four men and a woman, heaping coats on my arms, asking for wine.

I lay the coats over the desk in my office, then put crudités out on the table. As I poured wine, I introduced myself as "Annabelle, Professor Z.'s assistant," though in my head I thought, Apprentice.

Spence was telling the group that he had recently gone looking for Auden's apartment and what he found was a Mexican restaurant.

"Seventy-seven Saint Marks Place, between First and Second Avenue," Spence said with a laugh, and he tipped his glass slightly, spilling wine on Z.'s couch. I made a mental note not to fill the glasses so high. Then, very glumly, Spence recited some lines from Auden's "As I Walked Out One Evening."

" 'O plunge your hands in water, Plunge them in up to the wrist,' " he said, looking over at me. And I wondered if he was using poetry to send me a coded message: "Annabelle, Mr. Auden requests that you plunge your hands into a basin of soapy water and clean up this spill right away!"

I had expected the conversation to become deep and meaningful, that they would open their briefcases and take out their poems, much the way we did in our writing workshop.

Instead they spoke about margaritas and dental work, and shared strategies for getting out of jury duty. Maurita Collins, Z. said, had composed a brilliantly effective letter that got her a permanent exemption. Z. told me to get her a copy.

After the group was comfortably seated—before I even had a chance to clean up Spence's spill—Z. excused me so that I could complete my chores. As I was leaving for Bloomingdale's, I heard someone say, "Z. is a salonnarde in the great European tradition."

Annabelle in Bed

———

Imagine me, Annabelle, in bed. It is a platform bed, unvarnished pine. It is late afternoon, my hair is tousled, my skin aglow, my small breasts flattened against a pillow, and I am reciting:

> . . . *unnatural world, whorled, begotten, petaled—*
> *I see you and forget desire.*
> *I see you and succumb desire.*

Then Harry says, "Desire, whore, desire take me!" and leaps out of bed to find a poem he wants to share with me. Harry naked isn't what I expected at all. He is not a tall man, but he has a firm, muscular body. He carries himself with pride.

He opens a worn paperback, retrieves his glasses from the night table, and reads:

> *She stoops to the sponge, and her swung breasts*
> *Sway like full-blown yellow*
> *Gloire de Dijon roses—*

"It's a poem by D. H. Lawrence called 'Gloire de Dijon,' Annabelle." He runs a fingertip down the length of my body, then draws circles on my belly. "You have beautiful, swung breasts."

At this point, my mouth is numb from so much kissing. I feel raw between my legs. It's after three, and I still need to find a gift for Z.'s friend.

"Harry, what does it mean to be a 'salonnarde in the great European tradition'?"

"Let's consult the dictionary." He reaches up and pulls an imaginary book off an imaginary shelf and opens it.

He flips the pages, then says, "Annabelle, I'm sorry, but *salonnarde* is just not listed in my dictionary."

I had been in the literature section of Coliseum Books near Carnegie Hall. (I had gone there after buying hand towels for Z.'s bathroom at Home Decor.)

I was scanning the *G*'s, looking for a copy of Goethe's *Sorrows of Young Werther,* and there he was.

"Miss, may I recommend *The Kama Sutra* for your reading pleasure?" Harry said. He was holding a copy of James Joyce's *Ulysses*.

Maybe it was the comfort of finding a familiar face in an unfamiliar place.

Reader, I went home with him.

Then Harry is kissing my hair and he is inside me again. His eyes are closed; and he is trancelike, reciting in his deep, soft voice, " '. . . to all of them the same story was told: that I was going to be the great writer of the future in my country.' " He stops, readjusts his weight.

" 'Guide me, my saint, my angel. . . . Lead me forward. Everything that is noble and exalted and deep and true and moving in what I write . . .' "

A long pause, then Harry says, "This doesn't seem to be working. Let's try something else."

Then I am on all fours and Harry is holding my "Gloire de Dijon" breasts in his hands.

" 'To all of them, the same story: that I was going to be a great writer! Guide me, my saint, my angel. . . . Everything that is noble . . . and exalted! . . . and deep! . . . and true! . . . and moving! . . . comes, I believe, from you. O take me into your soul of souls!' "

And here, I gasp.

" '. . . take me into your soul of souls and then I will become . . . *THE POET OF MY RACE.* . . . I feel this, Nora, as I write it. My body soon will penetrate into yours. . . . O that my soul could too! O! O! My holy love! My darling—' "

An hour later in Z.'s apartment, I am retrieving coats and scraping dishes.

"The hand towels," Z. says. "Where are the hand towels? We are completely out."

"Yes, I know," I say. "I'm sorry. I went to Home Decor and bought some," then I sigh.

In my haste leaving Harry's apartment, I forgot them. What had I been thinking, having sex in the middle of the afternoon when I had so many pressing responsibilities?

"And the list of questions, did you work on the list?"

"No," I say. "I'm really sorry. The afternoon ran away with . . . the truth is, this afternoon I ran into an old friend—"

Z. says, "I have lunch with the president of the Society on Friday; I need that list of questions, Annabelle. . . . And the gift, do you have the gift?"

I shiver, suddenly remembering myself on all fours.

"Annabelle, you must remember, I am paying for your time."

"I'm sorry. You don't have to pay me for this afternoon. I'll go back out right away and get it."

Z. says, "Money is the issue, but it is also not the issue. If you had gotten here earlier, you could have walked over, bought the towels, and had the place ready before everyone arrived. You could have written your list of questions while you sat in a café this afternoon."

"I'm sorry," I say.

I am truly sorry.

It's getting late; I have reading to do for tomorrow's class. I feel fuzzy from so much sex. In a few hours I will be back on the Long Island Rail Road looking at the businessmen with their loosened ties, drinking beer out of paper bags.

"Annabelle," Z. says, "this isn't like you."

Suddenly I picture myself on Z.'s divan, my hand in her hand, confessing my trespass.

I'm not sure why, but it is in these stressful moments that I often feel very close to her.

"Professor Z., I've been commuting back and forth from Long Island every day. It takes over an hour each way, and then I have to change for the subway and the crosstown bus."

That's the moment when a key turns in the lock, delivering into Z.'s home a tall blond man, very handsome, and a young woman, late teens, with long, dirty blond hair, blue eyes, and lots of luggage.

They are the Z. family.

"We're home, we're home, we're home!" the man says, and pecks Z. on the cheek.

"Welcome home, you two. It's been a grueling day, but I can't wait to hear about the tour."

"Oh, you know—" The husband has found a pile of mail on the kitchen counter and is leafing through. "The Swedes pinned us in the corner and wanted to talk to us about their feelings. Athens was really the high point. Claire did beautifully there."

Z. says, "Claire, before I forget. I got a call today from my agent. He thinks he's found a publisher for your book."

"Oh, Mother . . ."

The husband drops the mail and says, "Listen, everyone, we've been down this road before. I say, 'Do not count your chickens before they are hatched.' "

He's quoting Aesop, "The Milkmaid and Her Pail."

I make a gesture with my hand; one that says, I'm leaving. I'm wondering why Z. hasn't advised her daughter to delay publication.

Then Z. says, "This is Annabelle, my new assistant."

The husband puts out his hand, which is large and covers mine completely. He has a firm handshake, and I wonder if he recites Joyce's letters to Z. during sex. My guess is he doesn't.

"This is my husband, Lars, and my daughter, Claire."

"Hi," Claire says.

"Annabelle, Claire is the author of *The Needlepoint Poems,* a wonderful first book that she wrote during her senior year at the Dalton School. She's attending Harvard in the spring." Z. looks proudly at her daughter.

The husband says, "It really is a fine school for the study of creative writing. So many famous literary figures pass through. Elizabeth Bishop, Robert Lowell, W. D. Snodgrass . . ."

Z. sighs. I think she would prefer her husband not talk about poetry.

"Well, Annabelle," Z. says. "Where do we stand?"

She walks me to the door.

"I'm going to Bloomingdale's now. Directly."

"Remember, something tasteful. Have them staple the bag shut."

"And then I'm going straight home to write my interview questions for the Emily Dickinson book."

"And we'll meet tomorrow at the university at nine A.M.?"

Nine A.M.? I want to be in bed with Harry at nine.

"Could it be a little later?"

Z. says, "I'll tell you what, why don't you go to Bloomingdale's now, and then meet me back here at, say, seven o'clock?"

"Seven o'clock?"

"Yes," Z. says. "Let's burn some midnight oil, and lay the state of American poetry question to rest. In the meantime, I'm going to give your commuting difficulties some serious thought."

Pompeii

———

In the Men's Department of Bloomingdale's, I know what I'll be talking about with Dr. Sanger:

How, in a state of postcoital bliss, I cleaned up a party I wasn't invited to; I shopped for another woman's lover.

After some searching I find the perfect gift: black silk boxers and a black turtleneck. It's a very New York look.

I have a brief fantasy: I am Z., and Spence is the man I love. I am rubbing my tongue across the top of an aperitif glass—there is the faintest taste of amaretto around the rim—and Jason Spence is removing his tie, unbuttoning his shirt . . .

"He looks good in black," I say to the woman ringing up the sale.

Harry does not wear black. His favorite piece of clothing is an off-white fisherman's sweater.

Then another fantasy: Spence is undressing and Z. is thinking of me.

One continuous solitary meal. I'm thinking back to the afternoon at the Metropolitan Café. She was the celebrity poet, and yet she had seemed wide-eyed, in awe of him. I had watched her surrender to his critique.

I call Harry from the street.

"Oh, hi," he says. He sounds half asleep. "Where are you?"

"Bloomingdale's."

" 'They toil not, neither do they spin,' " Harry says. It's a quote from the Bible that begins, "Consider the lilies of the field, how they grow."

"Harry, I have to do some more work for Z. tonight, but maybe when I'm done I could come over."

"Hey, you're sweet. I'll be out for a while, but you can let yourself in," he says. "I'll tape the key to the floor under the mat."

Walking back to Z.'s apartment with my packages from Bloomingdale's, I'm suddenly tired. The city streets are full of taxis, but I never think to take one. I need to save money.

I ring the buzzer twice. Z.'s husband answers. The apartment is noisy and now a bit disheveled, with open duffel bags and clothes strewn all along the hallway.

"I'm here to drop off the hand towels," I say.

"You mustn't let my wife work you so hard," Lars says, then, "Thank you." He reaches for the bag—one of those shopping bags that say "Big Brown Bag"—and adds it to the mess in the hallway.

"Z. had asked me to come back and help her with something."

"So come in, come in—is it Annabelle? You look tired. Let me get you something to drink."

I follow Z.'s husband into the kitchen. He points to the barstool at the counter and opens the refrigerator.

"Water would be great."

"I have tap water or sparkling water. As they say in Italy, 'with fizz or without.' "

"Tap water," I say. I've never been to Europe.

The music in the distant room has suddenly been turned up. A recurring lyric: "ant music, *ant music* . . ."

"Claire," the husband yells. "Lower it!"

Lars holds open the refrigerator door. He seems to be gathering his wits.

"Claire is so excited by the new wave. All she did in Europe was buy records. I believe we are listening to Adam Ant."

Watching Lars in his bare feet and ripped college T-shirt, in front of the refrigerator, talking about his daughter's music, I am suddenly in touch with a deep longing I have for family.

But it *is* weird being in Z.'s apartment with a husband and daughter. I had always imagined her home a stage where the drama of the writer was played out weekly and into eternity, but clearly, it's just another residence where a family goes about the business of daily living. Lars isn't what I would have expected at all. He is gentle, soft-spoken, with straight blond hair and a boyish face.

"My wife went to the deli to get some sandwiches. She'll be back soon."

It's hard to imagine Z. standing at a deli counter.

I say, "You're a writer?"

"Yes."

I take a sip of water; I'm nervous.

Lars sits down with his own water, drums his fingers along the counter.

"Are you working on something now?"

"Actually, I'm writing a memoir. It's set in Italy; in Pompeii—"

"Pompeii? Oh. That's interesting."

"You think so?"

"I like ruined cities."

"I do too," Lars says, now drinking his water.

"Pompeii is really the best of the ruined cities."

"Yes, it really is," Lars says. "I got the idea when Claire and I were on tour. I took her to various ruins, and suddenly I had an epiphany. I understood how to write the story of my life: ". . . As Lars Bovardine stands at the Herculaneum Gate with his daughter, Claire, he is suddenly drawn back to the visit that he and his pregnant wife, Elizabeth,

made to Pompeii. It was their first trip to Europe. They had just grad-
uated college, were mere children. In a month she would miscarry a
baby that wasn't even his . . ."

Elizabeth Bovardine.

Elizabeth.

Z.

She would miscarry a baby that wasn't even his.

"I've been working on it every waking moment since the idea came
to me." He rubs his eyes. "In the hotel room, in taxis, on the plane. . . .
It's my life story. *Mine*."

"I'd like to write a memoir," I say, "but I haven't lived enough."

"You will, Annabelle. Time will give you experience and perspective."

"It must be hard to write a memoir."

"No, not really. The trick is not to proceed chronologically. In my
first chapter, I intend to focus on a single moment . . . the moment that
we stood at the door to the ruins of that noble city; the moment before
I stepped inside, and discovered the House of the Tragic Poet, the moment before I took residence there for life."

The House of the Tragic Poet: It was such a great metaphor. I could
see it dying in the hands of a writer like Meg Cross. Lars certainly had
a lot of ambition. When I had time, I would look up his books in the library.

"There's an image I have of Pompeii, the moment it falls: a thick,
black cloud, and everyone is running like mad. Hot ashes, pebbles,
and the wild sea. . . . It's a maze in the dark and they can't see their way
out . . ."

Then there is the sound of footsteps. Claire is standing in the
kitchen, surveying us.

"Oh, hi," she says. "Mother said to tell you that she left some work
in a folder on your desk."

"I guess I better get busy."

"Are you her student?"

"No, not exactly," I say.

"Then who are you?"

Lars says, "Claire, is that polite? She's Annabelle, your mother's graduate assistant."

"Undergraduate," I say.

"Then you really must be very special," Lars says.

Z., the Adulterer

Then I am sitting in Z.'s dining room, alone, waiting for her to return.

It's odd that Z. has invited me over to work on her speech on the very night her husband and daughter have returned from a European reading tour.

I picture Lars settling down right now to work on his memoir.

Z. walks in, drops a plastic bag from the deli on the dining room table, and goes out for her briefcase. She returns, takes a yellow legal pad from the inside pouch, and puts the briefcase on the empty chair between us.

"Thank you for agreeing to stay, Annabelle. I am often at my most productive when I'm overtired."

Z. is unpacking the bag. "Tuna or turkey?" she says.

"Turkey," I say, and we begin unwrapping the sandwiches, opening the bags of potato chips, popping the soda tops. In her sparsely furnished dining room, sound echoes.

But the silence between Z. and me is what is most palpable.

I want to ask a question about her book-length poem "Flower Soliloquy," like, Did you plan for this to be a forty-page poem or did it just happen? Instead, I watch her eat. She takes a few small bites and chews. She doesn't seem to take much pleasure from her sandwich, and I wonder if she would have preferred the turkey. I take a bite of my own sandwich and look around. I think to myself that there are hundreds of people who would love to be in my place. If only I didn't feel guilty about taking her sandwich.

"Well, then," Z. says. "Let's talk poetry. I've been thinking about my address."

"Yes," I say, "me too. I was thinking that you could take an inventive approach. What if, instead of writing a straightforward speech, you approach the address as if you were answering a letter from a young poet? I've been thinking of some questions you might answer." I take a bite of my sandwich.

Now she's watching me chew.

"For example?"

I put my sandwich down.

"Dear Professor Z., I want to write poetry, but I'm concerned that there is little beauty in the world to write about . . . you know, the rise of the shopping center, the destruction of the natural environment . . ."

"Beauty," Z. says. "Is there anything left to say about beauty?"

"That poetry must be about beauty?"

"Yes! And everywhere you turn, you see a world of endangered beauty. Beauty, which has become endangered by sloppy writing, solipsism, and haiku."

"Then you could talk about the history of ugliness. You could trace it back to 1913, the year that Joyce Kilmer published his poem 'Trees.' "

"Remind me, Annabelle."

" 'I think that I shall never see a poem lovely as a tree,' " I say, then qualify myself. "But it's the last stanza that's truly ugly: 'Poems are made by fools like me, but only God can make a tree.' "

Z. frowns. I fear I have not been a good guardian of her psychic space.

We return to our food, then after some time, Z. looks up and says, "Tell me, Annabelle, what do my readers want?"

"Well," I say, slipping my right foot under me, so that I have some height in Z.'s high-back chair. "If I were coming to hear you speak, I would want to know what it is you love about poetry, and what you think about its future."

"Are you thinking that I should inject some hope into my state-of-American-poetry address?" Z. is tapping her pencil on her legal pad.

"Maybe you could talk about how poetry can change the world?"

"No, I think that's simplistic, sophomoric."

Then I say, apropos of nothing, "How is Mrs. Van Elder?"

"She's fine, Annabelle. Why do you ask?"

"I guess you never heard. When I was there, the teakettle shrieked, and her cat jumped off her lap, scratching her arm and ripping her sleeve. I offered to stay and help, but she wanted me to go. I'm afraid she blames me for the accident . . . and I was so nervous, I forgot to take back the four cans of seafood cat food that I picked up for her by mistake."

Z. says, "I find this deeply disturbing."

"I'm sorry."

"Make sure you resolve the cat food issue, Annabelle."

"I will. First thing—"

Z. says, "Poetry is in chaos. The spoken word is about to *devour* the written word . . ."

I reach for the legal pad and start writing.

Cat food
Devour

I like to think I inspire her.

"Annabelle," Z. says, "you never did tell me how your writing workshop went."

I hardly know what to say, so I say, "The truth is, I felt a little intimidated by Braun's graduate students. And I guess I overcompensated by rewriting this woman's poem at the end of the class. I don't think anyone appreciated it very much."

Z. says, "And Braun?"

"Oh, she's very professional," I say.

"Annabelle, you seem tense. Are you tense?"

"No, not really."

"Why don't you take a deep breath? You're making me nervous."

"I'm sorry. I'll try to breathe more."

"You know that part of your job is to relax me. So you need to be relaxed yourself."

"Okay, I'll try."

"I'm concerned that something is not quite right between us, Annabelle. You seem to choose your words carefully around me."

"No, that's not it at all. I'm just trying to discipline myself to say the right thing. Isn't being a poet about choosing the right word?"

"Annabelle, you can let down your guard here."

"Well, maybe I am a little nervous."

Z. says, "There can be no secrets between us. I need you to trust me, Annabelle. I need you to trust me in an absolute way. I want to know what you are really thinking. I want to hear your opinions."

Then Z. is looking at me and I am looking at her.

She had written of waiting at the edge of the garden for her beloved perennial to flower. In some ways, she is a patient woman.

"Can I trust you to be honest with me, Annabelle?"

"Yes, you can trust me," I say.

"Now, Annabelle, tell me what you truly think about Braun's workshop."

"Well, she seems extremely well read," I say.

"That should go without saying."

"And there is something very glamorous about her," I add, but sensing that this is not what Z. wants to hear, I hedge. "But her clothing is sort of out there. It was our first class and she didn't even wear a shirt under her jacket!"

"Are you sure?"

"Nothing, just a black bra. It's a look, you know."

"Lingerie?"

"Yes, a bra under a suit jacket. You have to be a little cold-blooded to dress that way," I say, but to Z. it's no joke.

"Is she honest in her criticism?"

"She's very honest, but she seems to approach each poem as if it were the same as every other poem. Miss Mary Mack is given the same treatment as a Shakespearean sonnet. Everything is regarded as art."

Z. says, "That phrase, 'everything is art,' do you mind if I use it in my speech?"

"Of course not."

She hesitates a moment, then says, "Annabelle, when you first accepted this position, I let you know that part of your job would be to help me 'preserve my writing time.' "

"I remember."

"This semester, I may be 'writing' away from home quite a bit. Perhaps my family will ask you questions . . . and you may feel the need to divulge my whereabouts."

"I would never do that."

"Annabelle, I'm going to tell you something extremely confidential. If this were the army, we would call this information classified. . . . Do you think you can handle this?"

At this moment, I'm feeling something akin to excitement, arousal maybe, and it's a bit unsettling.

"I can keep a secret, Professor Z."

"Well, then. As my apprentice—the person with whom I share the intimate details of my daily life—you need to know that I am involved with someone."

"A man?"

"Yes, a man. Of course."

"Sorry. That came out wrong."

"Yes, I'm involved with someone, and I think you might know who he is."

Now she is looking deep into my eyes, nodding. I'm nodding back. She lowers her voice and tells me that it's Mr. Spence.

"I'll need you to run interference for me. Can I count on you?"

"Of course," I say, but I feel uneasy. After all, I have just met her husband, and I like him.

I wonder what Dr. Sanger would say about this. I imagine her asking me if I felt compromised by Z.'s request. I imagine her asking me if a good mother would compromise her daughter.

Z. stands up and holds out her hand. "Can I count on you, Annabelle?"

She grasps my hand firmly, but this isn't a handshake; this is hand-holding.

"Yes, sure," I say. I'm holding hands with Z., the adulterer.

She squeezes my hand, then drops it.

"You see, Annabelle, there are things about marriage that are beyond explanation. What goes on between a couple often isn't obvious to anyone else.

"When I met my husband, he was an actor and I was a fledgling writer. We were each starting out, and we nurtured each other, and became the people that we are today. My husband is a well-respected stage actor. . . . I have my books and my university position. . . . And then, about two years ago, Lars decided to become a writer, and it's taken over his life. He's always writing. And when he's not writing, he's talking about writing, or he's looking at his watch so he can judge how much time he's wasted by *not* writing. Or he's reciting what he's just written. He's constantly producing drafts for me to read. I've told him a million times, nobody is interested in an epic poem called *The Last Days of Pompeii, New York*."

"Professor Z., is there such a place, Pompeii, New York?"

"No, there is not. The point here, Annabelle, is to upstage me," Z. says. "To show the world how easy it is to write a book of poetry."

"Then how did he get the reading tour if he hasn't published yet?"

"Lars is an actor with a great tenor voice. He has a booking agent."

"Does he read from his work in progress, *The Last Days of Pompeii, New York*?"

"Lars reads rambling monologues about God knows what. Years ago, Marshall adapted a piece from his book *Moses in the Promised Land* for Lars to read at a benefit for student scholarships. Lars liked being Moses so much that he decided to give it his own signature, so now he's performing Dr. Moses."

"Moses with a Ph.D. or Moses the physician?"

Z. says, "I try not to think about this, Annabelle."

"It must be terrible for you," I say.

"So, you'll help me?"

"As best I can."

"Thank you for having dinner with me tonight, Annabelle. By the way, I loved those little flower descriptions you wrote for me. They were so spontaneous, so natural, so far-reaching in their ambition! To look at a flower and think of a young girl's hair! Or Freud! You do have a sense of humor. You show such promise."

"Thanks," I say, feeling tremendous pride and the weight of the question that has come to haunt me even more than What is poetry?

"Professor Z., I know you are busy, but would you be willing to read my poem about Emily Dickinson?"

"Yes, Annabelle, certainly. But right now, it's hard for me to take on anything new. You know the pressure I'm under, and I'm working like a madwoman trying to finish *The Flower Dream Diaries*."

Because I am first and foremost Z.'s apprentice and my job is to protect her psychic space, I don't express my disappointment. I tell her I understand her predicament—being pulled daily in so many directions.

Then Z. gathers the potato chip bags and the soda cans off the table. I follow her through the dining room's swinging door. Before I know it, I'm underground, waiting for a subway to take me downtown.

Then I go to Harry's apartment, not thinking about what I'll wear tomorrow, not even calling my mother to tell her I'm staying at a girl-friend's place in the city. She knows I have no girlfriends.

Harry's apartment is a simple one-bedroom, one bedroom more than most New Yorkers get.

There's a note for me on his bed.

It is "The River-Merchant's Wife: a Letter," Ezra Pound's transla-tion of a poem by the Chinese poet Li Po. It's a love letter written to an absent husband. This is written on the top margin:

Yes, Pound was a fascist and an anti-Semite, but I love his transla-tion. Annabelle, make yourself at home.

Harry

He's circled this stanza:

At sixteen you departed,
You went into far Ku-to-yen, by the river of swirling eddies,
And you have been gone five months.
The monkeys make sorrowful noise overhead.

Suddenly I see why Jane's wind sock "calling the sailors home" poem fails. They are words disconnected from feeling. Here, there is a sorrowful noise, a woman's longing; a succinct description that does the work of a paragraph. I touch Harry's blanket, run my hand over his pillow. Am I falling in love?

Harry's desk is a typing table on wheels. In his typewriter—an IBM Selectric—is a piece of paper with this word in the center of the page:

G L O V E S

Hours pass. Perhaps Harry has disappeared into the River of Swirling Eddies. There is no television in his apartment. I begin the arduous task of writing the Emily Dickinson questionnaire. I come up with ten questions:

1. What is your favorite Emily Dickinson poem?
2. What is your least favorite Emily Dickinson poem?
3. Do you think Emily Dickinson was a feminine woman?
4. Do you think Emily Dickinson hated her mother?
5. Would Emily have been happier if she'd had children?
6. If Emily had been alive for the invention of television, what would have been her favorite TV show?
7. Was Emily Dickinson a smart woman?
8. Do you think Emily Dickinson had a sex life?
9. What would Emily Dickinson think of your poems?
10. Since Dickinson wrote, "Publication—is the Auction Of the Mind of Man," do you think she would feel exploited being the subject of this book?

Then I try to write a poem about a virgin. A virgin in her boy-friend's bed, I think, then give up.

Harry wakes me.

"Oh, my," he says, finding me naked. His clock says 5:00 A.M.

After sex, he puts on a pot of coffee.

"This is when I do my best work," Harry says. "I'm a raving in-somniac."

He wheels his typewriter into the bedroom.

"I'll be writing while I watch you sleep. Writing while you— Hey, how do you feel about giving me something to write about? How would you like to be my muse?"

"Tell me what I have to do."

"Touch yourself while I type."

"This gives new definition to the phrase 'touch type,' " I say.

Then I pull back the blanket and quickly get under the covers.

"You've never"—he makes a weird circling gesture with his fin-gers. "You've never done that for a lover?"

"Well, no," I say. "Not while they typed."

"It's good for me to know how you touch yourself."

"I'm shy, Harry." I yawn. "And I'm a little tired."

"Am I your first lover, Annabelle?"

I say, "Let me put it this way, Harry. I've never slept with a man be-fore in a bed."

It's been mostly cars and couches.

He kisses my forehead.

Harry at the typewriter: the clatter of keys and bells.

I'm thinking of that moment in Z.'s dining room. The darkness of the river. All the tiny points of light outside the window. Her hand, which was smooth and cool, holding my hand.

I don't know what Harry is working on, but clearly he is on a roll. I make a mental note to ask him what he's writing as I fall asleep.

Ben's Poem

===

Coffee top, table top, telephone, toothpaste!
Coffee top, table top, telephone, toothpaste!
Coffee top? Table top? Telephone? Toothpaste?
Coffee top—
Table top—
Telephone—
Toothpaste—

This is a passage from a book-length poem by Benjamin Adams, member of the graduate writing workshop, editor of a small downtown magazine called *New York Grit*.

Meg asks, "What exactly does that mean, 'downtown' magazine?"

Braun tells us that it's a literary movement that's happening as we speak. Young people are putting out their own magazines. Alternative consciousness is everywhere. The academy is not the only home for poetry.

Braun says, "Moving on now . . . who would like to read Ben's poem aloud?"

I raise my hand, and then, surprising even myself, I speak each

word with resonance and feeling, banging two fingers against the table
as I read. I imagine this is the year 2030 and I'm the last living Beat poet
reading in a smoke-filled café.

Braun says, "Annabelle, how did you feel reading Ben's poem?"

Today Braun is wearing a hot pink dress under her black suit jacket.
The dress is mod, circa 1965, with a huge oval cut out of its midsection.

When she leans over the seminar table, her hair swipes the various
papers that are scattered in front of her. She then proceeds to tie her
hair back with a ponytail holder. These are really commonplace ges-
tures, but I watch closely. I watch her because she is different from Z. I
wonder what I will look like fifteen years from now. I wonder what
kind of woman I will turn out to be.

"I'm sorry, can you restate the question?"

Braun laughs. "What were you feeling, Annabelle, when you read
Ben's poem like that?"

"I felt at one with the universe," I say.

The class laughs.

Braun says, "What a delightful way you have of putting that."

"You know," I say, "Virginia Woolf says that 'the most profound
and primitive of instincts' is 'the instinct of rhythm.' "

"Well, thank you, Annabelle," Braun says. "And let's thank Virginia Woolf, too, for sharing that deep insight with us."

Then Braun launches a discussion of the four words chosen by Ben.
We talk about the meaning of *coffee top, table top, telephone, toothpaste.*

If there is a flaw in his poem, we decide, it is the leap from *coffee top*
to *table top.*

"The reader can accept *coffee top,* but perhaps," Braun says, "*table top*
is too literal? Does *table top* force us to go back and probe the meaning of
coffee top? Should whimsical be followed by literal? I just don't know."

Meg says, "The word *toothpaste* is irritating."

Clearly, Meg does not like Ben's poem.

"Yes," Braun says, "it's thick and it's also full of mouth sounds, but
we must consider Ben's intentionality here."

I wish Braun would stand up again so I could see the flesh of her
midsection.

"Besides, I find the word *irritating* troubling, Meg. We must always remember to be diplomatic, to use neutral language when discussing poetry."

Obviously, Braun has never been advised to write like a whore.

Then, wanting to be the first to exercise diplomacy, I say, "I like Ben's use of dashes. The downtown poet taking on Emily Dickinson."

Braun says, "Yes, Annabelle, I agree. Ben's punctuation is mysterious." Then she gives us an assignment: "Why don't we all try to write a poem like Ben's?"

And we sit there in silence for ten minutes, then go around the room and read what we have written. Here are some of the poems:

Ant farm, beehive, steak knife, beach!
Ant farm? Beehive? Steak knife? Beach?

Bureau, Crucifix, Diaphragm? Cough!
Bureau? Crucifix? Diaphragm? Cough?

Iceberg, truck stop, holster, clock!
Iceberg? Truck stop? Holster? Clock?

What we learn from imitating Ben is that it is actually hard to write a poem as vivid and affecting as "Coffee top, table top, telephone, toothpaste!"

"Well," Ben says, "you only spent ten minutes on it. I've been working on that poem for years."

"For years?" Braun says. "You mean you've worked on this poem for years?"

"Yes," Ben says.

Braun says, "You've worked on this poem for years. How beautiful." Braun is looking at Ben in wonder; and the class is looking from Ben to Braun in dismay.

Braun says, "I am always moved by the men in my classes. It takes a very strong man to write poetry, a man who is not afraid to be in touch with his feminine side."

After class, Ben stops me in the hall.

"Hi, it's Annabelle, right? I've been meaning to tell you since our first class, I liked how you rewrote that cross poem."

Ben had a pierced eyebrow and black army boots. It was a time when piercing an eyebrow was considered facial mutilation, and people looked away in disgust.

"I don't know. I probably should have been more restrained. I'm afraid *I crossed* the line," I say.

Ben says, "Forget it. Listen, I don't know if you know about *New York Grit*. We have a reading series Thursday nights at the Mad Dog Café in the East Village."

He hands me a flyer. There's a two-drink minimum. He's also their bartender.

"It's an open mike. You can bring your own poems and try them out."

"My own poems are in sad shape," I say. "But thanks."

"Well, think about it. It's a good time."

I find Z. in the English Department, sitting behind her very large oak desk. She is reading the Emily Dickinson questionnaire. She looks over her shiny black glasses.

Today Z.'s black hair is bright and buoyant. She has had it cut.

"If *Emily* had been alive for the invention of television, what would have been her favorite TV show? Would *Emily* have been happier had she had children?"

She lays the questionnaire on her desk, takes off her glasses, and rubs her temples.

"What do *you* think Emily Dickinson's favorite television program would be, Annabelle?" Z. asks. She's incredulous.

I shrug my shoulders. "She lived in a different world. That's what I was trying to get at."

"And do *you* think she would have been happier having children?"

"I think she would have been a strange mother, incapable of performing the simple physical acts of motherhood—you know, making food, shopping, buying clothes."

"I see," Z. says.

"Imagine Emily Dickinson changing a diaper."

"And could you really see yourself asking Miriam Van Elder to speculate on Dickinson's sex life?"

"I hadn't really thought of it that way."

"Well, think of it that way, Annabelle! I don't mean to be harsh, but your questions are a little strange. What were you thinking when you composed that list?"

"I was trying to approach Emily Dickinson in a totally different way, from the right side of my brain."

She waves her hand in a dismissive gesture. "From now on use the left side of your brain when you do my work, please." From a folder on her desk, she takes out a sheet of paper. "Now, here's a list my daughter came up with. I think the two of you should collaborate on the questionnaire. You remember my daughter, Claire?"

Ant music. *The Needlepoint Poems.*

"Listen to some of Claire's questions: How does Emily Dickinson's work influence your own writing? How does her example influence your life? How does solitude affect your own writing process? It is said that Emily's poems are written to the rhythm of church hymns. How does religion influence your poems? Do you see what I'm getting at here, Annabelle?"

"I guess I was asking the person being interviewed for something different."

"Annabelle, your questions draw attention to themselves, and that's not what I am looking for. You must remember: We are working on a book that will bear the Society's logo. The Society for the Preservation of American Poetry is a name that carries with it the entire history of American poetry. . . . It is a history we must never toy with."

"It's sacred," I say.

"Yes, and do you see how simple and open-ended Claire's questions are? They ask the writer to speak about her craft, to speak to her calling."

She lays the paper down.

"In a poet, curiosity is key," Z. says. "But you must tailor your curiosity to the task at hand."

"I'll keep that in mind for the next assignment," I say.

Z. says, "A writer must think things through before committing words to paper. Find a question and *live* the question. I get the feeling that you just dashed off this assignment."

"No, " I say. "I've been living these questions for quite some time."

Z. is looking at the list again. Then she says, "Annabelle, do *you* think Emily Dickinson was a feminine woman?"

"No, I think she wore that white dress as a kind of costume, but underneath, she was without gender."

Z. says, "So you think that the issue of femininity *is* useful when trying to understand the work of women writers."

"Think of Braun," I say.

Z. says, "Let's limit our examples to the canon, Annabelle."

"Elizabeth Bishop said that if she'd been a man, she would have written more. She would have taken herself seriously as a writer."

Z. says, "A poor excuse for lack of output."

"But a question worth pursuing, don't you think?"

"A woman with means, complaining that the world has kept her from writing?"

"It wasn't the world so much as her own conflict about being a woman—"

Z. says, "I'll be honest, Annabelle. I don't understand that conflict. A writer writes. It's that simple." She lifts her briefcase from the floor and goes searching inside it for something.

As I'm leaving, I say, "But don't you think Dickinson would have been famous in her lifetime if she were a man?"

Her mentor, that eminent man of letters Thomas Wentworth Higginson, had advised her to delay publication.

Z. says, "It's a hypothetical question, one that we can never really answer ... so why speculate, why bother? Isn't it enough that we have Emily Dickinson's poems in print to this day?"

"Maybe," I say. "But she wanted to be famous in her lifetime. That was what she wanted."

"Annabelle," Z. says. "Let's leave 'femininity studies' to our friends in the Women's Studies Department. *What is poetry?* Now, there's a question worth pursuing."

Femininity Studies

If Elizabeth Bishop was saying, "I would have written more if only I had not had breasts," I was thinking: I would be writing more if only I had larger ones.

I have read that Nora Joyce was boyish-looking, of slight build. I am, too. I look like my father would if he were a woman; a plain woman, one who would never stand out in a crowd.

Claire looked like her mother. A beautiful, androgynous-looking Z. with short, spiky hair.

She had been Z.'s flower daughter, the subject of a book of poems.

SPINY GIRL
My daughter
is like the butterfly
milkweed,
a slender species,
simple and rising.

And who wouldn't love the ideal daughter? Claire was not yet eighteen, headed for Harvard, and poised to publish her first book of poems.

I couldn't compete. A poem about me would have been called "Wayward Daughter." I had stayed with Harry every night for a week, skipped my therapy, and left my mother to fend for her supper.

When I finally did go home, my mother was hurt and confused. She asked me where I had been. I told her I had stayed overnight with a friend.

And then I visited Dr. Sanger. I was sitting on her couch, speaking, but the words came out of a changed mouth. The mouth had sensual memory.

I could still feel that long afternoon of kissing, the way, after a while, it felt like I was no longer kissing but sucking. I tried to explain this to Dr. Sanger.

"So," Dr. Sanger said, "it sounds like you've discovered the joys of sex. Tell me, Annabelle, were you stoned?"

"No," I said. "I was just open to a new experience."

Dr. Sanger squirmed in her seat.

"I hope birth control is a part of this new life experience," she said.

I told Dr. Sanger that I was almost twenty-two; I was well versed in the practice of birth control.

Then I went back to my childhood bedroom and tried to write a poem.

I thought about the Frost poem I had failed to recite in Braun's class during our first meeting.

It was about a bird trying to sing by not singing. The bird's song asked something like What can I make of my life, being such a small bird?

I did not want to write about birds. I thought about the poets I admired, like the seventeenth-century religious poets. You just took out the *God* when you read a poem, and you got a love poem so deep, you thought the poet's heart was going to crack.

And I liked the Cavalier poets. When it came to sex, they did not mince words. There was Ben Jonson singing to Celia: "Let us prove, While we can, the sports of love." And Robert Herrick undressing his Julia with his eyes, liquefying her clothes.

It was the age of God and the virgin, and if a poet liked you and you played hard to get, you could end up naked, forever immortalized in his poetry.

But I wouldn't have wanted to be Celia or Julia. In the seventeenth century, there was no running water, just perfume to cover up bad odors. These poets were probably very smelly.

Then it came to me during therapy.

I would write a book called *DeFlower*. What is virginity? I would ask, and forty-eight poems later (the minimum needed to publish a poetry manuscript), the question would be answered. I would open my book with a quote from Sappho:

Can it be that I still long for my virginity?

Dr. Sanger said she wondered if the strains of adult life were proving too much for me. *Virginity* seemed a metaphor for childhood, and I was apparently still longing for mine.

Look at my relationship with Z., Dr. Sanger said. Wasn't she, after all, just another mother figure?

I disagreed.

She called it resistance.

At home, at my desk, I wrote some notes:

Virginity as impediment to freedom.
Chastity as virtue.
Virginity as prize.
Virginity as prison cell.

In my poems, I would answer the seduction song of the seventeenth-century poets. I would offer an intimate inquiry into virginity, that fleeting state of female sexuality.

I would call my first poem "Virgin in the Meadow."

I tried to write it.

There was a meadow of wildflowers and a virgin was lying in the center of it . . .

I was blocked. It is possible that I was overwhelmed by the confessional implications of the task I had set for myself. And flowers, I thought, were Z.'s terrain. My flower poem would be viewed as the work of a novice, a cheap imitation.

But, in truth, I did not care much about the virgin. I had considered my own virginity a liability and had gotten rid of it quickly. Since then I had spent years in therapy trying to reconcile my complex feelings about my own sexuality, which Dr. Sanger admitted she didn't fully understand but was trying to appreciate.

The Sylvia Plath soliloquy had landed me in Dr. Sanger's office, but there had been other troubling behaviors as well. That year—my sixteenth—my mother had gotten a call from the school librarian that I was spending too much time in the "anonymous" section of the library.

The anonymous section, I had discovered, was where the nameless authors lived, the ones who wrote the Victorian sex literature.

It gave my parents—who would divorce one week after my graduation—something else to fight about.

My mother had run into the librarian in the supermarket. Miss Adler had asked my mother if she knew what I'd been reading.

I'd been reading *Story of O.*

My mother borrowed the book from me that night and read it in one sitting. The next morning she told me that I was embarrassing her in front of her neighbors.

My father took me aside. "If you were my son, I'd tell you to sleep around. But since you're my daughter, I have to tell you I don't like what I hear about your reading habits."

Dr. Sanger's job was to liberate me from my unhappy parents and shore me up so I could go away to college. The early Dr. Sanger presented herself as hip. She chewed gum. She spoke the adolescent vernacular: "Shit, that really sucks," she'd respond to some minor hurt I'd brought in to examine.

From Dr. Sanger I learned to pronounce the word *sexual.* It gave me chills.

But now Dr. Sanger seemed tired.

"So you met a man in a bookstore and had sex with him," Dr. Sanger said. "And then you left to clean up a party. You made distance."

"The sex just seemed to go on and on. It felt like every nerve of my body was receptive and alive."

"Then why did you leave?" Dr. Sanger asked. "Why are you here, right now?"

I considered the question. With Dr. Sanger, I was always stepping into some psychological minefield. The minefield would invariably lead me to this insight: I wasn't honest with myself.

"Because I was scared," I said. "Because he's a man, not a boy. I've never been with a man before."

I'd only ever been with boys my own age.

Dr. Sanger said, "Annabelle, tell me, what would it have been like to spend some 'real time' with this man? Gone to the movies, then out to dinner? Whatever happened to dating?"

"But I couldn't stay. I had to go back and finish my work with Z."

"You couldn't say you had an emergency?"

"A sexual emergency?" I said.

Dr. Sanger didn't laugh.

"And then, cleaning up, I discovered that one of the guests had spilled red wine on Z.'s couch, and she was very thankful I noticed it."

"You're being evasive, Annabelle." Dr. Sanger adjusted herself on her seat so that she was now looking at me straight on. "Tell me, what is it about this man that makes everything so urgent? Is it his penis? Do we need to talk about his penis?"

I didn't answer.

"Because jumping into bed in the middle of the afternoon with a man you hardly know could be viewed as aberrant behavior . . ."

I wanted to tell Dr. Sanger that I was surrounded by aberrant conduct. I wanted to tell her about Braun's hot pink dress, the huge hole cut out of her midsection. I wanted to tell her that Z. was having an affair. But as much as Dr. Sanger was empathic, I knew that she didn't care much for the poetry world. She saw poetry as a mere map of emotion, something to fill a therapy session with. She would call these women histrionic, and tell me to stay away from them.

"I think it behooves you not to know him as the full-blooded, complex human being that he is."

"In bed," I said, "I'm like the speaker in Anne Sexton's poem 'Consorting with Angels'. I lose my common gender and my final aspect. I'm not a woman anymore—"

"Oh, stop that, Annabelle. You're using poetry as a way of avoiding your feelings again," Dr. Sanger said wearily.

When I was in high school, Dr. Sanger was the most sophisticated woman I knew. She'd been to graduate school and earned a Ph.D. But now I spent my days at a university where many people had Ph.D.'s, and only a few called themselves Doctor. It was hard to keep Dr. Sanger up on a pedestal.

I was watching her closely, memorizing her for some future time when she would be absent from my life.

"Am I using poetry?"

"Annabelle, sex without love is fucking. Good sex comes from caring. All I've heard about today is Harry's cock. You haven't even told me what you see in this man."

She was waiting for an answer, impatiently twisting her leather clog in the air.

Finally I said, "Harry has a good sense of irony and he likes poetry."

She sighed heavily, then her shoe dropped to the floor with a thud.

A Corolla of Fused Petals

I told my mother that there would be more overnights in New York City. I was looking for an apartment. It was too much, I said, to be traveling back and forth between urban and suburban cultures.

That was okay, because my mother was moving on as well. She was dating again. Leonard Gottlieb resembled my father in many ways. He was balding with a paunch. He took her to dinner with Adventures in Dining coupons. She would rush home from work and change her clothes. She had to be seated in the restaurant by six o'clock or they wouldn't honor the discount.

My mother told me that it was exciting, bucking the traffic to get to the restaurant on time.

"At my age," she said, "the men are few and far between. You take what you can get."

On the kitchen counter, there was a letter from Arthur Feld.

Dear Annabelle,

How lucky for you to have gotten in with the movers and shakers of the poetry world. Watch closely and take good notes. As a young poet, I apprenticed with the extraordinary Avi Singer, a difficult, exacting teacher, who taught me everything I know.

I will be reading on December 5 at Synagogue Beth L'Chaim on the Lower East Side—my first reading in New York City in years. Perhaps you will come?

I would love to hear more and, yes, have coffee, and here's a question: Would you consider teaching a class here next semester? I can pay you a small guest lecture fee.

Let's talk more about it when we meet.

Warmly,
Arthur

P.S. Your poem is brilliant. The young poet's identification with the cryptic Dickinson is the mystery of poetry itself.

I wrote the date of Arthur's reading in my calendar, and then, on the train, I wrote him a note:

Dear Arthur,
I will be the first on line on December 5.
Annabelle

I was on my way to Z.'s apartment to meet with Claire about the Emily Dickinson book. Then it was back to the university to meet with Z., and then with Braun for a conference about my poems. Afterward to Harry's apartment to study. He wouldn't be home until dawn.

"What exactly do you do every night?" I had asked him. "Are you a security guard or something?"

"I'm working on my dissertation," Harry said. "I found an all-night library."

So three or four nights a week, I would call my mother to say I was staying with a friend in the city. I would wander Harry's three-room apartment or sit outside on his narrow terrace. I would cook dinner, try to write poetry, do my homework, then read in his bed until I fell asleep. Then Harry would come home and we would make love. It was good sex, and Dr. Sanger would have been pleased to know that it came from a place of caring. Afterward, Harry would wheel his typewriter into the bedroom.

It was about that time that Z. told me she trusted me enough to type her poems.

I remember where I was: I was standing in the living room. It was one of those clear, bright mornings, and I was watching a small tugboat moving down the river.

"Annabelle, this will be one of the most confidential projects you will ever undertake for me. I have to know that you will never speak a word of this to anyone. If I had a pin, I would ask you to prick your finger and make a blood pact with me."

"Professor Z.," I said, "I would love to type your new poems. And of course I would never reveal anything about them to anyone."

"You see," Z. said, pulling a folder out of her briefcase, "I have come to realize that the physical work of typing draft after draft is standing in the way of further inspiration.

"And, on top of that, I have this gigantic callus on my middle finger. I should have tried to adjust my grip years ago." She stretched out her fingers. "It's finally just too painful to write."

I was looking at her fingers, long and slender. She had just had a manicure. I knew this because I had made the appointment. I said, "Perhaps you should get a special pencil grip. They sell these rubber things that you can put near the tip. I could go out and get you one."

"Thank you," Z. said. "But it's deeper than that. It's a chronic sort of pain." She was aggressively massaging her middle finger. "I hope it isn't tendonitis. I'd hate to have to wear a brace. Writing is so painful, Annabelle. I'd give it up if I could."

"You would?"

"Actually, I'd give up the rewriting. It's such a waste of time and paper. Back and forth from the paper to the typewriter again and again. . . . And ultimately you honor your first draft anyway."

"My Emily Dickinson poem—the one I told you about—I must have written it a thousand times."

She made a tight smile. "Sometimes it takes a thousand tries to make a poem. In the old days, I could do it all in my head, and I had the patience to follow a draft until the journey's end. But, Annabelle, this is something I wouldn't confide to just anyone . . . I'm tired in a way that I just can't explain."

"That's why I'm here," I said.

Z. laid a folder on my desk and said, "Sometimes a poem comes to me whole, and sometimes I simply have the blueprint for it. You'll see what I mean. I like my drafts to be double-spaced. I like two and a quarter inches on the left margin, and two inches on the right. I like my title to be typed in boldface, and there must be three spaces between my title and my first line. Never underline the title! Sometimes I will write questions in the margins or will put questions in parentheses in the body of the poems. Those questions will be for you to answer on a separate piece of paper, attached to the poem with a paper clip. Never staple these documents together. Use large paper clips, never small ones."

Then I was alone in Z.'s apartment with her poems.

MASCULINE FLOWER
He is black or blue.
He is the powerful, upright flower.
The one who commands attention
from the other flowers.

Then this in the margin:

A.—Please research masculine flowers.

THE FLOWER LOVER
A masculine flower absorbing rays.
Something about spreading pollen.
A woman,
Two flowers swaying,

Something about the nightshade family.
Her surreptitious wanderings— (describe more fully)
What I love about his body (couch it
in flower metaphor), sex and after sex.
An image here about seeking and finding
the body/essence of the flower.
Describe the coolness of the garden
on summer evenings.
(Stanza break)
Last line must make a leap from the garden into eternity.

A.—Please research nocturnal wandering plants; fill in metaphor of body with real flower body part; find image which represents seeking and finding essence of flower body.

How could the flower poet know so little about flowers? I had assumed that after so many years Z. would be the expert. She held the highest honor a university could bestow—an endowed chair in creative writing—and yet she seemed incapable of writing her own poems.

Or perhaps she was so successful that she no longer had to write her own poems. She could simply hire out for research and inspiration.

I wondered how many other assistants had been entrusted with the evidence of Z.'s artistic decline. I imagined myself to be the only one.

Dear Professor Z.,

On the question of "masculine flowers," it is my understanding that each flower has a stamen (a male part) and a pistil (a female part) . . . so no flower is completely masculine—at least I haven't found one yet—but I will keep looking.

I wrote these lines for "The Flower Lover":

Flower-body metaphor: *What I love about the two-lipped flower*
is its corolla of fused petals.

Seeking and finding image: *I spread the dark, veined petals, and marvel at the stamen's rounded tip.*

The only wandering plant I could find was the wandering jew—but I didn't think you wanted to bring religion into your poem.

Annabelle

A Poetry Family

And then there were Claire's poems. Shortly before I met Claire, I had read her manuscript, *The Needlepoint Poems.*

It had been presented to me as one of Z.'s editing projects. I had found it on my desk one morning with this note:

Annabelle,

Please proofread copy to original, noting, with keen eye, line breaks, misspellings, and anything you think seems out of order. Write notes in margin in blue pencil. And do let me know what you think.

Z.

There was no blue pencil, so I went out to the stationery store to buy one. And then, as I was leaving the store, I saw *Sirens*. A magazine devoted to women's poetry, it contained poems by several notable women writers. The editor was Judith Hammer, and I copied her address from the masthead. This might be the place for me to publish my poem about Emily Dickinson. I would send it out.

But my excitement was soon tempered when I found a poem called "Cross Women" on page 47. "Here is the introspective Meg Cross," Ms. Hammer had written in the magazine's introduction, "musing on matriarchy and crosses, and, by extension, religion, which is, at its core, patriarchal."

Meg's poem was another look at Cross family history, published, it seemed, as it was first written, without much editing or revision.

CROSS WOMEN

Double crossed and tripled crossed,
I cross myself with the sign of the cross.
My mother, like Jane in that haystack,
crossing herself with a "cross-your-heart."
Once I crossed against traffic.
The road was treacherous
like the women of the Cross family, angry,
petulant, black iron crosses
hammered into the street.
I was very cross
and so I wore a Celtic cross.

Why would an angry person wear a Celtic cross? Meg's poem defied logic.

But whatever I thought of her poetry, there was Meg's name, emboldened in eighteen-point type. I had yet to learn that the poetasters would always be out there, publishing their long poems in magazines, winning awards and recognition. They were the squeaky wheels of the literary world, generating reams of paper, wearing down the editors with the sheer magnitude of their product.

In an interview Z. said that she wrote every day, rising at 6:00 A.M. and returning to her desk in the early evening to review the day's output. Indeed, there were always new poems to type in my folder.

Apparently, there was a writing gene that inclined you toward prolificacy, and judging from the abundance of poems in Claire's manuscript, Z.'s daughter had inherited it.

MOTHER

My mother blooms like a flower
in the center of the needlepoint.
It is pink. Yellow loops go round it.
One black thread is eye.
My mother stitches for eternity
with reading glasses perched,
one lone cigarette
burning in her ashtray.

STITCHES

Some are ornate and complicated,
like the lotus position.

SOLILOQUY ON NEEDLEPOINT

In her bedroom my mother frames
the flowers with more minute flowers.
She uses hot pink, bright orange.
The center is the golden rose.
What flower is mother?
What flower is daughter?
Once, a great poet dropped
two lilies on my nightstand.
When I woke,
they were rice paper.

I gave Claire's manuscript a critical eye, finding some errors in punctuation, some questions of syntax. I left my queries in blue pencil, in the margin, as Z. had requested. If I had been honest, I would have said that I was unsettled by *The Needlepoint Poems*. It seemed to me to be an homage to the perfect mother and, as such, seemed false. But I knew to be careful. I wrote this note:

Professor Z.,

These poems are interesting because women have been sewing forever, so they represent a link to that "feminine" tradition.

Through the course of these poems, we watch the poet transform the ancient "womanly art" into a twentieth-century poet's art.

Annabelle

In the days since Claire had returned from Europe, she had pierced one ear all the way up to her cartilage and in the other was wearing a diamond stud. The day we met, she was wearing jeans and a tight black T-shirt. She looked like a sexy thug.

I told her that I had read her poems and I had liked them.

Then she asked me if I had a book, and I told her, no, I was in a therapy group to cure my addiction to writing, so I was hoping to be poetry-free soon.

It wasn't a funny joke, but Claire acknowledged it anyway with a laugh.

We were working together on *Emily Dickinson at One Hundred and Fifty*. I was the "coordinator," and Claire was the "field assistant." As Z. explained it, I would be arranging the interviews; Claire would do the "legwork." The "legwork" was meeting the poets at their apartments, offices, or a restaurant and asking the questions that Z. had culled from the list Claire and I had come up with. Then I would transcribe Claire's tape. After Z. made her edits, I would retype the interview.

Years later, the computer would make this an easy task. But at the time Z.'s Emily Dickinson book was a process of cutting and pasting, retyping and applying rubber cement. I was grateful that her Smith-Corona had built-in eraser tape.

Most people would have disliked Claire off the bat, but I actually felt a certain tenderness toward her. Despite the many privileges, it couldn't have been easy to be Z.'s daughter.

In Z.'s "Narcissus Poeticus," Claire was her beautiful reflection.

NARCISSUS POETICUS

I am the flower impossible to please,
And you are my echo.
Faithful blossom of the golden cup,

White daffodil daughter,
You fill me.
You fill me.

But in real life, Z. hardly seemed to see her.

And I thought it odd that there was so little physical affection between them. Shouldn't Claire and Z. have at least hugged each other the night Claire returned from Europe? Then there was the matter of Jason Spence—the masculine flower radiating light—rending the precious bond Claire knew as family. As the keeper of her mother's secret, I was, of course, complicit in her betrayal.

"Annabelle," Claire said, "tell me what Braun is like as a teacher."

I was sitting in Z.'s living room at a huge mahogany desk with red-and-yellow inlay. I had just gotten off the phone. (There was no phone in my office.)

I had to think.

"Do you like her class?"

"I like her class. She's a good teacher, I think, a very evenhanded one. She helps us find what's good in every poem."

What could I say? That I hated Meg Cross's poem and wished Braun had hated it too?

I said, "How was the interview?"

"It was okay," Claire said. "But I have to go back today. We didn't finish."

We looked at each other—the servant and the landowner's daughter—and I looked away.

"Mother isn't exactly an admirer. She thinks her poems are facile."

"Aren't everyone's these days?"

"Mother thinks there is some important work being done."

Claire climbed onto the edge of the desk. I moved some papers out of her way.

"I think Braun doesn't like Mother."

"What makes you say that? In class she said Z. was her favorite living poet."

"When someone really likes Mother, they treat me differently. Deferentially. But I felt Braun was like, I think I like you even though you're the flower poet's daughter."

At that moment, I felt like Claire's big sister.

"Listen to this excerpt from Braun's interview," Claire said.

Beside the desk was a canvas bag monogrammed with the initial Z. Claire took out the tape recorder.

I think Emily was a sexy woman. She did write one of the most erotic poems of the nineteenth century. . . . You know the one I mean? "Wild Nights! Were I with thee Wild Nights should be Our luxury!" Oh.

"Braun likes that poem a lot," I said, but what I was really thinking about was the "Oh." What did it mean?

"I think Braun's getting a little punchy going back and forth to Boston every week," Claire said.

"Braun commutes?"

"Braun's got a beautiful old house in Boston with a big bay window. She loves to sit there with her cat and write in a leather notebook she bought in Venice.

"It's on the tape." Claire pressed the fast-forward button, and we listened to the tape recorder's high-pitched, garbled speech, and then to Braun.

My first retreat was Alice Bolton's Praise Poetry! workshop. You've never heard of Praise Poetry! Claire?

Claire stopped the machine. "Have you, Annabelle?"

I shook my head.

We sat around for a weekend and everyone wrote all the time and when we met as a group, we read our poems and simply praised each other. There was no "negative" criticism allowed.

Claire's small background voice said: What was that like?

Braun sighed. Oh, I was young and naïve— In the end, I felt like a member of a radical poetry sect. The cult of the positive poets. (Laughter) Poets against unhappiness. I can't explain it, really.

Claire said: What happened if some negative criticism leaked out?

Braun said: No one dared. It was all about love, Claire. We loved our words and we loved each other. Each poem was born into an outpouring of love, a poetry family. How I loved those retreats! A big house full of poets and their new poems. A fire blazing all day, coffee brewing on the stove. You had your notebook open and sat there all weekend, waiting for your visitation from the Muse. . . . And when she finally came and you read your poem, it was accepted with open arms.

Claire shut off the tape recorder.

"Isn't she great?"

"Love," I said. I tried to imagine Z. leading such a retreat. At the end of the weekend there would just be a few remaining attendees, writing like whores.

"Yeah," Claire said. "Pure love."

I sighed.

"Claire, do you want to go with me to the Mad Dog Café? They have an open mike on Thursday nights."

"When?"

"This week or next. Ben, in my class, invited me. It's the *New York Grit* scene. They do poems like this." And I smacked two fingers on the desk and said, "Coffee top, table top, telephone, toothpaste!"

"How deep."

"The idea, here, is to be cutting-edge, to be different. Anyone can read."

"Are you going to read, Annabelle?"

"No. I thought I'd go and take in the scene."

"You don't like reading?"

"Claire, to be honest, I'm like that character in the Jane Austen story . . . 'I cannot act.' " Which wasn't true, exactly, because nightly I had been playing Nora Joyce to great acclaim.

"Oh, *Persuasion*! That book changed my life! But, Annabelle, if you're afraid to read, you're thinking too much about your own poem. . . . Reading in Europe with my father, I really learned how to do it. It's all about the intonation; it's about 'presentation'—because the Europeans don't really know what you're saying. You have to remember that, Annabelle. When you get up to read, you need to remember that *nobody really knows what you're saying*. Just dress the part."

I said, "Thanks for the tip," then worried for a moment that my tone betrayed a touch of sarcasm. After all, who was Claire to be giving me advice? I went digging into my backpack for my list of errands.

Z. had asked me to pick up some dry cleaning and then make a trip to the thrift store. She was donating a bag of clothing. I was to meet her after these chores were done, at 3:30 in her office.

Claire said, "Have you ever gone to the readings at the Inner Sanctum?"

"No," I said. "I don't go to many readings."

"I'll take you sometime if you want. I go all the time."

"Oh, that's so nice of you," I said, and for a moment I felt really touched that Z.'s daughter wanted to be my friend.

"It's a gay bar. Wednesday is Poetry Slam. Anyone can read."

"Oh, no thanks," I said. "I'm not—"

"Hey, that's okay. I'm not either. Just curious."

"You know," I said, "the truth is, I've never been to a gay bar before."

"Never?"

"It kind of scares me."

Claire said, "Well, that's okay. It used to scare me, too. But then in Europe, my father started to take me. . . . In Amsterdam, we found a place called the Tight Squeeze. And in Sweden, a bar only for women, and only after nine o'clock . . ."

Was Lars gay? Could this be one of those things about Z.'s marriage that were beyond explanation?

I said, "Your father took you?"

"My father's a very open person. His idea is that before I make a decision about anything I should educate myself as fully as possible, whether we're talking about gender or what college I should go to."

"I could never imagine my father taking me to a gay bar or any bar, or even a museum, for that matter. My parents are so . . . limited. My mother especially."

"Annabelle, in case you haven't noticed, my mother is limited too."

Shoes

===

In the center of Harry's bed—his bedspread was an old velvet quilt—
were two black boxes tied together with a white bow. Inside the first
box was a beautiful pair of butter-soft leather gloves. In the second, silk
opera gloves.

There was this note:

Annabelle,

So sorry that you haven't had gloves this fall. Wear the leather
(so very soft) outside and save the white ones (a little rough against
your skin?) for special occasions—in the night table drawer. I will
be home early Friday night. Can you bring some heels and memorize the attached? (James gave Nora gloves; this was her reply.)

Harry

In the same envelope, there was this:

dear Mr. Joyce how can I thank you for your kindness the box of
Gloves which you sent me are lovely and a splendid fit it was a

great surprise to get such a nice present I hope you are quite well, and will be very pleased to see you I hope you will write to me and let me know when I am to meet you.

Like masturbating to Harry's typing, the request both repulsed and compelled me. But where to find heels? If only I had a girlfriend with whom I could share my heart, we could walk arm in arm down the wide boulevards of the Walt Whitman Mall and shop for shoes together.

Z. in her office. Behind her is Washington Square Park, the arch. It is a balmy day in early November. Outside, mothers are pushing strollers; some are pushing their children on the swings.

"Come in, come in, and shut the door, Annabelle. . . . Did you pick up my suit, was it ready?"

"Yes, it's hanging in the hall closet. Professor Z., I have something to ask you."

Z. says, "Hold that thought. My throat is parched from teaching all day. So many profound questions to answer. Can you get me a glass of water?"

In the hallway at the watercooler, I stare at a bulletin board plastered with invitations calling for academics to submit their papers for publication. I am behind on my reading. I need to finish *The Sorrows of Young Werther,* so I can start *The Death of Ivan Ilich.*

I hand Z. a cup of water, then settle in.

"I ran into your friend Braun Brown at a restaurant today," Z. says. Her hair has fallen into her eyes, and she pushes it back behind her ears.

"You mean my teacher?"

"Yes. Your *teacher* says you've got quite an imagination. She says you're a writer who can call up the voice of Emily Dickinson."

"Yes," I say. "In my poem, Dickinson actually asks a riddle."

"I told Braun you've never showed it to me."

"Would you like to see it?" I open my backpack and quickly search through but don't find it. I take a deep breath to relax myself, then say, "I think Braun's been generous to me because of my relationship with you. For instance, this afternoon she's giving me a tutorial, even though I'm not enrolled."

"What's this tutorial on?"

"We're writing confessional poems."

Z. sits upright. "Tell me."

"Braun thinks confessional poetry can help a writer clear her psyche. She says that if you bring forth what is within you, it will set you free; otherwise, it will destroy you."

"Yes," Z. says, "I've heard that before."

"Do you ever write confessional poems to clear out your psyche?"

Z. smiles. "I'll be honest with you, Annabelle. I don't really believe in the concept of a psyche. And if you want my true opinion, it's a phrase that's bandied about here a little too freely."

"Do you believe in the unconscious?"

"I've never given it much thought," Z. says, taking off her glasses and placing them on her desk. "On a more important subject, Annabelle, I want to thank you for that wonderful line about the two-lipped flower."

"You're welcome."

"You have made an important contribution to my poem 'The Flower Lover.'"

"Oh, I wanted to tell you: I'm still researching the nocturnal wandering plant issue."

Arms folded, Z. recites,

What I love about the two-lipped flower is its corolla of fused petals.

These are my words. What does it say that I can mimic Z. so easily?

"Thank you, Annabelle. However you did it, you've managed to master the one-line poem. Exquisite.

"How do you feel about doing more research for me? I've got back-to-back meetings for the next couple of days and no time to do it myself. You could go back to the gardens or, if you want to save time, pick up a gardening book. I need you to identify some masculine flowers and write down your associations. . . . I realize that between working for me in my apartment and in the department, you're pretty booked these days, but this is a great chance for you to exercise your writing muscle. You know I'm happy to pay you extra for these descriptions."

So far Z. has paid me about three hundred dollars for writing flower descriptions. And, sad to say, I don't have a new brown bomber jacket to show for it yet. Along with my commuting expenses, I have a car in my mother's driveway that I'm still making payments on, and I owe Dr. Sanger $405 for the last two months of therapy.

I'm wearing the ratty pea coat I've had since high school.

"And don't struggle too much. Just write down the first thing that pops into your head."

Now she's cleaning her glasses with a chamois cloth. She looks at me with naked eyes. "And here, I'd like you to be graphic. Evoke the glorious masculinity of the flower. Can you do this? You must let me know if you're ever made uncomfortable by what I'm asking." She looks toward her door. "You may not know that there is a sexual harassment case brewing here, and we have all been asked to be very circumspect in our work with our students."

I wonder who it is.

"No," I say. "I'm not at all embarrassed by masculine flowers. I just felt overwhelmed suddenly by everything I have to do. I fell behind in my reading for the Psychological Novel, and I haven't been taking good notes and don't know how I'm going to pass the midterm if I haven't read the books."

"Annabelle, is your intention to be a scholar or a writer?"

"A writer—"

"Then you really need to keep things in perspective . . . flex that writing muscle as much as you can."

"I'll get on it right away. Braun says that I should try to write more realistically."

"This is very important work, Annabelle. But it's not about realism. It's about metaphor. Subtle, evocative metaphor."

I say, "I'm really flattered that you would ask for more flower research—"

"Yes, I would do it myself, but I'm very busy writing my address for the Society. . . . Now, you said in your note that there is no such thing as a masculine flower, but I want to defy horticulture. I want to create a kingdom of masculine flowers. And I need your help."

"I'm happy to do it. Honored, really. Someday, I'll be reading one of your books and maybe there will be a word or phrase that I can trace back to my influence."

"An influence is a record of an affinity," Z. says warmly.

It's why I love her.

"So have the masculine flower research for me next week, will you?"

Then, just as I am about to get up to leave, Z. says, "Annabelle, this morning I fear I might have left a pair of black pumps on top of the donation bag I gave you to drop off at the little thrift store around the corner. Did you see them?"

"I don't remember seeing shoes," I say, reaching into my backpack for Z.'s tax receipt.

"Velvet with a fraying heel? I need them for my reading at the Folger Library."

"Sorry, I didn't see any shoes."

"Then they must have been inside the bag. Annabelle, would you go back and ask Mrs. Hanson, the proprietress, if she would be so kind as to let me have my shoes back. You can tell her that I made a mistake, that I need them for a reading."

"I didn't know the Salvation Army had a proprietress," I say.

"What?"

"The Salvation Army, I didn't know—"

"I asked you to drop my clothes off at the Little Thrift Store Around the Corner, that little thrift store down the street?"

"Oh," I say. "When I saw the note, I assumed—"

"You never saw that little store on the corner called the Little Thrift Store Around the Corner? Annabelle, how can you expect to be a poet with such limited powers of observation?"

"Really. I guess I've been preoccupied with so many things, I didn't give this my full attention."

"Think, Annabelle, think! Would I give my clothes to the Salvation Army? I can't believe you did this to me! Well, go. Go now! Go back to that store and see if you can find me my black velvet pumps—stiletto heel, silver horseshoe on top, matte belt buckle. . . . Tell them you made a mistake. You didn't really mean to give the shoes away. And if that doesn't work, find them and buy them back."

"What if they sent them out to a warehouse or something?"

"I don't care what it takes. Just get the shoes back. And when you do, call!"

Quickly, I gather my backpack, my pea coat, and my new brown gloves.

"Professor Z.," I say, "I will bring back your lucky shoes."

The Poem You Won't Let Yourself Write

The thrift store was a locus of human misery, a place where even the Flower Poet Z. had no cachet.

Because when I said her name, the clerk stared at me absently and pointed to the ladies' shoe department, four shelves to the right of the cash register.

At the Salvation Army, I met the shoe women, a subculture of New Yorkers whose desire for footwear is so intense that they scour the various thrift stores in search of the otherwise unaffordable shoe.

And now they were my competition.

The shoes were in a heap on the floor. "Welcome to Shoe Mountain," said a small woman in a dirty sheepskin jacket, but I chose to ignore her. One by one, I took the dusty shoes from the pile and organized them in pairs on the floor. My task was a grim one.

I was not happy to be touching strangers' shoes. I imagined the past owners taking them off after a day's work, massaging their bunions.

I didn't find Z.'s lucky black shoes.

I called Z. from a pay phone and told her. She hung up on me before I could ask her to transfer me to Braun's line. I wanted to tell

Braun that I would be late for my tutorial, but I was so thrown by Z.'s anger that I spent my last dime calling the wrong number.

On the subway downtown, I berated myself for delivering the bag to the wrong thrift store. I made a list of all the things I had done wrong so far: letting Mrs. Van Elder's teakettle shriek, forgetting the hand towels at Harry's house . . . I worried that Z. would fire me.

When I finally got back to the English Department, it was after five. I knocked on Z.'s door and there was no answer. When I discovered that Braun too had gone, I banged my head against her door and started to cry.

It was in this state that Braun—wearing a simple black dress with a slit up the side—found me.

She unlocked her door and pointed to a chair. She handed me a tissue box.

Probably because our class had been on the confessional poem, I felt comfortable bringing forth what was inside of me in front of Braun. I cried some more, then blew my nose a few times and took a deep breath.

Braun said, "Annabelle, did something happen?"

I said, "I tried to call you, but I got the wrong number."

"Annabelle, that's no reason to be so upset. Something must be terribly wrong."

I shook my head no and said, "Have you seen Z.?"

Braun stuck her head out the door and looked down the hall. She shut the door behind her.

"Is this about Z.?"

I closed my eyes for a moment and then answered, "I really can't talk about it. It would be a betrayal of confidence. . . . It's okay. Really. I can take care of it. It's my problem."

Braun said, "Annabelle, when I find my student banging her head on my door, it's really not okay. And it's my problem, too."

"I took an oath of confidentiality," I said.

Braun said, "I respect that, but think you should nevertheless talk to me or talk to the dean. Your behavior concerns me."

My forehead was beginning to throb. I wondered if I had bruised myself, if there would be a bulge.

I said, "This morning I dropped off a bag for Z. at a thrift store and took it to the wrong one. I was late because I was searching for her velvet shoes in Shoe Mountain, and I couldn't find them."

"Shoe Mountain?"

I said, "I gave Z.'s clothes away to the Salvation Army instead of the Little Thrift Store Around the Corner, and then she wanted her shoes back."

Braun was nodding.

"So I went back to the Salvation Army, and I couldn't find them."

"That's it?"

"No. I told her and she hung up on me . . ."

"What did the shoes look like?"

"Black velvet with fraying heels, a silver horseshoe. I really want to keep my job."

"Do you really?"

"She's not always like this . . ."

Braun was quiet.

I said, "Z. will never see her shoes again."

Braun said, "Z. can survive the loss of her shoes, Annabelle. What matters is that you managed to get here today despite all you've been through. This shows me how committed you are to poetry."

"Thank you," I said. I blew my nose.

"Did you bring your confessional poem?"

"I keep trying to write it, but nothing comes. I tried to write about a virgin in the meadow. I really want to write about virginity, but I feel so blocked."

"Write a poem using *I* as the first word. Did you try that?"

"Yes, and nothing came."

I was too embarrassed to look at Braun, so I looked down at my sneakers. They looked shabby and pathetic. I should have been out shopping for my own shoes, high heels to wear while reciting Nora Joyce's thank-you.

Braun said, "Annabelle, you need to write about the shoes."

"I'd rather forget them."

"You've been wounded, and now it is time to heal. . . . I think Z.'s shoes might be the vehicle for your healing."

"I can't write that poem." I rubbed my forehead.

"Annabelle, you must write that poem to put that terrible, hurtful experience to some good. The poem is so alive; it's right here." She put her hand over her heart.

Braun said, "The shoe has a tongue and a sole. . . . There's a stranger walking around right now in Z.'s shoes. Who is she? Think about that."

Braun picked up a pen from her desk and examined the writing across its side. It was a cheap ballpoint, the kind they give out at the Holiday Inn. She put it down on her blotter.

I pictured Z. kicking off those shoes in her living room, walking in stocking feet into her bedroom, where Jason Spence was sitting on the edge of her bed, reading the *TLS*.

"Annabelle, you strike me as someone who is much too obliging in your life and in your work. Great art pushes the limits of acceptability. It makes us uncomfortable. You must push yourself to the edge of the abyss and beyond."

And then, sitting there, I began to wonder about Braun: Where did she come from and who did she know? There was something electric about her presence, her long, wild hair, her hazel eyes, her face tilted in such a way as to convey empathy. She seemed without a dark side.

"Maybe you could try an experiment: Write a poem about her just for yourself. You don't have to show it to anyone."

"I can't."

Braun said, "What about her name? If you could move beyond your own agitation for a moment, you would see that you have the makings of a very rich topic right here. Think of T. S., e. e.—all those men who were boldly defined by their initials.

"Now, think about a woman who casts off one of her initials. What does that mean to you, Annabelle?"

"A poem about the letter *Z*?"

"Allow yourself to penetrate the mystery of that letter."

"I shouldn't be talking about her like this."

Braun said, "Really, Annabelle. This is not about Z., it's about you. The poem you won't let yourself write is the most urgent one of all."

Harry's Book

About this time, late fall of my junior year, Harry brings home two antiquarian books.

The first volume is *The Sentiment of Flowers,* a delicate leather book with gilt around the edges.

"Annabelle, look at this book. Have you ever seen anything so sensual?"

I take it in my hands, turn the pages.

"Gentle. Gentle," Harry says. "It's nearly a hundred fifty years old."

"Harry," I say, "I know how to hold a book. I've been holding them all my life."

"It's for you."

"Really?"

Then he shows me *Choix des Plus Belles Fleurs*. This book has large engravings that look like the botanical prints hanging in Z.'s living room. In *Papaver somniferum,* the huge red-and-purple head of the poppy is pictured from behind. The flower's green fleshy bud hangs next to it.

"They called this process color stipple engraving," Harry says, lightly touching the picture. "This is the work of the artist Pierre-Joseph Redouté, who lived from 1759 to 1840. Redouté actually defended his right to use this particular process of engraving in a court case. He said it gave his prints the softness and brilliance of a watercolor."

"How do you know this?"

"I read it."

"And you're really giving these books to me?"

"I heard that you were studying flowers."

He sits down at his desk and sits me on his lap. He unbuttons my pajama top, which is actually his pajama top. A kiss on my forehead, my neck, and now he is touching my nipple with his index finger. A touch so light, it's startling. This must be a nipple stipple.

It's lovely to be sitting on Harry's lap. There's the Empire State Building in the distance, coffee perking in an old aluminum pot on the stove.

I touch Harry's mop of curls. "Dear Mr. Joyce," I whisper, "how can I thank you for your kindness? The box of gloves which you sent me are lovely and a splendid fit."

Harry closes his eyes, and he shakes his head as if to free himself from the dream of the gloves. He nuzzles my neck, then gets up for coffee.

"Annabelle, I want you to read something. You've asked me where I am every night. The truth is, I've been driving every night to Marshall Greene's abandoned farmhouse in High Falls, near Stone Ridge, across the Hudson. I've been working on a novel."

"You have a car?"

"A relic."

"But you said you were at the library writing a dissertation on Joyce."

"Annabelle, you should know better. I'm not an academic."

"But, Harry, aren't you afraid of getting caught? You could get arrested for trespassing."

"Isn't trespassing the writer's work?"

"Very clever, Harry," I say. "Are you really breaking into a dead man's house every night, sitting at his desk, writing your book?"

"Yes, but why should it matter where I'm writing it? I want you to read my novel."

"How do you get in, through the window, like a cat burglar?"

"No, I have the key. When I was Marshall's assistant, I took care of Thomas Wyatt. The dog, remember, his dog? I still have the key."

"I'm surprised they haven't changed the locks."

"Only the IRS could catch me—but they won't be there for a while."

He opens a cardboard box and pulls out his manuscript. I had expected he would have thousands of pages, but it looks very thin. It's called *Harry's Book*.

CHAPTER 1

He was an old man who sat alone at a desk in High Falls, New York, and he had gone eighty-four days now without stringing together a paragraph.

In the first forty days, his assistant sat beside him in that room, but the university had sent his assistant back to campus, back to the copy machine, back to the graduate lounge to grade papers.

Harry settles down with his coffee.

It made the assistant sad to see the old man returning to campus, his hair disheveled, a book in one hand, a briefcase in the other.

The briefcase was scuffed. The handle was taped together, and swinging back and forth in the writer's hand, the briefcase looked like a flag of permanent defeat.

Now the writer is dead and the young man sits at the writer's desk, writing these words.

"Wow," I say. "It really deconstructs itself." I read on. From what I can see, it's a story about a man (Harry) sitting at the desk of a famous dead writer (Marshall Greene), writing a story about a man sitting at the desk of a famous dead writer, writing.

> The old writer was portly. His long white hair had once made him seem like a girl, but that hair was long gone. His face was mapped with lines.
>
> "Marshall," the assistant had said to him, "I could stay with you tonight. I could sit by your desk and egg you on the way it used to be. Remember how you once went ninety days without a sentence, and then you wrote and wrote for three weeks?"

"I need you to come," Harry says. "The story's going nowhere without you. You're my muse."

"No way," I say.

"No one will ever find out, Annabelle. I promise. Come with me to Marshall's house and write your own book, if you want."

"Harry, *Harry's Book* is a paper trail."

He's crushed.

"No, really, I think it's very inventive—writing about writing. But, Harry, do you think they'll let you finish your book about breaking and entering in jail?"

"Thursday night?"

"I can't."

"I'll set you up in a little room with my typewriter."

"I don't work on a typewriter."

"Come with me, Annabelle, please. The house is in probate. It doesn't belong to anyone now. No one will ever know. Just once?"

I think about what Braun has said about great art pushing limits. And I think of Arthur Feld telling me that I have a gift, and I should make use of it.

"Okay," I say. "I'll go with you on Thursday night, but first you have to come with me to Arthur's reading."

"Remind me who that is, Annabelle."

"Arthur Feld," I say, and while I'm describing my former poetry teacher, Harry goes into his study, then comes back with a Rolodex. A metal one, a bit rusty, with big black knobs.

"Look at this, Annabelle. This is Marshall's Rolodex, the wheel of fortune," Harry says.

He pulls out a card: the editor of *The New York Literary Review*.

"Do you want to write book reviews?"

"I've never written one; no experience," I say.

"It doesn't matter. We can draft a letter from Marshall asking to put you on their reviewers' list. I do a great Marshall Greene signature. *Dear Sir, I would like to draw your attention to the critical work of Annabelle Goldsmith. Ms. Goldsmith is a gifted writer, whose work has appeared in numerous periodicals. She is especially suited to review poetry—*"

"Harry, don't you think people will be suspicious getting a letter from a dead man? His obituary in the *Times* was half a page."

He says, twirling the Rolodex, "Reviewing poetry will give you a power base."

"They'd trace the letter back to you, and both of us would go to jail. And believe me, they wouldn't let us share a cell."

"You can be so down sometimes, Annabelle. Look, I want to tell you something, and you have to promise never to tell anyone. Ever."

"Okay."

"When Marshall died, I realized that I never got a letter for my dossier from him."

He looks at me. "I know. I know. It's terrible. He suffered a gruesome death, smashed beyond recognition by a speeding train, and I was only thinking about myself."

"Go on."

"I became obsessed. Why hadn't I asked Marshall for a letter! How many days and nights I sat beside him in that fucking freezing cold office— 'So, Harry, listen to this sentence, better to use *a* or *the*?' Then, 'Why, Harry, why the *the* and not the *a*?'

"I paper-trained that dog, washed its piss off Marshall's carpet for chrissake— And I hadn't even asked him to write me a letter of recommendation! I was loyal to the point of invisibility, Annabelle. Don't let this happen to you with Z.!"

He gets up and walks to the bathroom. I hear the snap of the medicine cabinet opening and closing.

Now he's standing in front of me with his arm outstretched. "Look at this."

It is a small bottle of Percocet prescribed to Marshall Greene.

"A week after Marshall was buried, I was so distraught I was going to down them in the English Department. My plan was to do it first thing in the morning, before anyone had arrived. I saw myself in that corner lounge . . . lying on the dirty green sofa. I wanted Maurita to find me there, eyes open, the empty pill bottle in my hand . . ."

"Harry, that's so angry and sad."

"And that was the moment I realized Marshall would have asked me to draft my own letter anyway. So I wrote it, forged his signature, and sent it off to Career Services."

"And no one ever questioned the letter arriving after Marshall was dead?"

"Not one person."

"And you aren't afraid that something bad is going to happen to you?"

"Like what?"

"I don't know. It just seems so . . ." I grimace. "It's so wicked what you've done. It's forgery—forgery involving a really famous person. You know better than that, Harry."

"Don't be so pure, Annabelle. Marshall used me . . . and now I'm using him. You need to figure out how to make use of Z. People use people. Z. knows that. Do you know that I used to find Marshall dates? He liked a young poet just starting out. He would have liked you," Harry says, and he puts his arm around me and gives me a squeeze.

The Rumor Mill

―――

Hours later, Z. is opening a package that I have brought her.

"Oh, my," she says as she opens *Choix des Plus Belles Fleurs*. She is standing near the window, about to draw the blinds.

The midday sun is illuminating the stain I discovered on Z.'s striped couch after last week's salon. It is a faint red stain, amorphous, left behind by Jason Spence.

Z. says, "I saw this years ago in a bookstore in Paris, and I've regretted all my life that I didn't have the money to buy it then . . ." She's turning the pages. "And the colors are so vivid, so alive. And not a single plate is missing!"

"A friend of mine found it at a used-book store, and I've decided to pass it on to you. I guess it's my way of apologizing for the lost shoes."

A nod of acknowledgment. She's holding the book to her chest. My sacrifice to the poetry goddess.

Z. says, "Thank you, Annabelle. Thank you so much! Now, before I forget, here's your list of errands for the day. . . . Maybe you could make a trip to one of those department stores where they sell the kinds of stain removers they advertise on TV . . . Stain-Out or Stain-Go?"

"I've seen that ad. . . . They say you can find it at Mays, Fourteenth Street and Union Square."

"Who was sitting on that seat last week, do you remember?"

I tell her I didn't notice. Why ruin the illusion of a perfect love?

"Out, out damn spot!" I say.

The corner of Z.'s lip rises.

She motions for me to sit down.

This is the exact place where we had tea the morning I signed on for my apprenticeship.

I can see myself reflected in her glasses.

"Annabelle, I want to speak with you about something that's been on my mind. I think you may have wondered why I assigned my daughter the task of interviewing poets for our Emily Dickinson book."

I nod my head. I sense this is a question Z. does not want me to answer.

". . . You see, since she's come home from Europe, Claire's been a little odd." Z. is groping for words. "The other night I found myself in a panic. All that piercing! Who in their right mind goes out and pierces four holes up their ear? And, of course, you've noticed her hair. Today it's sticking up and pointing in every direction. Has the Statue of Liberty suddenly come into vogue? Because my daughter looks like she is wearing her crown. Clearly, she's going through something. I just worry that, at the end of it, the impression she will make on my colleagues at Harvard this spring is that Claire Bovardine is not like everyone else. Claire Bovardine is not normal."

I reflect on the phrase "not normal." What is Z. really thinking?

"I don't know," I say. "Maybe it's just about style."

"No, I think there's more to it than that. I had hoped that the Emily Dickinson project would absorb Claire until she leaves for school in January, but she just seems to be going through the motions."

"She's going back to interview Braun Brown this week."

"Annabelle, if you knew anything about my daughter which struck you as troubling, would you tell me?"

"Of course," I say, although it occurs to me that I've promised Claire not to tell Z. anything.

"This is a strange thing to ask. I'm sorry. But I feel so unequal to what is happening with her. Poor Claire is in pain and I am completely shut out."

"Is Claire in pain?"

"But for a few mishaps, your devotion has not been lost on me, Annabelle. I know I can count on you. Can you be there for my daughter as well?"

"Sure," I say, then, without missing a beat, "I wanted to ask you about the Emily Dickinson project—my poem?"

Z. says, "Your poem?"

"Yes," I say. "The one Braun told you about. I want to know if there's a chance we could include it."

"Of course there's a chance." Then, still preoccupied, Z. says, "By the way, Annabelle, how are you coming with those masculine flowers?"

Obviously Z. isn't going to make an editorial decision today.

So I reach into my backpack for a folded piece of paper with a mess of spiral notebook edges, and say, "I have two more descriptions. You know, they were harder to write than I thought."

Z. holds the paper in her hands for a long time, then she clears her throat, and this is what she reads:

> *A delicate blue flower hanging on a slender stalk.*
> *A flower has one goal, producing seeds.*

Z. says, "That's it?"

"Well, I have some ideas, but nothing's finished. I'll bring you more as they come to me."

Z. says, "You were off to such a good start, Annabelle." She reads the first one again, "A delicate blue flower hanging on a slender stalk . . .

"I like the 'delicate blue flower,' but the slender stalk? Avoid alliteration, Annabelle. It weakens your poetry. Now, the kinds of 'hanging flowers' we're talking about—yes, they're bluish, but are they delicate? I don't think so. . . . A metaphor only works if we can visualize the object."

"Maybe I didn't spend enough time on these. I mean, I was looking at a flower book and this is what came to me, so I wrote it down."

"Meaning you spent no time on revision? . . . And your second idea: A flower's goal is producing seeds . . ."

"Here I was trying something new. I was trying to be precise, without ornamentation."

"I see." She hands me back the paper. "Annabelle, is this your best work? You do know that I need your best work."

I say, "It's just that I've been a little distracted. The truth is, I have a new boyfriend, and I've been commuting from my mother's house on Long Island. . . . He's a novelist."

"I have a friend who owns an apartment building in the Village. Maybe I could help you there. . . . Let me talk to her. . . . Meanwhile, I think we should reexamine this 'masculine flower' idea. Maybe there's not enough material out there to generate a book-length manuscript."

"Professor Z.," I say, "of all the assignments you've given me, this has been the toughest. I mean, I didn't have this much trouble when I was doing my flower research in the garden."

"Then by all means, go back to the garden."

"I just don't know if that would help. The truth is, I look at a flower and I don't think *man*. I think *woman*."

"Are you telling me, Annabelle, that there aren't enough masculine flowers to fill a book?"

"Well, I've even considered the orchid, which comes from the Greek word for testicle, but I'm not making great progress."

"A flower named for a testicle?"

"Yes, from the Greek word *orkhis*."

"And this doesn't inspire you?"

"Believe me, Professor Z., I've really been trying. I even set up a desk in the student lounge with all my botanical books so I could compare sources."

"I don't see how you could possibly concentrate there, with all the whispering that goes on. You must know that our English Department has one of the most pernicious rumor mills in the country."

I want to say, "Yes, I've heard you eat your assistants," but instead I feign ignorance.

Z. says, "For example, the other day, I was dropping something off on Maurita's desk when I turned around and a group of graduate students were laughing behind my back."

"That could mean anything, don't you think?"

"Annabelle, what are people *saying* about me? It really is incumbent upon you to let me know."

"I thought it was my job to protect you from this kind of thing, but if you really want to know . . . Once I heard someone at the Xerox machine say that you and Mr. Spence were seen having lunch together at a restaurant. I mean, it didn't register as malicious. It sounded more like this person just went out to lunch and saw you at another table."

"Seen having lunch?"

"Maybe those weren't the exact words. It was hard to hear—"

"Were they whispering?"

"Not in a bad way . . ."

"Who? Who?"

"A couple of grad students, maybe."

"Graduate *creative writing* students?"

"I think so."

"And was there more?"

"The only other thing I remember is that the word *hotel* was used."

Z. gasps.

I make a mental note never to speak the word *hotel* again.

"To the student body, I am clearly an object of ridicule."

"Because you were seen having lunch at a hotel restaurant? Professor Z., I saw you together, having drinks at the Metropolitan Café, so what's the—"

Then Z. gets up and walks to the window. Her back is toward me. She is standing perfectly still, and then I notice an almost imperceptible shaking of her shoulders. I can tell she is crying. I want to give her a tissue, but I feel it would be intrusive.

"Annabelle, you may think that I'm overreacting. But when I hear something like this, I am reminded of what the tragic poet Delmore Schwartz once said: 'Even paranoids have real enemies.' "

General Ink

———

Within a week, I saw that "being there for Claire" involved typing her letters. And she, too, was leaving work for me in Z.'s folder.

> Annabelle,
>   *Please* take this stack to General Ink, and make two copies of each poem.

> Annabelle,
>   Can you type these envelopes and letters for me? Please attach poems to back of letter with paper clip for me to sign.

While I sat in the maid's room typing, Claire's father, Lars Bovardine, milled about the house in his sweat clothes, holding a sheet of paper and reading with expression: "The owner is a man of taste and cultivation, but there is nothing to show he was a poet. Outside his house, there is a garden. The scent of flowers floods the house of the tragic poet—"

The slamming of the refrigerator door.

"At the end of the wall, there is a chapel, the temple for Lares. This house of tragedy is my temple. . . . The temple of Lares, Lararium. Who is the tragic poet? . . . Lares, a tutelary god? Who guards my house? I do."

How did Z. get any work done, I wondered.

I typed:

Dear Mr. Scott,

My first book is about to be published, and my mother, Z., remembering your kindness in publishing her very first poems, suggested I write you about the possibility of your reviewing my book in *Poetry: America!* I have enclosed my galleys.

I deeply appreciate your consideration.

Sincerely,
Claire Bovardine

Since my head-banging tutorial with Braun, I had been trying to write a poem about Z.'s lost shoe, but to no avail. Most of my time was spent thinking about Harry's bed, with its view of the Empire State Building; Z.'s husband, barefoot, in a college T-shirt; and Benjamin Adams, with his pierced eyebrow, reciting "Coffee top, table top, telephone, toothpaste!"

In order to be poets, Arthur Feld had told my class, "we must first be lovers." But I couldn't imagine my crazy love of men making a poem that would be of interest to anyone.

I was defeated before I even sat down to write. How I wished I had a mother like Z. pressing me forward.

Annabelle,

Can you transcribe this tape? When you're done, can you put the pages in an envelope and slide them under my door? Thanks so much for your help.

Claire

Part 2 of the Braun Brown interview started with static and Claire saying, "Testing. Testing. Is it working?" Then the voice of Braun Brown: "You know, I wrote my dissertation on Stevens."

"Really?"

"Yes, Stevens's use of snow in his poem 'The Snow Man.' "

"You wrote an entire dissertation on snow?"

Braun laughs. "Yes, it was an influence study."

There's a glitch in the tape where the tape recorder has been turned off, and here, it begins again.

"Shall we talk about Emily?" Claire says.

"Yes," says Braun. "Let's talk Emily."

"Now here's the kind of question my mother hates: Do you think Emily Dickinson was a feminist?"

Braun says, "Such a big question straight off. What did the word *feminist* mean to a woman in the nineteenth century?"

Claire says, "I'm not sure. I'll have to look it up in a nineteenth-century dictionary and see if there's a definition. So forget that question. Tell me, do you think Emily would have been happy having children?"

"She was so deeply in love with Gib, her nephew, and grieved so over his death. So maybe, yes. Not happier, but perhaps she would have had more happiness in her life."

Claire says, "I think Emily Dickinson was a lesbian."

Braun is quiet. Perhaps she is taking in Claire's spiked hair and earrings, those telltale signs of sexual awakening.

"What's your evidence?"

"Her letters to her sister-in-law, Sue. When they stopped being close, Dickinson's writing suffered."

Braun says, "You sound like quite the scholar of Dickinson."

Claire says, "Mother has asked me to do some research."

Braun says, "Well then, every scholar knows you need to be cautious about making a leap from the page to the bed."

"Or the bed to the page—"

Nervous laughter?

Then Braun says, "Claire, I'm doing a weekend workshop in December. It's a retreat for the students in the writing program. Would you like to come? It could be a lot of fun for you. You'll get a room in my house and a funky old desk to write at."

"What's the focus?"

"It's an intensive on confessional poetry. I want everyone to spend a weekend writing anything they want. I want to shape a group of poets to be fearless writers, writers who are not afraid to engage their passion—"

"So, they work all weekend on their poems?"

"Yes, and I have a good friend staying with me who has a two-week appointment at Wellesley. She's agreed to lead the seminar . . . Gay Farinette—"

"Gay, is that really her name? C'mon."

Claire may have been brilliant, but she led a sheltered life.

Braun says, "Oh, you should take a look at her poems. . . . Here, borrow my copy. . . . So, would you like to come? Maybe you could collaborate with me, help me organize the weekend."

"Sure, but I've got to tell you, I've never studied with a woman named Gay before."

Braun laughs. "You might learn something."

Claire says, "Maybe you can teach me?"

Silence. Sexual tension, but who can say? Someone should turn off the tape recorder.

Then Claire says, "Okay, you're going to think this is extreme, but have you ever slept with a woman? My mother says everyone does it at least once. She slept with her thesis adviser when she was in college."

The sound of Braun clearing her throat. "Claire, people do things for all sorts of reasons."

"Mother says it's normal, but you quickly grow out of it. Do you think that's right?"

"Well," Braun says, "I can only speak from my own experience, but I think it's different for everyone."

There's distortion, the noise of papers shuffling. Claire says, "Have you ever slept with a woman, Braun?"

Braun says, "I'm in a terrible predicament here. I want to speak openly to you about what it is you might be going through, Claire, but I can't. . . .Your mother feels I am too familiar with my students as it is. Dr. Marks, our department chair, told me this."

"What?"

"She saw me in a coffee shop with a student . . ."

That's the moment Lars walks in with a sheet of paper, and I turn off the tape recorder.

He stands before me and reads, "He stood at the Herculaneum Gate. He had an epiphany. His life as he knew it would change. . . ."

Lars smiles down at me with his most theatrical smile.

I smile back, but it's not enough.

"What do you think of that?"

"What is the Herculaneum Gate?"

"It's not clear?"

"Some gate in Pompeii?"

"Yes, the door to Pompeii."

"Maybe take out the last line," I say. "I think you should end on the word *epiphany*." He coughs twice, then reads, "He stood at the Herculaneum Gate. He had an epiphany."

Epiphanies and interruptions, I think, turning the tape recorder back on. The story was just getting good.

There's a long pause, then Braun says, "Getting back to Emily . . ."

"Yes, Emily," Claire says. "Too many poems and not enough words. A little boring sometimes, don't you think?"

"A necessary poet," Braun says. "An important poet. A poet of the heart and mind."

The sound of Claire turning the pages of her legal pad. "Here's the kind of serious question that Mother likes: It is said that Emily Dickinson composed her poems to church hymns. How does religion influence your writing, Braun?"

"Well, perhaps we should talk about how the strict moral code of Puritan New England shaped Emily Dickinson's writing, Claire. . . . I think we are all still struggling to write against that."

Claire says, "All of us who aren't flower poets, that is," and laughs.

Braun says, "Yes, the confessional road is a tough one. Take it from someone who wrote a book called *His Mistress*. I put my desire out, front and center, and now the idea that I'm a person without moral character has come to haunt me."

"Sorry she's making your life miserable," Claire says, and the tape clicks, the story ends, static.

A Misplaced Alphabet

Why am I so devoted to Z.? That's what I'm thinking in the car after Arthur Feld's reading.

Then Harry says, "Annabelle, did you bring the gloves?"

"Was I supposed to?"

"Were you supposed to? Oh, Jesus Christ."

He makes a series of angry turns out of the city. Then we are suddenly alone in the dark on Route 87. It's quiet. Harry says, "It's just when he read those 'Women Undressing' poems. I thought my head was going to explode."

He clears his throat, affects a weird accent.

" 'Now I will read from my recently published chapbook, *The Woman Undressing Poems:*

Woman undressing
beautiful with lion,
Beautiful, yellow woman, your dress undoes me
you ask, what is art,
woman undressing.

I say, "Not funny, Harry. And the poems— You're making them worse than they are. I liked them."

"Really?"

It embarrasses me to say this: "I think Arthur Feld is a fine writer, a sensitive man."

"I'd like to dedicate this poem to my beloved wife, Lucille, whose warm body has sheltered me for the last twenty-eight years. Lucille, please stand up for the audience—"

"Shut up, Harry."

" 'Woman undressing, beautiful with rabbit. Big, white, furry woman alone in the forest. . . .' "

"You're an asshole, Harry. You fawn over Joyce. No matter what he writes, you hang on his every word. 'Can I fuck you up the ass, sweet Nora?' "

"Yes, but Joyce is a great writer, Annabelle. Arthur Feld is not. And, for your information, what he said was something like this." Harry clears his throat.

"It is my love for you that allows me to throw you down on your soft belly and fuck you like a hog riding a sow. I glory in the stink and sweat that rises from your ass."

"Why would you memorize such a thing?"

"I don't memorize; I paraphrase, distill the essence. And what's the big deal? It's beautiful and tender and playful." He takes his eyes off the road for a second and looks at me. "And it's art."

"Look, the gloves are one thing, touching myself—well, okay. But forget it if you think I am going to get fucked up the ass on Marshall Greene's bed so you can write about it in your memoir. It's not in the muse's job description."

"It's not a memoir, it's fiction," Harry says. "And why are you so argumentative, Annabelle? I brought my little red Valentine typewriter so you could work on your own poems."

"You can't write poems on a typewriter, Harry, even if it is the Olivetti that ushered in the design revolution."

"There's a space for you in Marshall's house, a little guest room with a chaise longue and a lady's writing desk. . . . It's small and compact like a lady."

"I'm not impressed."

Harry takes a hand off the steering wheel and touches my face. "I'm sorry. I shouldn't have made fun. Arthur is very important to you."

And, here, I shut my eyes. I feel miles away from home. I'm missing Arthur and I'm missing my mother. I'm wondering if I've cut her out of my life too hastily.

"He's the reason you're at the university, right? He helped you get that scholarship."

"The Edgar Allan Poe Fellowship." To say this still fills me with pride.

"You know I love you, Annabelle, and I haven't loved anyone in a long time."

"I haven't loved anyone either," I say, which isn't entirely true. I've secretly loved Z.

I'm thinking about Arthur's reading. How he settled down with his books in the sanctuary of that dilapidated synagogue on the Lower East Side and read from them one at a time, until he was left just holding sheaves of paper, poems he had written that morning. I had never been to a reading at a synagogue before; there was something holy about it.

"It just felt a little sad tonight. Arthur looked so . . . desperate in that green bow tie. So desperate and excited to finally be reading in New York City."

"Well," Harry says. "That's making it as a poet, reading in the Big Apple, even if it happens to be in a synagogue."

"No, Harry. Reading at the Society for the Preservation of American Poetry is making it."

The auditorium that night was half full, but for an unknown poet like Arthur, the auditorium would always be half empty.

"Harry, can I tell you something? I love being in New York City, but sometimes I miss my old life. I miss Dr. Sanger."

"Why don't you call her?"

"She'd tell me to come in and talk, and I'm just too busy."

"So tell me," Harry says. "What seems to be the problem?"

"I feel like I don't belong anywhere. I'm always inhabiting someone else's life, whether it's Z.'s or yours."

"You could move in with me."

"Thanks, Harry."

"You could move in with Z."

"And work around the clock refreshing the supply of hand towels? I don't think so. . . . Can I read you a poem, Harry?"

"In the dark?"

"Actually, I wrote it in my head, so I know it by heart. . . . I thought it through before committing it to paper. . . . Braun asked us to write a confessional poem." And I recite,

MISPLACED ALPHABET
I was A to her Z;
and I to her C.
I was finite to her indefinite,
and known to her unknown.
To get to Z,
you must travel
through the alphabet.
The road is a trail
of misplaced, broken letters.
I am a small letter
setting out for the capital.

"Annabelle, that's good," Harry says. "Original and kind of funny."

"You think?"

"Yeah, and it's poignant at the same time. . . . But I'm sorry you feel so out of place."

"I just feel so isolated, keeping so many secrets. Harry, if I share something with you, would you keep it confidential?"

"Is something wrong?"

"Z. has this husband who is always writing—"

"Lars."

"He's an actor, Z. said."

"Yes, once at a scholarship event, he performed a monologue Marshall wrote for him. . . . He was in his glory, having just won the Critics Circle award—"

"Now Lars is writing a memoir."

"I'm sure it will be a blockbuster."

"Apparently, he had an epiphany once in Pompeii when he and Z. were just starting out together, and recently he went back and had another one with Claire. . . . He keeps reciting this one line."

"Really, an epiphany?"

"Something like, 'Lars Bovardine at the Herculaneum Gate. He had an epiphany.' "

"Joyce coined that word, *epiphany,* did you know that?"

"He said they were young and starting out—"

"It was Stephen Dedalus in *Portrait of the Artist as a Young Man* who had the epiphany."

"And Z. asked me to keep an eye on Claire."

"The beautiful, exotic Claire."

"Z. is upset because Claire came back from Europe and spiked her hair and pierced four holes up her ear in a day."

"I'll keep an eye on Claire if you don't want to."

"Hey, shut up, Harry. . . . So getting back to Claire. I'm helping Z. put together a book called *Emily Dickinson at One Hundred and Fifty.* Originally—because it was my idea—I was supposed to interview all these famous poets about Emily Dickinson, but Z. had Claire do it instead. At first I was hurt, but it turns out to be her way of keeping an eye on Claire."

"What does that mean?"

"I don't know. She's asked me to help her, help Claire. This is hard to explain."

"You're helping her help Claire?"

"I'm the apprentice in life and in art, what can I say? . . . So I'm transcribing this tape that has Claire interviewing Braun Brown."

"The beautiful, exotic Braun Brown."

I sigh because I can't reveal to Harry the whole truth: that in a strange act of aggression, Claire has told the rival poet that her mother once slept with a woman.

So I say, "They're talking about Emily Dickinson being gay. And then there's this flirting. It's hard to explain. Braun invites Claire to this retreat she's going to have and tells her that she's invited a poet named Gay. You might learn something from her, Braun says. And then Claire says in a provocative way, 'Maybe you can teach me.' It's a strange moment, rife with sexual innuendo."

"Wouldn't you have had to be there with them to know?"

"Maybe," I say. "But Z. asked me to keep an eye on Claire, to let her know if there's anything that seems 'not quite right'—"

"Annabelle," Harry breaks in, "I listen better with coffee. Do you see that thermos in the back?"

It's a big plaid thermos, an old-fashioned one. The coffee, coming so late at night in the darkness, feels good. He takes a few sips, and then I drink some.

Harry's car is a small, beat-up Chevy. He needs to feel like he has the freedom to leave the city at any time.

I touch Harry's arm. He's wearing his rough fisherman's sweater. He's been wearing it every day since the weather turned cold.

I like being with Harry. I like how adventurous he is. Harry lives Arthur Feld's motto. He takes the world by its reins.

I'm hoping to learn by his example.

We're quiet for a while, passing the coffee back and forth, then I say, "You know, I think Z. was right to think that Claire is going through something, because she is. She told me that she's been going to gay bars with her father as her escort. But back to the tape—it ends on a weird note. Braun is telling Claire that Z. is trying to get her fired. Braun says that she was seen having lunch with a student."

"That's not what I've heard," Harry says.

"I need to know what you've heard," I say.

"Well, they say that Z. saw Braun and a young man entering a room at the Hotel Manhattan. Supposedly Braun was fumbling with the keys and laughing. Ms. Brown has said what she does in her private time is private and she doesn't feel the need to explain."

"I wonder who it was."

"A graduate student."

"Ben? She loves Ben. She thinks men who write poetry have a feminine side. What do you think?"

"I think Braun and Z. were both doing it in the middle of the afternoon at the Hotel Manhattan, that's what I think."

I wanted to tell him not to be a know-it-all. I knew for a fact that Z. frequented the Plaza, not the Manhattan.

I said, "All you think about is sex, Harry."

"Annabelle, sex is there to distract you from the real issue, which is that Ms. Brown is a visiting professor who is about to be offered a tenure-track position, and Z. doesn't want her to have it."

"How do you know?"

"I've been sorting mail for the department. There are some letters I'm required to open, and in the case of a recent one marked 'confidential,' I accidentally slit the envelope."

"I don't believe it. Z. wouldn't do that to Braun."

"Are you sure? Doesn't she have a boyfriend who needs a job?"

I don't answer.

"But tell me this, Harry, if Z. is out to kill Braun's career, then why would Braun befriend Claire, invite her to our retreat?"

"Annabelle, I'm starting to think you haven't learned anything about the poetry world."

Breaking and Entering

⸻

An hour later I wake up at the old converted farmhouse of the great, dead writer. Harry is carrying me in his arms.

"Hey—what is this?" I'm a little disoriented.

"I wanted to carry you across the threshold."

And he does, fumbling for the keys in his pocket and kicking open the door. Inside, the house is dark. It has an old wood smell.

He carries me up the stairs, which evokes in me a series of complicated feelings. I feel like I am his baby; he is my father. I feel that he is all-powerful and I am weak. I like feeling weak.

"Okay, down you go. Don't touch the light switch."

"No lights?"

"I have battery-operated lamps in the rooms, flashlights in my car, and there are some candles. I'm trying not to raise suspicion by jacking up the electric bill."

"That's why you brought me the manual typewriter."

"Right. Annabelle, you should see the view from up here. Mountain peaks from every window. Too bad we'll have to be gone before daylight."

We put our things down in a central room, which was once the bedroom of the novelist Marshall Greene. The room's a bit messy, with papers on the floor and jeans and a bathrobe draped across a chair.

"It's as he left it. I've only changed the sheets."

"A real Marshall Greene fan would sleep in them," I say.

"They were pretty crusty."

"This is creepy, Harry. Where are we?"

"A town called High Falls."

"The fictional town in your book?"

"Yes," Harry says. "We're in the middle of a fiction, Annabelle. Now, I'm going out to the car to get a few things. When I come back, will you be undressed and lying on the bed? You're shivering. I'll put the heat on."

The creaking of one door, the slamming of another one. How to undress in the house of the dead writer? On the floor is a huge stack of papers. This must be another Marshall Greene manuscript. The cover page says "Saul."

I've never read a book by Marshall Greene. I don't understand prolificacy, these writers writing a dozen 850-page books. Who has that much to say?

Emily Dickinson wrote 1,775 poems, the equivalent of two Marshall Greene books.

It's a disturbing thought.

Books line one wall of Marshall Greene's bedroom. There is a door on either side. I sit on the bed. I hear feet on the gravel, the slamming of a car door.

I'm wearing a simple black scoop-neck cotton shirt. I take it off. I unsnap the waist of my blue jeans.

I kick off my black boots, put all my clothes neatly in a pile in the corner of the room. Then I pull back the comforter. The sheets are flannel and feel soft against my skin. Once under the covers, I take off the last of my clothing: underwear and bra. I am no longer an accomplice in the crime of trespassing. I am a criminal, a stark naked criminal.

When I hear him walking up the stairs, I take the comforter off. As he wishes.

Entering the bedroom, Harry says, "My, my, my . . ."

He lays a cold hand on my stomach.

"I want to do lots of things to you tonight, but I also have to write."

"Woman undressing, alone in dark farmhouse . . ."

"Have you forgiven my mocking your teacher's poems?"

But before I can answer, we kiss.

Harry detaches and pushes open a door across the room.

"This is the study of the great writer."

There is a desk with a typewriter.

"And this," he says, walking over to the far side of the room, and pushing open the door, "this is where you will work."

He picks up a flashlight and illuminates a chaise longue, a wall full of books, and a small oak writing desk.

"A house designed for making love and then going to your desk and writing about it."

He lights some candles, sits on the edge of the bed. I've covered myself with a blanket.

"Will you be my model, Annabelle? I want to work from you as a painter would, not from memory, but from sight and touch."

He's stroking the length of me, then settles on my nipples, making them hard. What I really want to do is talk. I want to talk about Emily Dickinson, Lars Bovardine, Claire.

He kisses my face, runs a hand down my back.

"It was nice of you to promise to introduce Arthur to Z.," Harry says.

"I don't think he'll go to her reading," I say.

Arthur had brought his wife and daughter over to meet me. He had told them that I was his "success story," that I was "in with the movers and shakers of the poetry world," and that I would be one someday, too. That was when, overcome with gratitude and guilt, I told him I would introduce him to Z. at her reading at the Society in the spring.

"You should call him and take him up on his offer; teach his class."

"What would I teach?"

"For my first class of the semester, I always teach Roethke's 'My

Papa's Waltz.' You could spend an entire class on that poem. You talk about metrics, form, the dance of the father and son, and then you talk a little bit about child abuse."

"I don't have the time to go out to Long Island, Harry."

He looks at his watch. "Hey, Annabelle, it's getting late. Could you lay this way for me? I want to sit at my desk and watch you."

A perfunctory kiss on my forehead.

"You want me to touch-type?"

"Yes, while I sit at the desk and write."

"While you sit at Daddy's desk and write?"

From his open bag on the floor, he takes out his dog-eared paperback of Joyce's letters.

"Here," Harry says. "Read this." It's James writing to Nora:

"'I am your child as I told you and you must be severe with me. Punish me as much as you like. I would be delighted to feel my flesh tingling under your hand.'"

"I want to spank you," Harry says. "I want to write about it."

"Now, right now?"

"Okay, maybe later."

Then Harry is sitting before the typewriter of the famous, dead writer. The heat comes up in a rattle of old pipes.

I turn myself on the bed so I'm facing Harry. I spread my legs. I want to give him a show, but it's dark. I want to distract him from the idea of spanking me, or do I? All of this is so new and exciting.

While I am touching myself, I'm thinking about what Claire said about Emily Dickinson being gay. I wonder what she wrote in her letters to her sister-in-law. I'm thinking about Claire interviewing Braun Brown—that space between them that I can't decipher, the silence and the nervous laughter—is it a sexual space?

Harry alternates between looking at his typewriter and looking absentmindedly between my legs.

I love the sound of the keys hitting the page. The more I think about it, the closer, I think, I am to coming.

"You're not as inhibited as you used to be," Harry says.

Harry's book Harry's book Harry's book—

The typewriter keys come down in a torrent. He must know I am about to come.

"Just hold it there. Good. Now, let's stop. I want to show you what I've been writing."

I cover myself with the blanket. I'm aroused, on fire.

I lean over Harry's shoulder. The view from the window is desolate, black country. This is what he's written:

Now the writer is dead and the assistant sits at the writer's desk, writing these words. Once he had paced downstairs, waiting for the writer to emerge. It was a gray morning, and finally the writer did emerge, red-faced, unshowered, belligerent in his early morning sobriety.

The assistant had come with mail from the department and he had made coffee. The writer took it with a smirk. They worked together at the desk.

"Type while I talk," the writer said. The room was stuffy, or was it cold? There was a woman in the center room and she made a lot of noise. The assistant typed—

"Now read that back to me," the writer said.

The assistant read, "dr4str eue w;eofjw 3020fs;kj e dkgoieg sosos;g eos." A crazy scramble of words.

"What? Have you lost your mind? Fuck you, you lowly piece of shit."

The writer poured himself a shot of whiskey and then another and another.

He threw the glass across the room. The assistant jumped. The writer began to rant.

"Screw you!" he screamed. "Ruining my book. You don't have the talent to wipe my ass."

The assistant typed. The typing soothed the old man. They fell into a rhythm. It was like old times.

"Harry," I say. "Did this really happen?"

"Lots of times. I don't know why Marshall couldn't get a Dictaphone like everyone else. He had a thing for hearing the typewriter when he wrote, but—maybe it was the drinking, who knows why he couldn't type it himself? I wasn't a good secretary; I could barely keep up."

"I wonder why he didn't just fire you," I say.

"Because . . . see that manuscript on the floor over there, 'Saul'? I practically wrote that book."

"Marshall, once you couldn't string together a sentence, now you're a belligerent drunk," the assistant types.

"Once you were a belligerent drunk, and now you're dead. And there's another woman in your bed.

"Here's the rival, outliving you, you fucking pig."

"Well, Harry," I say. "I guess I know what we're doing here, but I'm a little disappointed. I thought I'd have a bigger role."

He puts his arm around my shoulder and hugs me to him. "Oh, you will later. But do you like it?"

"Yeah, and it could get really mystical, Harry. Imagine Marshall coming back from the dead and watching you at his typewriter."

"That's a thought."

"But do you really think *pig* is the right word in this case? It seems a little vulgar, Harry."

At that, he leads me to the edge of the bed, bends me over, and undoes his belt.

"But, seriously, I can't wait to read what happens," I say.

And suddenly there is the realization: No one will ever publish *Harry's Book*.

Caught Napping

"You fell asleep," Z. says. "Here, have some tea."

"Thank you," I say. "I guess I was tired."

She had found me in my narrow office, dozing with my head on the desk.

"Why don't you take a nap in here?" she said, opening the door to her study.

Hours later, I wake to hear Claire and Lars speaking, pots banging in the kitchen. Then Z. pushes the door to her study open with her foot and puts a tray down on her desk.

"I can't remember if you take milk and sugar."

"Just sugar."

I look around the room. There are flower paintings hanging everywhere. I am in Z.'s garden.

"Do you live with your mother, Annabelle?"

"Yes."

"And you're still traveling back and forth every day from Long Island?"

"Yes."

"No wonder you're tired. . . . We have a house on Long Island, too."

"The other Long Island," I say.

"Sag Harbor," Z. says. "An old ramshackle cottage at the water's edge."

"But sometimes I stay overnight with a friend who has an apartment in the city."

"That's convenient."

"But not ideal. I don't have my own desk."

"Writing without a desk! That must be hard for you, but I truly appreciate the effort it took to write those twelve masculine flower descriptions. Art is struggle, Annabelle, and the rewards are great if you persevere. You thought you had nothing to say! Well, you proved yourself wrong. You really have a knack for metaphor after all."

She takes a paper from her desk and reads: " 'Your long leaves your large buds your soft hairy stem: flower.' "

"I tried," I say.

Z. says, "Apparently. You are so eloquent and precise sometimes. I look at what you've written and think: Here is a writer with promise."

Z. in her shiny black glasses reading me my own words. It's almost more than I can bear.

If only I had my Emily Dickinson poem with me, I'd whip it out and ask Z. again about including it in the anthology.

The room is turning pink from the light of the sunset on the water.

"You collect flower paintings?" I say.

"Yes," Z. says, sipping her tea. "I have forever."

"They say that if someone collects nothing, that's as telling as what he or she does collect."

"An odd thought."

"I read it in *Smithsonian,*" I say. Z smiles politely. She cannot be provoked into deep thought.

"I found my first painting in the trash." Z. points to a black-and-gold one hanging above her desk. The flowers are chipped away so what remains has the abstract look of a piece of spin-art. "It's my habit, whenever I do a reading, to browse in the local antique shop.

"Annabelle, that beautiful line: 'The Flowers of the Forest are a weed away.' Do you remember that one?"

"Yes. That was Miss Jane Elliot. Actually, I've done a little research, and I think her name might be Jean."

"Are you sure?"

"Not one hundred percent, no."

"I'd like you to be sure. You see, I find myself obsessed with that phrase, 'a weed away.'"

"It's very mysterious. I know what you mean."

"When I'm not writing my own poems—when I'm not working on my address to the Society—I'm thinking about that line. I have a book in mind, one that pays homage to the weed. But I need someone to do the groundwork. . . . Perhaps you would like to take a week in Sag Harbor. You could live in our guest cottage, take long walks in the dunes—and write me some of those lovely raw descriptions. . . . Tell me, Annabelle, how do you do it?"

"You mean how do I write?"

She's nodding, smiling.

I say, "Well, I guess I find a word, like *raw,* for example, and just do a riff on it. 'Raw: the green, uncooked stem of the half-eaten flower.' At the same time, I might be thinking about something like Freud or nervous laughter, so that gets mixed into the line as well."

"Your mind is very fertile, Annabelle."

"I should show you my poem about Emily Dickinson," I say. "But I forgot to bring it. I wish I had something new I could show you. These days, I'm having a terrible time with my own work. I've written a personal poem for Braun, but I'm afraid it's a little too personal."

"Of course real poetry cannot be evoked by a classroom assignment. It comes from within."

"Professor Z.," I say, staring into my teacup. "I want to write about virginity, but nothing seems to be coming."

"You want to write about virginity?"

"Yes, but I feel totally blocked."

"In that case, you must write about the opposite. That often works for me."

"You mean sex?"

"Wrap it in metaphor if you must . . ."

"You see, my idea was to write about virginity from a woman's point of view. And saying it in a way it's never been said before."

Z. says, "Is that your interest, to make it new? How are you defining *new*, Annabelle? Is that a word Braun uses?"

"She didn't say that exactly, no. I think her thing is that we should break from tradition—go out on the proverbial limb—"

Then I look up and see Z. before me. She is dressed in black and bathed in the silver light of the river. She looks almost celestial, too glamorous to be true. "Annabelle, our poems tell us what they are," she says. "They come from a place inside us. The only tradition that exists for the writer is the one she makes for herself."

"It's the waiting that's so hard . . ."

"Poetry is not about the agonies of the soul, Annabelle. Sit down and write. Something will come. If virginity is your passion, you will find a way to write about it. Poems—even about virginity—come from passion."

I consider this. A rush of memory. Last night Harry actually became tender, taking his time with me, waiting at each juncture for me to relax more and more—and then . . .

I shiver.

"Are you coming down with something, Annabelle?"

"No, I don't think so."

"Then let's get on with things. Tell me, Annabelle, have you been in touch with Jane? She was supposed to have produced that paper on Emily Dickinson and jewelry."

"It's in my folder. She just gave it to me."

"And?"

"Jane opens with a discussion of the cameo that Emily Dickinson might have worn had she worn jewelry . . . a cameo of three muses. Then, briefly, she discusses jewelry of the Victorian era. She concludes with an analysis of 'I heard a Fly buzz—when I died.' "

Z. is shaking her head. "It sounds like hackwork."

Poor Jane. Her name will endure, but her scholarship will not.

"And Claire?"

"I'm scheduling some interviews for her."

And here's where I say, "I think I can make a unique contribution to this book. . . . I want to do a handwriting analysis of Emily Dickinson. I could analyze her letters, her poems. Everything."

"Annabelle," Z. says very gently. "Didn't we talk about selflessness? I thought we talked about this when we first discussed your responsibilities."

"Yes, but wouldn't this be a way of helping you?"

"I love your ideas, Annabelle. I love the idea of analyzing Dickinson's handwriting. But please, remember, as tempting as it is to get caught up in the thrill of these projects, your job here is to assist."

I force a smile. I'm becoming thick-skinned.

"Now tell me why you think Claire is resisting my Emily Dickinson volume."

"Well, at this point, I think Claire's true interest lies with Poetry Slam."

"Poetry Spam?" She rolls her eyes.

"No, Slam. It's a contest. You perform your poem, and then they rate your presentation on a scale of one to ten. The person with the highest number wins."

"What does the winner get?" Z. asks. "The Bollingen Prize?"

"Cash, I think, for traveling around to other slam contests."

"I see," Z. says.

"The slam circuit has its own celebrities. I don't think Emily Dickinson is one of them."

"Because to understand Dickinson is to connect to Dickinson. You must endeavor to study every last revelatory word. Poetry is a struggle, and the sooner you and Claire understand that, the better. Sacrifice, struggle, dedication: This is the life of poetry. . . . Now tell me, Annabelle, what's the latest gossip in the English Department?"

I should say, "That you are out to kill Braun Brown's career," but instead I say, "I haven't heard a thing . . . career suicide, you know?"

"Do you really think I go around killing careers, Annabelle? Is that what you think?"

"No, but people are cautious around me."

"Is Professor Brown cautious around you?"

"A little."

"That's because you're loyal, Annabelle. Which reminds me: I believe I mentioned my friend Carol Martin, who owns some real estate. . . . I may have introduced you to her at one of my soirees?"

"I've never really been to one of your soirees, Professor Z."

"Anyway, Carol is known for her research on folk art."

Then I remember. I had photocopied an article in *The Journal of Higher Education* about a harassment suit filed by Martin's former students claiming that they had to sew two hundred quilt squares each for her in order to get their grades. In court papers Martin had been accused of running a sewing business under the auspices of an art class called Women, Textiles, and Labor. The students had hours of taped phone conversations with Martin in which you could actually hear sewing machines in the background.

"Carol owns a rent-controlled apartment building in the West Village," Z. says, "and is looking for a responsible tenant for one of her studios. Immediately, I thought of you."

"I would love to live in the Village," I say. "It's been a dream of mine for a long time."

Z. says, "There's just one glitch, a finder's fee for this apartment. Carol uses that money to maintain the building. Believe me, Annabelle, this is not the kind of business I would ever involve myself in—passing money under the table—but it occurred to me that you could use 'a room of your own.' "

Now the voices of Lars and Claire are quite audible, and a pungent waft of something—roast beef, chicken, potatoes au gratin?—floods into Z.'s office the minute she opens the door.

"I'm not sure I can afford the fee. It probably puts it out of my range."

Z. is writing down the phone number. "Let me take care of the finder's fee for you, Annabelle. Consider it a housewarming gift. . . . But you'll need to come up with the security deposit. She'd like three months in advance, which is nearly nine hundred dollars."

It was a time when rents in New York City were exorbitant, and apartments were scarce. Everyone my age had at least one roommate.

"That's so much money."

"Annabelle," Z. says, "I don't like to interfere in the lives of my apprentices, but I know that you are very resourceful, and I think you should find a way. There is no substitute for independence."

I take the phone number, and as we walk to the door, Z. straightens my collar and says, "Take care of yourself."

Then she is suddenly all business.

"Now, getting back to the weeds," Z. says. "I'd like you to make them a priority. And please go back to the library first thing and confirm for me: Is the 'weed away' author Jane or Jean?"

Sirens

———

That night I decided to go to my mother's house. It was dark when the taxi drove into Mapleleaf Court and pulled up the driveway. There was a light on in the foyer, but oddly, my mother wasn't home.

I went back to the pink room at the top of the stairs, got into my bed, pulled down the covers, and fell asleep.

I wondered if I was pregnant. I wondered if I was avoiding Harry. I wondered how I would pay for an apartment in New York City. I wondered if I would also end up sewing quilt squares.

When I woke up the next morning, I had my period. My mother was smoking cigarettes at the breakfast table.

"Nice to see you again," she said.

I poured myself some coffee.

"Z.'s friend, a professor, has an apartment that she might rent me."

"Your teacher certainly takes good care of you—"

"She's concerned because I've been run-down. I'm tired, Mom. I've fallen behind in my coursework."

"Annabelle," my mother said. "Where have you been every night? Are you seeing someone?"

I sipped my coffee. "Harry. His name is Harry."

"Is he in your class?"

"No, he was the Marshall Greene Fellow, but Marshall Greene died in a car crash, so he's trying to figure out what he's going to do."

My mother said, "Does he work?"

"He's writing a novel."

"Oh," she said, and there was something in her voice. I got the feeling she didn't like what she was hearing.

"Dr. Sanger called here twice, Annabelle. I told her that you didn't have a phone, that you've been staying with a friend."

"I should call her."

"She seemed a little concerned."

"It gets busy mid-semester . . ."

"I'm also a little concerned. I ran into Elisa's mother in the mall. She says Elisa just finished Katie Gibbs and already has a job in the city—"

"I'm not going to secretarial school, if that's what you're thinking."

"Your father won't support you forever, Annabelle."

I said, "He's not supporting me now."

Then she stubbed out her cigarette and stood up. It was time to dress for work.

"Call her, Annabelle. Because if you don't want to see her anymore, I'd like to see her."

"My therapist?"

"She's fine with that. She reminded me that we all started out together in family therapy."

"And look how far she brought us," I wanted to say, but I didn't want to hurt my mother's feelings by pointing out how fragmented our little family unit had become. I said, "It's okay, Mom. I really haven't got time anymore for therapy."

I hadn't the resources either, but I didn't want my mother telling Dr. Sanger that. After all, Dr. Sanger said I could owe her money forever, but taking her up on her offer seemed a step in the wrong direction.

"And your car, what do you want to do with your car?"

"Mom, am I terminally ill or something? I thought I was just away at school."

"I'd like to see Dr. Sanger."

"Then see her. What do I care? Tell her I say hello."

"Don't forget your mail," she said, pointing to the counter.

And there, mixed in with my student loan bill and the latest copy of *Poet & Poem* was a letter from Judith Hammer, the editor of *Sirens*. She wrote to say she was happy to inform me that she would be publishing my poem, "Mask of the Poet," in her special Literary Women issue next winter.

Mrs. Finster, an agent for Z.'s friend Carol Martin, was a birdlike woman with an English accent. She showed me the studio apartment on Horatio Street—a fourth-floor walk-up—which cost $298 a month. Because it was rent-controlled, the rent could go up only in small increments.

The apartment was one long, narrow room with a fireplace.

"This place has good spirits," Mrs. Finster said. "The former tenant was an actress, and last month she got the call she'd been waiting for her entire life."

Judith Hammer, editor of *Sirens*. "Dear Annabelle Goldsmith, I am pleased to inform you . . ."

"Broadway?"

"No, Hollywood."

I opened the closet. There were six sewing machines lining the floor.

Apparently this was where Carol Martin ran her academic sweatshop.

I said, "Do you know this couplet by Wordsworth? 'And now I see with eye serene, the very pulse of the machine'?"

Mrs. Finster smiled. "You know, you remind me of my own granddaughter in your wool coat, so very businesslike and young."

And so that is how I, who had once wandered the Walt Whitman Mall in Long Island for cultural stimulation, moved to the onetime capital of literary Bohemia, the place where Edna St. Vincent Millay lived in a room narrower than mine and had a million love affairs.

A Critical Time

Annabelle,
Urgent!
Please see me.
Rap three times on my door.
Z.

Dear Annabelle—
I would like to speak to you about doing some research for me. I am interested in learning more about the Villa of Mysteries. I have gone out for a paper. Will return soon.

Lars

Annabelle!!!!
Have you done the tape yet? Can you talk to me before you do it? THANKS!!

Claire

I rapped three times on Z.'s door as instructed.
"Good, Annabelle. You're here." Her yellow terry-cloth bathrobe

was tied with a red sash. A mistake? What was she doing in a bathrobe in the middle of the afternoon? There were circles under her eyes. Her hair was tied back in a ponytail and held in place with a pink barrette. It was a strange, disheveled look, with strands of hair falling out all over the place.

"Annabelle, I want to show you something." She walked outside the door, and in doing so, bumped into me. She was not wearing her trademark black glasses.

"Here," she said. "From now on when you knock on my door, you do this." She drummed her fingers three times on the door. "That's your knock."

"Thanks," I said.

"Now look at this." She was shaking some papers.

It was a course outline, "Women Poets: The Miltown Years." Braun Brown was teaching it.

"Your good friend has proposed a new course and is teaching it this spring."

I sat down on the edge of the chaise longue.

"Is this a problem?"

"That she's trivializing women's literary history? You ask if this is a problem?"

"Well," I said, "maybe Braun plans to teach it in a serious way but just gave it a witty course title to get students interested."

"The study of poetry is one big stand-up comedy routine . . ."

She tossed the paper across the room. It glided to the floor.

"And even if she is going to approach it in a serious manner, it's a terribly sexist notion, after all. Our literary foremothers as a bunch of depressed housewives? What nonsense!"

And once again I asked myself, What is poetry?

"And how about this class: Confessional Poetry in the Age of the Talk Show? In this rigorously academic course, Professor Brown asks, Is there a place for confessional poetry in the age of sensationalism?"

The truth is, I would sign up for both of Braun's classes if they were offered. I wanted to know more about depressed housewives—after all, I was raised by one—and I wanted to know if poetry could matter in a world dominated by the sound of pop music and television.

"I was at a Curriculum Review meeting this morning, and before I knew it, we were voting to approve these two absurdities. Well, I was shocked. What was the faculty thinking?"

I picked "Women Poets: The Miltown Years" off the floor and handed it to Z.

I wanted to tell her the news, that I was getting my first poem published, but it hardly seemed the time.

"How can I be taken seriously as chancellor of the Society for the Preservation of American Poetry when I teach at a university that reduces the study of literature to a joke?"

I said, "Then again, if she gets students interested in poetry, isn't that a good thing?"

"Don't defend her, Annabelle. *Do not* defend her! Is anything sacred anymore? Is poetry sacred?"

"I think poetry is sacred," I said.

"Obviously it isn't to your friend, the poet laureate of pop culture. Next she'll want to teach a class on the 'sham-a-lam-a-ding-dong' poets."

"But, Professor Z., don't you think the idea about confessional poetry being embedded in the television culture of confession is sort of interesting?"

"Maybe at T.V.U. or some junior college where they teach people to be newscasters. Let her join the faculty there."

"Actually, Braun's calling for a new confessional poetry. One that embraces the use of metaphor," I added, hoping Z. might feel flattered by that.

"There's that word *new* again. Anyway, believe me, there is nothing *new* about confessional poetry."

Z. reached into the pocket of her bathrobe, pulled out her glasses, and put them on. Then she removed the barrette that had been holding her hair in place, put it in her mouth, pulled the stray pieces of her hair back, made a new ponytail, and clipped it in place.

Order restored.

"Annabelle," she said, "I want to counter this confessional poetry movement with real scholarship. I need you to help me research a course curriculum about women poets that is truly erudite. A class that tells us where we are going and where we have been. Something only I could teach. My signature course."

"What about the home? Didn't you write household poems once?"

"What's your thinking about this, Annabelle? A class about women poets and the home? Did Dickinson write any household poems?"

I couldn't think. The talk of course curriculums had made me anxious. I was so behind in my own classwork, it was laughable.

Z. said, "This is what I would like you to work on: a curriculum which studies the rise of the household poem. You can go all the way back to Sappho and bring it to modern day. I want art. I want drama. Above all, I want you to find me an unknown poet." She pulled her sash tighter. "I want you to find a poet, lost to history, who we can bring back to life. . . . I want to find her and publish her in *The New York Literary Review*."

Then, simply to change the subject, I said, "I wanted to thank you again for that apartment. It was really generous of you to think of me, and to cover that key money. For the first time in my life, I'm completely on my own."

"You're quite welcome. I'm glad it worked out."

"Professor Z., I don't want to presume on your generosity, but I was wondering if I could take some time off in the next few weeks? I've fallen behind in my reading for the Psychological Novel, and I need to do research for my final paper. I plan to pay homage to the garden, using it as a metaphor for the eighteenth-century imagination."

Z. yawned.

"This can't be done on evenings or weekends?"

"I also need to be free during the day to have my phone installed and my futon delivered."

Z. said, "This is a very critical time, Annabelle. You can't move in during intersession?"

"I guess I could," I said. But now I was thinking about my train ticket. I didn't want to pay another month for commuting when I was already paying for the apartment.

Then Z. went into the kitchen and came back with three plastic bags filled with dirt and weeds.

"Before I forget, I wanted to give you these. . . . I couldn't imagine you'd find the time to go out to Sag Harbor, so I had Claire pull these for you last weekend. I want you to start by researching weeds indigenous to the South Fork of Long Island."

I could hear the waves crashing against the winter shore.

"This time I'd like you to go way out in your descriptions, Annabelle. Be expansive. I haven't left you too much work, so you could really do it right now in your office. . . . You could lay the weeds side by side on your desk and compare them. . . . Now, Annabelle, in the event that Mr. Spence calls, tell him I'm on my way. Or better yet, call the Edwardian Room at the Plaza, and tell Mr. Spence that I'm running a little late."

Weed

———

I put the weeds on the farthest corner of the desk, called the Plaza, and went through the mail. There were letters to answer, letters to throw out. We did not answer letters from writers (unless they were famous) or letters from people we did not know. In the beginning I read every errant, sad poem and letter that came Z.'s way. I pitied the writer who wrote looking for a reply to some deeply felt emotion—an exchange like Rilke's *Letters to a Young Poet*—from Z. Now I simply slit open the letter, read the first line, thought, Life is sad, and threw it in the trash.

I picked up one of the plastic bags. The afternoon light in Z.'s apartment was blinding. Apparently Claire had dug down hard. I had sand, dirt, and even roots to write about.

Wordsworth said that poetry was "emotion recollected in tranquillity." I felt nothing about the hairy weeds Z. had brought me back from Sag Harbor.

I wrote in my notebook:

WEEDS
Someone has pulled out my eyelashes
and left me with sand.
Out, vile jelly!
Where is thy lustre now?

I needed to get to work on Z.'s curriculum. I went to the bookcase in the living room, pulled down an oversize book about Sappho, and flipped through. Sappho didn't write many poems about the home. She seemed to spend a lot of time outdoors watching women dance in ethereal bliss.

There was a line drawing of two women in a garden. One woman was reaching out and touching the other woman's nipple with her fingertip. Like Adam touching God on the ceiling of the Sistine Chapel.

Briefly, I thought about the power of great art. I remembered the nipple stipple.

I wrote in my notebook:

THE HOME AS GOD

Then I thought of something I'd learned in Braun's class: that Anne Bradstreet was the author of the first book of verse to be written in the New World. That book was *The Tenth Muse Lately Sprung Up in America*. Z. could begin her class with Bradstreet's poem "Upon the Burning of Our House." It would be a class about burning passion, a class about making a home and destroying it, a class about the burning passion to write.

Then I noticed a book turned backward, spine to the wall, on the bottom shelf. How odd, I thought as I pulled it out. It was *His Mistress*.

I turned to the title page. There, in Braun's loopy handwriting, was this inscription:

FOR LARS,

WITH LOVE FROM

She'd circled the title, "His Mistress." There were lines radiating out from it, turning it into a sun.

Then, at the bottom of the page, she wrote these words:

(SEE PAGE 27)

I flipped to page 27. She had circled

The good love conjugates "to lay."
The good lord conjugates "to lie."

Suddenly, I felt sick.

Maybe Z. was right to be wary; maybe Braun *was* trying to topple her kingdom.

Then there was the sound of a key turning in the lock. It was Lars, Claire.

"Annabelle!"

"Annabelle!"

They were excited to see me, and for a moment I felt like a member of the family.

"Annabelle, I need to talk to you," Claire says. "Can we go in my room? Let's get a soda from the refrigerator."

Lars puts his newspaper down on the kitchen counter. "Then you and I will talk some other time about my research."

"Yes," I say, following Claire down the hall.

"The Villa of Mysteries," he says, his voice rising at the end of his sentence.

Claire's room is very juvenile. White furniture with pink flower decals and, on the wall, a framed needlepoint of three flowers. On another wall is a big yellow smiling face. The smile is composed of small black stitches, so it's not exactly a perfect curve. It's a smile with some quirky angles, but it's close enough.

"My mother did those," Claire says, pointing.

I try to imagine Z. as a young mother sitting on the couch doing needlepoint while her small daughter watches *Sesame Street*. It's a stretch.

"She's very talented," I say.

"I don't know if you listened to that tape or not, because I didn't see any transcription."

"I heard some of it."

I'm thinking about Lars's copy of *His Mistress*. Did I put it back where I found it, backward on the bottom shelf? And did he leave it that way so that Z. would find it and read the inscription?

Claire pops the top off her soda and sets it on the night table.

In Claire's room there's a stereo, a telephone, and a Peter Max poster of a guy on a drug trip. It's a recent acquisition, Claire says, an antidote to the childish decor.

"I heard almost all of the tape, actually."

Even the flirtation and that betrayal of your mother, I want to add.

Now she's showing me a slip of paper.

"Could you call them for me, Annabelle, and tell them all about the retreat? We need everyone to fill out a form. They have to write their meal preference—vegetarian or not—and who Braun should call in an emergency.

"Here are their phone numbers. All of the graduate writing students need to be called. Meg from your class and Jane, who's doing an independent study with Mother. Tell them you need to know right away whether they can make it or not. I would call them myself, but my mother wouldn't take well to my doing this for Braun."

"So, let me understand this. Braun's invited you, and you agreed to do some work for her, but you're asking me to do it for you?"

"Yes. That's right. You're a jewel, Annabelle."

I look at Claire, who I'm supposed to be keeping an eye on. Today her hair is Mercurochrome, brushed down and parted on the side. Even if I had more courage, I wouldn't dye my hair that color.

"I don't like keeping secrets from your mother."

"It's not a secret. She doesn't need to know everything, you know."
Then Claire says, "Braun is teaching Joni Mitchell, The Troubadour
Poet, that Saturday afternoon. It is so anti-Mother, don't you think?"

"Anti-Mother?"

"It's so not her generation. Mother hates experimental poetry. She
had a terrible time with the 'language poetry' movement. She went to
one of their Buddhist retreats and refused to say Om.

"After that, she was so traumatized, she only wrote about flowers."

"I thought she went to England and fell in love with the flowers at
the Royal Botanic Gardens."

"That's not what Mother's biographer says."

"Mother's biographer?"

"Yes . . . though it's kind of at a standstill since she interviewed Mimi.
Mother says Mimi's not lucid. They'd been hoping to do a small volume
on Mother's early years, and then another on her middle years. . . . Did
you know that Mother once studied with Gay Farinette?"

"Braun's Gay Farinette?"

"Yes, when she was in college, on an exchange program in England
she took her poetry workshop. . . . Mother says Gay's a poetry cockroach. She survives despite one bad review after another."

Claire goes to the stereo, finds an album, removes it from its cardboard jacket, and holds it along the edges. "This is poetry."

Woke up, it was a Chelsea morning,
and the first thing that I heard . . .

Joni's voice is young and high. She reminds me of Snow White
singing to the birds in the Disney movie. Claire changes the record.
Now Joni's singing "Rainy Night House." Her voice is dark, almost
melancholy. She's a complicated woman.

We listen for a while, then Claire says, "What's wrong with this picture, Annabelle?"

I don't know.

"No weed." She reaches into a drawer and pulls out a plastic bag,
retrieves a joint, lights it, and inhales.

"You're going to smoke that in here?"

"No?"

"Claire, if we get caught, I'll get fired."

She passes me the joint.

"You wouldn't be the first," she says, exhaling. "There was Susan Lester, fired for typing her poems on Mother's typewriter."

"I would never do that," I say, but in truth, I would like to do it once just to see what it feels like.

I try to remember the last time I got stoned. I inhale, hold it for a few long seconds, exhale.

"Mandy Rogers, fired because she couldn't learn the difference between ripe and rotten. Her fruit shopping drove Mother crazy."

"Sour grapes?"

"And kiwi."

"Claire, do you think your mother is threatened by Braun?"

"Mother takes great offense at women who glorify the male body, who make men seem virile and powerful in their poems." Claire leans in. "She calls them cocksuckers."

I can imagine Z. saying *cockroach,* but I can't imagine her saying *cocksucker.*

"But Braun also likes men with a feminine side," I say.

"You know, Mother says *His Mistress* is as if the women's movement never happened . . . and Braun is just a big exhibitionist getting off on being the object of a man's desire, and the reviewers love that."

"I thought she hadn't read it," I say.

"Of course she's read it."

"Does your father like Braun's writing?"

"We heard her in Boston—Mother doesn't know this—and he was really quite taken with her. He had her sign a book."

FOR LARS, WITH LOVE . . .

The text as body, a postmodern construction.

Reading as infidelity.

"Braun says at department meetings Mother is cold and uncollegial." Claire inhales again.

"Do you think that maybe Braun is *reading* into it?"

Claire exhales. "Mother says of Braun: 'Great poets are all alike; every mediocre poet is mediocre in her own way.'

"And Braun is really tired of those flowers. I'm a little tired of them, too. Everyone's tired of Mother's flowers, Annabelle."

Claire was Z., without Z.'s refinement. She was pretty and smart, but she had not yet learned how to hide her aggression.

Taking a toke, I say, "Claire, I'm worried about making all those phone calls. I don't want to get caught working for Braun. I mean, I don't want to sound paranoid, but what if your mother hears me on the phone?"

I could make the calls from my own apartment, if only I could find the time to get my phone installed.

Claire gets up and opens the window. Even from the penthouse, you can hear city sounds.

"What if you one day publish a murder mystery where Braun Brown is decapitated by a flower poet, and my mother decides to sue you? That's what you should worry about, Annabelle."

We're laughing, and then we stop abruptly. Such a violent, unsettling fantasy. We're stoned.

I take another toke and say, "You can say what you want about Braun, but she is interested in helping people become good writers, don't you think?"

Claire says, "I don't know. Maybe she's going to get us all together and steal our ideas or turn them into a novel or a memoir. . . . Mother had an assistant once, fired for publishing such an essay in a little magazine."

I exhale. "While she was working for her?"

"Yeah, pretty crazy if you ask me. But it was a hilarious piece."

Claire throws some pillows on the floor, and we lie down, our hands behind our heads, and listen.

"Betrayal," I say. "I think Joni is singing about betrayal."

"No, I don't think so."

. . . To see who in the world, I might be . . .

"I think she's remembering a younger version of herself, sleeping with this guy and wondering who she was then."

I feel the minutes pass, and then I wonder if they were really minutes.

"Yes," I say, "Joni Mitchell is a lot of words. Interesting words; poems that weave themselves into stories. Like the Peter Max poster, only the words are long, beautiful sentences that turn around and around in her head."

Claire says, "Did you ever feel so thankful to somebody that you wanted to kiss them, Annabelle?"

I think of Arthur Feld. I hugged him once, but I can't say I've ever wanted to kiss him.

"No," I say. "But when I smoke pot, I do feel things in my lips."

"Me, too," Claire says. Her mouth is slightly open. She's about to inhale. "Sometimes, I feel like I want to kiss my therapist . . . you know what I mean?"

I can no longer imagine kissing Dr. Sanger, but I can imagine kissing Z.

"I know the feeling."

Claire exhales.

"Mother sent me because I might be gay. . . . And my therapist loves me for who I am. She told me so."

I say, "Claire, whatever you do, don't kiss your therapist, okay?"

I don't want to have to describe the encounter to Z.

Then Claire is sitting cross-legged. She has an intense look, which I recognize as Z.

"Mother's been in a mood. She's been raging since Friday night. She had a faculty cocktail party. Father talked Braun's ear off. 'August twenty-fourth, A.D. seventy-nine,' he kept saying. And Braun just stood there the whole time, listening, smiling. . . . He really has a thing for her."

"August twenty-fourth?"

"The day Mount Vesuvius unleashed its fury . . . and the city of Pompeii was buried under ash."

Where was I last Friday night? I'm trying to remember; then other thoughts fill my head and I can't hold on to them.

"I think my mother is seeing someone . . . and I think it's Jason Spence. What do you know about this, Annabelle?"

I sit up abruptly. "Really, Claire, do you think she'd tell me?"

"She's just been so weird lately. Ever since we came back from Europe. She's so distracted. You know what I mean?"

"Well, I think you have to give her a break, Claire. . . . I mean, she was just named chancellor, and she has to write an address on the state of American poetry."

"It's Spence, isn't it?"

"Out, out damn spot," I say, but what I meant to say is "Don't put me on the spot."

Then Claire gets up to change the record, lifts the arm of the stereo, and drops it, scratching the record.

. . . help me I think I'm falling in love again . . .

"Mother has just come out of her 'white heat.' She'd been writing all the time, hardly sleeping, leaving her study only to use the bathroom and eat . . ."

The image of Z. in her bathrobe, desperate for a course curriculum to rival Bruan Brown's Miltown Years comes to mind.

"So she has this party, and then she goes crazy afterward because how could Braun come to her party and stand in her living room and eat her food?"

It's something I'm wondering, too, since finding that book Braun inscribed to Lars.

Claire's found a soft pack of cigarettes; French, Gitanes. The cigarette burns sweet and acrid, not what I'm accustomed to. She inhales.

Exhaling, she says, "And Spence just stood on the terrace the whole time drinking martinis . . . wouldn't talk to anyone."

Is that any way for a job candidate to behave?

"Claire," I say, "what's the real story about Ben in the hotel room?"

"I know what Mother tells me. She says he won't come forward to file a sexual harassment complaint because he's afraid for his grade."

"Is that true?"

"Well, Braun says what happened was perfectly innocent: Ben is making a movie about the downtown poetry scene, and he rented a hotel room for the shoot, and Mother, coincidentally, was in the hotel lobby when Braun and Ben were checking in."

The Plaza is located in midtown, I want to say, but instead take another toke.

"But what was Mother doing in the hotel lobby in the middle of the afternoon? That's what I want to know."

I exhale. "Having tea?" I look down at the joint. It's finished. I lay the roach on the edge of the night table.

"I just hope it isn't Jason Spence. That guy walks around like he's God's gift to poetry. And you want to know something else, Annabelle? I came home the other day after getting my ears pierced. Mother took one look at me and started to cry."

I think of Z. standing at the window during our talk about gossip, that nearly imperceptible shaking of her shoulders.

I say, "She's a poet, Claire. She feels things deeply."

"Come on, Annabelle." Claire flicks some ash from her cigarette into her empty soda can.

"I'm surprised that they would all come to the party if there was so much tension."

"Yeah," Claire says. "Mother says they're all parasites. They eat off her. It's a feeding frenzy."

There's silence, then Claire says, "Who are you, Annabelle?"

"Who am I?"

"Yeah, who are you? Where did you come from?"

"What do you mean?"

"Are you related to someone? How did you get here?"

"I got the Edgar Allan Poe Fellowship. Arthur Feld helped me."

"Arthur Feld?" Claire says.

"My teacher at LICC."

"So, are you like a nobody . . . someone who just happened to get assigned to Mother?"

"Not exactly a nobody, but I did get assigned to her," I say, and think of my poem "Mask of the Poet," which has just been accepted by *Sirens*.

"I wondered if you were related to Jason Spence—like his niece or something—because you both showed up here around the same time."

"No, I don't even know him. I mean, I've met him."

"Are you like a lost person or something?"

"Do I seem lost?"

"Maybe. It's more like out of place."

"Sometimes I do feel like an outsider, like I don't belong."

Claire stretches out her arms.

Photo beauty gets attention
Then her eye paint's running down

"Can I ask you something, Claire?"

"Sure."

"Does your mother ever take you shopping?"

"What?"

"For clothes?"

"Does my mother take me shopping for clothes? She used to."

"How did it feel?"

"Are you like a really, really sad person, Annabelle? Did your mother die when you were very young or something?"

Now I'm embarrassed.

"No, I have parents, but they've been spending all their time and money suing each other for divorce."

"Do you need money, Annabelle? Mother will lend you whatever you need."

"I can't ask her. She's already helped me enough with the finder's fee for my apartment."

"Do you have anyone else?" She leans closer, reaching for the soda can. We're in such close proximity that it makes me shudder. "Do you have a boyfriend?"

I feel the weight of a lag between her question and my answer.

"My boyfriend?"

"Yeah, who is he?"

"His name is Harry. He's a graduate student, and . . ."

"Not Marshall Greene's Harry?"

"Do you have a boyfriend, Claire? A girlfriend?"

"Don't change the subject. It's Harry Banks, isn't it?"

"Right. Harry Banks. And now I'm leaving."

"No shit. Mr. Harry. I wondered what happened to him. Now, there's a strange story. Little Mr. Harry . . . He could play Marshall Greene better than Marshall could play himself."

Mentor, Tormentor

I'm about to leave the apartment. I have the door open. I have a foot out the door, in fact, when Lars calls out to me.

"Annabelle, do spend ten minutes with me now in my office. . . . Or better yet, here, let's sit at the counter. Can I make you an espresso?"

I take off my coat and drop my backpack.

Then Lars is opening cabinets and slamming them, and unscrewing the canister of his aluminum pot.

Lars looks different today. His blond hair has been trimmed into a crew cut with lots of sharp angles.

I get the feeling something is awry. If I've learned anything about the Bovardine family, it's that hair is the barometer of their emotional life.

"I also make a fabulous cappuccino," Lars says.

He puts two demitasse cups in front of us—very delicate, bone china, decorated with light green and pink flowers. Inside each cup is a tiny silver spoon. The top of each spoon is decorated in intricate fili-gree work.

"I've had such a day. First yoga, then the mind doctor. I couldn't meditate in yoga—and I told this to the mind doctor, and he asked me if I was anxious."

He retrieves the pot from the stove and pours the espresso. I drink. It burns my tongue. But the espresso is good. It helps to clarify my thinking.

FOR LARS,

WITH LOVE FROM

HIS MISTRESS

"The language of these mind doctors is so unromantic. I'm afraid they've polluted polite society with their jargon: anxiety, depression, therapy, relationship . . ."

"Relationship? I think that's a nice word."

Little Mr. Harry!

"Yes," Lars says, "but now it's also a dirty word, a clinical description of a natural human occurrence . . ."

Lars has lost his train of thought. He's somewhere else. Maybe it's the marijuana, but I'm beginning to feel like I'm losing my boundaries, or perhaps I've had no boundaries all along and now I'm finally noticing.

"I've started another story. It's a roman à clef about New York City survivors—five feminists onstage in the dark after an earthquake has destroyed Manhattan. They're the only people left in the city."

"Why feminists?"

"It's dark humor, Annabelle, very dark. But maybe it's as the mind doctor says . . . maybe it's some 'passive-aggressive acting out' against my wife."

Like leaving a book inscribed by her rival upside down and backward on the bookshelf, I think.

"Then maybe you want Z. to be onstage reading as New York City falls. Have the ceiling break through. Have an angel crash through the ceiling," I say, only because I'm still stoned.

"No," Lars says. "I wouldn't feel right about that."

"Then have a skinhead crash through the ceiling."

"Yes," Lars says, glumly, turning his spoon in his cup. "An undesirable person crashes through the ceiling during my wife's reading, covering her in dust. The curtain falls."

We sit in silence.

I wonder why he doesn't leave her.

"I want to write 'The House of the Tragic Poet.' I have the entire manuscript laid out in my mind's eye, but I can't move beyond the title."

"Maybe you're trying too hard," I say. "Sometimes it helps to write the opposite. Write about your life in New York City right now, at this moment."

"I've tried that. It doesn't work."

"Try starting every sentence with the word *I*."

"I've tried that."

"Write what you know."

"Pompeii," he says, longingly.

"Does your story open at the moment the volcano erupts?"

"Oh, no," Lars says. "Nothing so dramatic. In this draft it begins at a bucolic place—a college, the gates of the college, at the very moment that Mimi Van Elder introduces us."

"You were introduced by Mrs. Van Elder?"

"Yes, Mimi is an old family friend. . . . My story begins with a kiss. I kiss my wife. My young, vulnerable, romantic wife."

I look at my watch. I should go home.

"She had just returned from Europe. She'd been sent there to get away from . . ."

He looks at me for a moment, as if contemplating something.

"Vivian DePresto."

"Who?"

"Every story needs a villain: Ours is Vivian DePresto, Vassar's distinguished professor of English literature. A woman studied in Shakespeare and the art of seduction.

"Imagine my wife at seventeen, the gifted English major with her high school prizes. I wish I had a picture of her. . . . But she's hidden every photograph.

"Now, Annabelle, imagine Elizabeth at the feet of Vivian DePresto in her little cabin on that mountain in Ithaca. . . . O, Icarus, who floated too close to the sun!"

"What a powerful opening," I say. I want him to say more, but I also want him to shut up. I fear I am no longer running interference; I am colluding in the disrespect of my mentor, the Flower Poet Z.

"Let me get you some more espresso," he says. When he returns from the stove, he says: "Where was I?"

"At the feet of Vivian DePresto in the cabin."

"Yes, in the cabin, in front of a wood-burning stove. Vivian with her jug of margaritas, refilling the glass of my dear young wife, lighting that fateful marijuana cigarette. . . . Promising to send that young girl's poems to *The New York Literary Review,* telling her how much weight the name, the return address of Vivian DePresto, carried on an envelope."

"Really? They smoked marijuana?"

"What followed was a loosening of inhibitions . . . Vivian DePresto slurring her words, reciting her convoluted poetry in that dark cabin lit by a single candle. . . . You see," Lars says, "she did not believe in electricity or running water."

I nod.

"My starry-eyed wife sitting at her mentor's feet, listening to the drunken, garbled speech DePresto put forth as poetry, waking up the next morning naked, in her teacher's bed."

She had slept with her thesis adviser.

"Elizabeth, calling that woman night after night, happy just to hear DePresto's voice—listening for hours to those drunken meanderings that later would comprise yet another volume of DePresto's wretched poetry. 'Have you sent my poems to *The New York Literary Review?*' my wife would ask."

Will you read my Emily Dickinson poem, Professor Z.?

"And then, having pried open her heart, DePresto refused to return her phone calls." He lowers his voice. "Ultimately, Mimi found Elizabeth in the hallway of the English Department, hysterical, banging her head against DePresto's door. And so, you see, her mentor became her tormentor."

Lars pauses. Because he's an actor, he knows the moment to look for applause. This is it.

"That's funny, Lars, 'mentor, tormentor.' "

"So Mimi stepped in and sent Elizabeth to Oxford on an exchange program. She gave her five hundred dollars and helped her find a flat. She connected Elizabeth with the London poetry set. And there Elizabeth published her first poems and fell in love with the natural world. And when she returned to America, DePresto was gone, banished from the college, forever."

Lars is at the refrigerator. He's showing me two small blue bottles. He likes a glass of water with his espresso.

"With fizz or without?" he asks.

Now he's pouring the seltzer into two glasses he's retrieved from the cabinet.

"From then on, Mimi watched over Elizabeth like a mother hawk, giving her those glowing reviews—saying, 'Elizabeth Bovardine is the poet of her generation'—calling all those others who were writing about their abortions and their love affairs pornographers. As Mimi rose in stature as the country's preeminent literary critic, my wife's fortunes rose as well."

And now I understand the cat food, the carbon paper . . .

"And so my wife came home from England pregnant with the child of an esteemed Irish poet—and even so, I fell in love with her . . . and then, because I am noble and true, I married her."

He takes a long drink of water.

I imagine Z. my age, pregnant by an Irish poet, and in desperate straits, about to marry Lars Bovardine, the actor.

Oh, sullied flower of the untouched, perfect blossom!

Perhaps this is why her poems idealize love.

"Can I ask you a question?"

"As long as it's not too intimate."

"How did she get the name Z.?"

"Our family secret!"

"Sorry. That was wrong of me. I shouldn't have asked."

"No, I shouldn't have teased. You're very sensitive, I can see that. Well, here's the story: When my wife was a student in England, there were two other Elizabeths in her class. It drove everyone crazy, so one day the three Elizabeths got together and decided to draw straws for the names Elizabeth, Liz, and Z. My Elizabeth got the shortest straw, and so she became Z."

"Was that Z. so very different from this Z.?"

"Oh, the Villa of Mysteries! Time is so mysterious," Lars says. "It buries us all."

"Archaeology and excavation, that's how Freud says we get to the past."

"By the way, Annabelle, my wife says you are an excellent research assistant."

"Well," I say, feeling proud and embarrassed all at once. "I really do enjoy it."

"If you have the time—and I would pay you handsomely—I'd like to call upon you to find out everything about a picture called *The Frightened Woman,* which hangs on the wall in the Villa of Mysteries in Pompeii. It's a picture of a winged demon who is flagellating a younger woman."

"Oh, my," I say. "Sure, I'd be happy to research that for you."

Then I ask Lars if he can lend me nine hundred dollars. Part of it could be an advance payment for my research. I tell him that I will pay him back. I tell him that Z. helped me find the apartment, and it all happened so quickly that I took it without figuring out exactly how I would manage to pay the rent and a three-month security deposit. I tell him I've applied for a credit card and am waiting for it to arrive.

He asks me if this is one of Carol Martin's apartments and expresses disgust that she would require such a large deposit from a young person just starting out in the world.

Mimi Van Elder had not only assuaged his wife's suffering but launched her literary career. He wonders why Z. isn't more benevolent toward her own students.

I don't tell him that Z. is covering the key money.

We decide that Lars should mail me a check. We agree to be discreet about our work together.

Then Lars asks me how this sounds, a book starting with a man sitting at his desk, writing at the exact moment his kingdom is destroyed.

Lars says, "Imagine a society so affluent that it constructs a house for a tragic poet. A society that pays someone to live there—just so every once in a while there is someone in residence, someone to remind them of their deepest sorrows . . . this is the house of the tragic poet."

And then there is the sound of the lock, the jangling keys, Z. dropping her bags, and the awkwardness of Lars and me.

I should have left an hour ago. I should never have smoked pot with Claire. I have no work to show for my time here.

Z. has found the mail.

"Lars was just telling me about the Villa of Mysteries," I say.

She looks up. He's out of the kitchen. Perhaps he's sitting at his desk now.

"The Villa of what?"

"Of Mysteries."

She wears a black silk blouse, a gray flannel suit, and carries a briefcase. The barrette is gone. Her black hair is swept back over her forehead and held in place by a headband. I want to look like Z. someday: the artist as tailored, professional woman.

She looks up over her black glasses.

"You know, Pompeii."

Z. says, now slitting open an envelope, "Lars will talk your ear off."

"Yes," I say. "He's very passionate about his writing."

I'm waiting for a response. Or am I standing there because I feel like a shoplifter who's thinking about returning what she has pocketed?

"Lars will talk your ear off," she repeats.

She had told me that the issue of confidentiality was paramount to our work together, that there would be "poems, drafts, questions." I might have questions, but I was not to ask questions.

I had asked Lars how she became Z., and he had answered me. In a cabin in Ithaca, her young heart had been broken.

In the poem "Flower Power," Z. had touched the "she-flower," and the "she-flower" had touched her back, as once she had touched the "maiden pink."

Was "maiden pink" a veiled reference to Vivian DePresto?

Were there other women as well?

I begin to sweat.

"Annabelle, have you written on those weeds?"

"No, not yet."

She shakes her head.

"Annabelle, you told me you were going to write about those weeds."

"I know, but I misplaced the bag of weeds you gave me. Fortunately, I've found them again."

"Annabelle, I gave you those weeds for inspiration, not for their particularity. You can find a weed anywhere. Go to Central Park. Go to the Lower East Side. Annabelle . . . I feel you are resisting me."

"Oh, no," I say. "It's not that. It's just that what I wrote after I found the weeds seemed kind of morbid."

"Go down to the bookstore and buy a couple of field guides if that will help. Charge them to my account.

"Now," Z. says, "tell me again, which Jane wrote 'the Flowers of the Forest are a weed away'?"

"Miss Jane Elliot, I think."

She shakes her head in disgust. "I thought you were going to find out her name."

"I will, this afternoon—"

Z. cuts me off. "But you are sure it is Miss?"

"During the seventeenth and eighteenth centuries, women writers were known as Miss, Mrs., Lady, Princess, or Duchess. A formal title appeared as part of the author's name."

"Are you sure of that, Annabelle?"

"Pretty sure. . . . Well, not a hundred percent, no."

"I need certainty, Annabelle. And be sure to get me her book."

"She only published one poem," I say. "I don't think there is a book."

Z. says, reaching for her briefcase, "By now you should 'know,' not 'think.' If there's no book, I want you to be sure of that."

"I'll go to the library. I'll start researching right away." I smile to try to smooth things over, but I'm stoned. I should not be operating dangerous machinery.

"Wonderful. I'm itching to get to work on a new manuscript, but I'm counting on you to do the groundwork."

"I'm good at groundwork," I say. "It's just finding the time to do it that's a little tough right now."

"Annabelle," Z. says. "Poetry is inspiration, but it is also discipline. Have you forgotten that? At this time you have three outstanding assignments: weed research, coordinating Claire's interviews for the Emily Dickinson book, and creating a course curriculum. It seems you haven't completed one of them. You have a new apartment, so you should not be under so much pressure. What *are* you doing with your time, Annabelle?"

She doesn't realize that I haven't moved in yet. In some ways, I think, she is oblivious to my struggle.

"When you were blocked on writing about 'masculine' flowers, I gave in and told you to write whatever you could. But writing about weeds, why should that be so difficult?"

The Trouble with Harry

—

I was afraid of Z. because I had violated our nonintrusion pact.

I was afraid of Harry because I had seen his dark side. Just last week, I had been Nora to his James, reciting, "I am your child . . . and you must be severe with me."

Next thing I was over his knee in Marshall Greene's office, and Harry was saying, "Do you want this? And do you want this?"

And, in truth, I didn't know exactly what I wanted.

"Enough," I said, pulling away. "Stop!"

Then Harry stopped and made slow circular strokes around my bottom, where it really hurt. When it was over, he escorted me out of the study and closed the door.

The next night when we arrive at the farmhouse, which is dark, of course, and cold, Harry goes right to the typewriter in Marshall Greene's office and thunderously types. I remind myself that I'm here because being with Harry is strange and exciting. I'm here because I am hoping to feel something so exhilarating that I am driven to write poetry. And, also, I'm here because I think I'm attracted to Harry. I might even be in love with him.

And then this feeling comes over me. I want to be in my own apartment. Even though my futon has not yet been delivered, I want to see what it feels like to spend a night there.

Harry's book Harry's book Harry's book.

I take my flashlight and shine it on his face.

"Annabelle, honey, I'm coming to a very critical moment. Please."

I return to the bedroom, throw my flashlight up a row of books. It's the usual academic fare—lots of critical theory. There's a row of Marshall's novels, and I pull out the first book, *Lilith and Eve in Paradise*. It's filled with marginalia.

Lilith and Eve in Paradise, one of Marshall's shorter books. It's 550 pages. Folded inside is a book review. This is the last line: "Lilith and Eve, two cartoon characters lost in a garden of words."

"Drop that book, you're under arrest!"

Startled, I drop it and turn, but of course, it's only Harry.

"Do you know what he said when he finished the Anna Livia piece?"

"Who?"

"Joyce. He said he had hardly energy enough to hold a pen."

"You've finished?"

"Yes. I've finished."

"Good, because I really want to go home."

"How about once more for victory's sake?"

I hug myself. "No, Harry, I'm really cold."

"Annabelle, I'm done! I'm done!"

"Great. I'm glad you're done, Harry. This book has been your dream."

"I wrote at a clip, knowing I'd never have the chance to come back here again. And thanks for the other night, and listen, I'm sorry about it, too. But, Annabelle, that scene really makes the book! Imagine,

Harry in the book finally gets to exorcise the masochism that has permeated his life in this place."

"Great," I say. "But at whose expense?"

"I'm sorry you're unhappy with me, Annabelle."

"What are you going to do now? Send it out?"

"Actually, I've got a call in to an agent on Marshall's Rolodex. But first, I want to dedicate this book to my darling, Annabelle . . . my love, my inspiration.

" 'O! for a Muse of Fire, that would ascend the brightest heaven of invention!' " Harry says. "That's Shakespeare, King Henry V."

Then I ask myself this question: Do I want to continue being Harry's muse of fire, or do I want to do my own work?

"You're tired of me. You can say it."

"Did I say that? No, I just want to go home. I want to be in my own apartment. I want to spend a night there by myself."

"It's the spanking. Isn't it?"

"I'm alone in this godforsaken place with you, Harry. It feels so strange. These trips up here at night feel like some form of bondage."

Harry puts his arm around me. The other hand is holding his manuscript.

"When we go home, we'll reverse our course. Go back to the glove thing."

"I wasn't good at the glove thing, Harry. I felt foolish."

"No, you were very good. You really were."

When we first started with the gloves, I would stand at the side of Harry's bed in my Nora Joyce costume and Harry would admire my body, praise my recitation, and coax me into bed.

But here in the Marshall Greene farmhouse, with Harry constantly at the typewriter, there was no time for such tenderness.

I would walk around Marshall's study, reciting "Thank you for the gloves, Mr. Joyce, they are lovely and a splendid fit" while Harry typed. I was naked except for my white gloves and high-heeled shoes and a black lacy garter belt he had gotten me from God knows where. The room was illuminated by candlelight. And Harry would tell me to stop, and sometimes he would ask me to bend over and retrieve some-thing from the floor and hold that pose. The farmhouse floor was caked with dirt, and it made me sneeze. At the end of the evening, my feet hurt from the high heels.

Now I wondered how my character would come off in *Harry's Book*.

"Being here is like wearing a dead man's shoes," I say. "Can we go?"

I hear the scurrying of a mouse.

"Okay, Annabelle, go. Go start the car while I pack up."

He's picking paper off the floor and stamping about. One of Mar-shall Greene's manuscript stacks has fallen over.

"Are you mad at me?"

"I need to leave this place untouched."

"Because I really do like your story, I just want to get out of here."

Outside, I start the car and make smoke rings with my breath. For sev-eral minutes, I examine the crystalline formations on the windshield.

"Move over," Harry says, slamming the door. Now he's mumbling to himself.

"Listen, I just wanted to be in my own apartment . . ."

"Yes, but I finished and I did not get the feeling that you were truly happy for me." He jolts the car into reverse.

"Hey, if you want happy, next time give Mrs. Nabokov the gloves."

Much later that night, when daylight was a couple of hours away, Harry dropped me off at my apartment on Horatio Street. It had been a quiet ride home. I told him that I would like to be on my own for a while. There was no kiss good-bye. Harry was distracted, having real-ized only minutes earlier that he had left his copy of Joyce's *Selected Letters* in Marshall's farmhouse, and it was too late to go back for it.

My apartment was a mess, with suitcases and shopping bags and boxes of books clogging the tiny space. I'd been moving out of my mother's house piecemeal, bringing something else into the city every day. A coffeemaker I had purchased days earlier sat in front of the fireplace.

It was a black-and-silver chrome four-cup Mr. Coffee, and I unwrapped it and put it on the kitchen counter. I didn't really want coffee—I needed to get some sleep so I could be reasonably coherent when I went to work at Z.'s—but I made it anyway. The sound of the coffee splattering into the carafe was like a poem in that empty room. I drank thinking how good black coffee could taste when you made it yourself in your own apartment.

Then I took my clothes out of the suitcase and spread them on the floor. I covered myself with my pea coat. There were monks who slept every night on concrete pallets. Certainly for one night I could manage. And sleeping on my own floor beat sleeping in Marshall Greene's bed any day, even if Harry had changed the sheets. On the way to work the next morning I would stop by the futon store and make an urgent plea for delivery.

The Flower Dream Diaries

Z. says, "Annabelle, I have a luncheon meeting at the Plaza today. Have you seen the black stockings that were hanging up over the towel rack in the blue bathroom?"

I am hunched over the file cabinet in my office, organizing Z.'s RSVP file.

"Stripped of meter, who can I be? The dress, the sandal, the elegant hose. . . ," I want to say.

These are lines from my Emily Dickinson poem.

Instead, I say, looking up, "Sorry."

I don't frequent the bathroom at the end of the hall, the one to which Z. is referring.

"And by the way, how are you doing on my curriculum challenge to Women Poets: The Miltown Years? Have you worked up a syllabus for me yet?"

"Oh, I found you a poet," I say, turning to the desk for a folder. "You wanted a poet lost to history and I found you Margaret Sangster, author of *Poems of the Household* and *Home Life Made Beautiful*. She was the editor of the *Christian Intelligencer* in 1876."

"A Christian woman!"

"Do you know Claire has a friend who was kicked out of a religious study group when she delivered a sermon in her underwear?"

"What does this have to do with my course, Annabelle?"

"Sorry . . . In your course, Sangster is part of a movement aimed at glorifying women who made home life beautiful. The book that you could say inspired much of this was *The Angel in the House*."

Z. says, "Why is that title so familiar?"

"In that article you told me about, 'Professions for Women,' Virginia Woolf says that for a woman to be a writer she has to kill the angel in the house, that part of herself that is utterly unselfish and makes sacrifices for other people on a daily basis—"

I notice Z.'s fingernails. The tips are white, the nails themselves a shiny flesh tone. How I envied the woman who got to hold Z.'s hand as she gave her that manicure.

"Annabelle, I love your idea. It would make a wonderful dissertation, but it doesn't sound scholarly enough."

"But the housewife curriculum reflects poetry in its purest state— a time when there was no stereo, no television, and no telephone. People had to read—if only out of desperation—and they turned to poetry."

Z. says, "I don't mean to offend you, Annabelle, but is this the kind of thing that if you saw it listed in a college bulletin, you'd think, There's a class I have to take? I want to teach a course on unconventional minds, women writing outside the social norms. For instance, find me a poem by a woman written a hundred years ago that talks about sex in a subtle way."

"There was a ton of literature written by unnamed authors that was quite erotic."

"Yes," Z. says. "Not pornography. I'm talking literature. I want to remind my students that there are poems written by women that sanctify the body."

"Well," I say, "there was Aphra Behn. She wrote a very unconventional poem called 'To the fair Clarinda, Who made love to me, Imagin'd more than woman.'"

"A lesbian," Z. says, then, "Annabelle, this may not work. I want you to start again. I want to teach a very serious class this spring called Great Women Thinkers. I need you to find me some very serious poets."

"What about a class called Billie Holiday and the Harlem Renaissance Poets? I could put that one together fairly quickly."

"Did Billie Holiday write poems?"

"No, she was a jazz singer."

"Annabelle, I'm concerned about your lack of focus."

"Well, she was a junkie with a terribly sad life. When she was a young girl, she scrubbed floors in a brothel. That's when she first heard the music of Louis Armstrong . . ."

Z. rubs her temples in a circular motion with her fingertips.

". . . she was a heroin addict, a prostitute, but her songs were heartbreaking . . . She sang like a whore pining for her john," I say, but Z. is not amused.

"Is this about poetry or prostitution, Annabelle? Quickly."

"It's really about passion. Billie Holiday would be the cultural context—the fabric upon which you could examine the Harlem Renaissance poets. For example, you could talk about the vision of Langston Hughes." And I tell her about his poem "Harlem: A Dream Deferred," which asks if a dream deferred dries up "like a raisin in the sun" or "festers like a sore—and then runs."

"No," Z. says. "I don't want to talk about festering sores."

"Or you could do his wonderful 'The Negro Speaks of Rivers.' I could lend you a tape I have of him reciting it."

"Am I even allowed to say *Negro* in the classroom?" Z. asks. And then, very abruptly, she says, "Annabelle, where are my stockings? Oh! I just can't bear this! You're not helping me! I have to be there at twelve-thirty and this is a terrible hour to hail a cab. Would you please go into every bathroom and systematically search out my stockings?"

A less noble person would feel degraded, but I take Z.'s assignment as a challenge.

The bathroom at the end of the hall is tastefully papered in blue and mauve stripes. There are no stockings there, but there are hand towels.

In Z.'s bathroom, I find moisturizing lotion, toothpaste, a diaphragm case, a half-smoked cigarette in an ashtray, and Valium.

This is trespassing, the writer's work.

Lars's bathroom is covered in architectural drawings of Pompeii. No surprise there, and no stockings.

Claire's bathroom: a mess, with spilled nail polish, dirty cotton balls, and an open tube of bacitracin oozing onto the countertop. No stockings, but leaving, I see spread-eagle on the night table the book she borrowed from Braun, Gay Farinette's *14 Suicide Lane*. I close it and lay it flat, and then, on second thought, decide to check the inscription. I open to the title page. It says:

> TO BRAUN,
>
> I LOVE YOU,
>
> GAY

Perhaps she signs all her books to women this way, her name being Gay. It wouldn't surprise me.

Now Z. is at her desk. She has changed her clothes and is wearing slacks.

"No stockings," I say.

Z. says, "I may have thrown them out."

In the intense late morning light, Z.'s hair seems to have a reddish hue. Has she dyed it?

"Annabelle, when was Miss Elliot published?"

"She published 'A Lament for Flodden' anonymously in 1755. In 1871 it appeared in an anthology called *Songstresses of Scotland*."

"And is her name Jane or Jean?"

"It's Jane. I'm certain."

"Thank you," Z. says, "for finally resolving that mystery for me."

I'm waiting for her to ask me to start a used-book search for *Songstresses of Scotland,* but instead she says, "Annabelle, I want you to go to Bloomingdale's today. Here is some money, and here's what I am looking for . . ."

I take in a whiff of her perfume. It's something you can get only in France. I know this because I've ordered it for her.

"I want you to buy me every extant pair of Bloomie's sheer black stockings, size A/B."

"Consider it done." Then I say, "Professor Z., would it be okay if I took Monday off? I'm going to a poetry retreat this weekend."

"With Claire?"

"Yes," I say. "I don't know how much she's told you, but it's an intensive workshop. Gay Farinette is leading it. Braun says her book *14 Suicide Lane* is a classic."

"Annabelle," Z. says, "is Braun now teaching a class on 'hyperbole'?"

She is putting a folder into her briefcase.

"Professor Z.," I say, "I finally got my poem accepted to a magazine."

Z. says, "Well, hats off to you, Annabelle. Here's to your publication."

I want to tell her about the magazine, the excitement of opening the letter, but clearly this is not the time. I see myself in her office at the university next week, starting that conversation before we get down to the business of poetry.

Then, very proudly, Z. says, "It's a red-letter day, Annabelle. I have just completed *The Flower Dream Diaries*. It's almost ready to go off to my publisher."

"But I thought you had just started that."

"Well," Z. says, "I wrote it, it seemed, in one sitting. . . . It all came so quickly; it was of a piece."

I wonder if I will ever write with such ease.

I tell Z. about the sensation of reading a poem you've never read before, how thrilling it was to sit down and read *Flowers of Fate* for the first time.

"I would love to read your new manuscript, Professor Z.," I say.

"Well," Z. says, "I'm afraid this one needs a bit more fine-tuning before it goes out into the world . . . but would you like to proofread my *Selected Poems*? I realize you are going away, but the galleys are due back early next week and they could really use a cold eye."

"I'd be honored. I could proofread them this weekend, on the train."

Z. says, "Though it's not the same as holding a book of poems in your hands. The galleys are long and cumbersome, and I wouldn't want it to interfere with your *workshop*."

"No," I say, "really, it's an honor. I could even start reading now."

Then she says, standing up, putting the strap for her briefcase over her shoulder, "Annabelle, let the proofreading wait for the weekend. Right now the trip to Bloomingdale's is more crucial."

Secrets

=====

We were nine women sitting around a fireplace in a Boston town house. Ben had excused himself from the retreat, citing a prior obligation. He tended bar at the Mad Dog Café, and weekends were his most profitable time.

Gay Farinette sat on a rocking chair; Braun stood by her side.

Braun said, "And now I'd like to introduce you to Gay Farinette, the first lady of confessional poetry."

Everyone clapped.

"Gay was kind enough to agree to give us all a weekend of her time. . . . You may not know this, but Gay has been the teacher of some of our most celebrated poets, including Claire's mother, the Flower Poet Z."

Gay said, "I'm honored to be here. But the truth is, we owe this weekend to Wellesley, where I am visiting, and the poetry of frequent flier miles."

More laughter.

"Gay is already familiar with your work," Braun said. "I took the liberty of sending her samples."

Gay said, "Where's that girl, the author of that book you sent me? The book about the crucifixes."

"Oh, that would be Meg," Braun said.

Meg waved her hand and smiled.

"And the one who wrote that poem 'Song of the Sailor's Whore,' where is she?"

Jane raised her hand.

"Girl, you're cooking with Crisco," Gay said.

Then Braun laughed. "Such an earthy metaphor, Gay, . . . so modern, yet woefully outdated. . . . Now, shall we go around the room and introduce ourselves?"

"Yes," Gay said. "Let's break through the great wall of solitude."

She told us that she was Gay Farinette, the author of a book of poetry called *14 Suicide Lane,* which was published to "grave indifference" in the 1960s.

How was it that Robert Lowell and Sylvia Plath could get so much attention for turning their miserable lives into poetry and Gay Farinette could be completely ignored?

Hers was a lesson in perseverance: While the other poets were at home practicing the fine art of asphyxiation, Gay began a course of therapy with a famous—now dead—Kleinian analyst. And that was why she was alive today.

So when the world was once again hungry for confessional poetry, Gay Farinette was right there with three more elegant volumes: *Poems for Dr. Klein, My Heavy Heart,* and *Let Grief Come.*

"Life is mostly unhappy," Gay said. "It's one big, grievous burden, and only art can redeem us." She had a pen in her hand, and she pointed it at each one of us.

When it came time to introduce myself, I looked up in confusion. I couldn't decide whether to call myself Z.'s assistant or Z.'s apprentice, so I said nothing.

Braun said, "Annabelle, do you want to say something?"

Finally I said, "I'm Annabelle. I'm auditing Braun's class this se-mester."

Gay said, "Welcome, Annabelle." Then to the group, "This will be a weekend of reclaiming our lost voices, of facing down our inhibitions and turning them into poetry." She nodded kindly at me.

"This weekend," Gay continued, "we midwife a new kind of po-etry. A poetry of the body and soul; a poetry of secrets and revelation. Bring it forth and it will save you. Keep it in and it will destroy you!"

Meg said, "Our secrets?"

Gay shouted, "No more masks! No more mythologies! Did Muriel Rukeyser die in vain?"

Braun said, "Muriel said, 'If one woman told the truth about her life, the world would split open.' "

Gay said, "And I say, let's split the world wide open! Only when we tell all our secrets will we be free."

Braun said, "Some of you may not want to give up your secrets, at least right away, and I respect that. And many of you will tell your se-crets and feel self-conscious afterward. But I want you to know right now that all of us are in this together. . . . Nothing that goes on in this house goes any further than the front door. This weekend we work with the knowledge that everything said here is confidential. I can't emphasize this enough! Confidentiality yields trust; trust yields safety. Trust in the world, a feeling of safety, these are the foundations on which we build a home for poetry.

"Now let's begin by taking a deep breath, sitting cross-legged with our palms open. Our palms open to receive positive energy. Exhale."

Gay said, "This weekend we're going to write a poem about a secret. Something you've never told anyone, that means a great deal to you."

My crush on Z.? I thought, but this wasn't the place for that revela-tion.

Braun said, "First, let me start by telling you my secret. My secret is that I won't be returning to the university this spring—"

A collective gasp of shock and disappointment.

"As some of you know, this semester has been a tough one for me, with allegations flying back and forth—"

Ben and the downtown-midtown hotel room.

I looked over at Claire, who was pulling at the cuticle on her middle finger. She was probably used to this sort of thing. The world seemed either to idealize her mother or condemn her.

"So, I'm going to take some time off next semester to work through my anger." Braun laughed. "Maybe I'll get some good poems out of this."

Gay patted her hand. Would Braun ever get another teaching job anywhere?

Then Braun said, "Why don't you bare your soul for these young women, Gay? Show them how it's done."

Gay said, "My secret is a tender young man thirty years my junior, a former student, who lives in my flat. The world thinks he's my secretary, but he's never so much as typed a letter."

Braun said, "Thank you, Gay. Now, let's go around the room and reveal a secret. Any secret. It doesn't have to be the one you're going to write about."

Around the room, there was the usual garden variety of secrets: incest, adultery, drug addiction, and blackmail.

Jane's secret was family money. Meg sometimes wished she were a man. My secret was my gloves and high heels, my recitation of Nora Joyce's letter in the nude.

But Claire's secret was the strangest.

Claire said, "My secret is that when I read with my father, I dress like a nurse."

Gay said, "You read your poems dressed like a nurse?"

"Yes."

Claire glanced over at me.

"Does your mother know about this?"

Claire said, "No, it's a secret."

Gay adjusted herself in her chair. A sudden look of distress passed across her face. Braun saw it and said, "We are here to offer each other love and support. No one is judging you, Claire."

"It was acting, and it was my idea," Claire said. "He dresses like a doctor. He does these monologues. He does his Dr. Moses. And I'm his nurse, Esther. I read my own poems."

Gay Farinette said, "And you read about . . . ?"

"I read about my mother's needlepoint," Claire said.

Then Gay said, "Do you like reading your poems dressed as a nurse?"

Claire shrugged her shoulders.

Gay said, "Then why do you do it?"

"I don't know."

Braun said, "Well, Claire, there's an undercurrent in your story that's rather dark. This weekend is your chance to dig in and mine it."

Let Y = Z

―――

That night in bed, I couldn't sleep. In Braun's creaky, old house I thought I heard the sound of typewriter keys hitting the blank page, and I felt aroused.

Claire was asleep in the bed across from mine.

I liked Lars. I did not like to imagine him in a hotel room in Europe watching his daughter dress up like a nurse.

Even if she was performing with a father who was dressed like a doctor, it still made no sense for a nurse to be onstage reading *The Needlepoint Poems*.

Clearly, Z. had more than Claire's hair and piercings to worry about.

I decided to go downstairs and, while the house was quiet, try to write. Then I would call Harry. Sitting in Braun's living room with my notebook on my lap, I felt a sudden rush of words I could not contain in my head.

THE SOLUTION OF POETRY
Let x = *my mother.*
Let y = Z.

If infinity = question mark,
and New York is equidistant from Boston,
then
is the sum of my distance from Long Island =
to the sum of my distance from Z.?
Can u ever = y?

It wasn't the Poem of My Virginity, but still, I'd written another poem. I decided to celebrate with a cup of tea. I went into the kitchen and put a pot of water on to boil. Then I heard footsteps on the stairs. It was Gay Farinette in flannel bathrobe and slippers.

Gay ruffled through the magazine holder. "Jet-lagged?" I said.

"I'm looking for something trashy, an American emblem of bad taste, and all I find is a precious little journal called *Poesy Art,* and another called *Wordsmith.* Everywhere. Even in the bathroom, poetry."

"I don't understand reading in the bathroom," I said.

Gay said, "I like a woman who's not afraid to express her opinion." She sat down on the couch and patted the seat next to her.

Gay took my hand. Her hands were soft and knobby. She was massaging my fingers.

I didn't know what to say, so I said, "Do you like Emily Dickinson?"

"Well, of course."

"What does she mean to you?"

I was listening for the teakettle. I didn't want it to shriek.

Gay said, "What does she mean to me? I suppose different things at different times. . . . 'After great pain, a formal feeling comes' is a poem I always associate with migraine headaches, which I used to suffer from as a child. The 'formal feeling' being the moment the pain is miraculously gone and you can carry on with your life."

Then I got up off the couch and went into the kitchen. I found some peppermint tea and made each of us a cup.

Gay said, "Do you have a poem to read me?"

"My own?"

"Yes, of course."

"I have something I was just working on. It still needs polishing."

"That's fine," Gay said.

I opened my notebook, "Let x equal my mother," I said. Gay took a sip of her tea.

"Brilliant," she said. "An equation. A stark, beautiful, intelligent line. The universe revealed in a single line!"

Perhaps this is what Braun meant when she told Claire about her writing weekends, feeling that each poem she wrote was welcomed into the world with an outpouring of love.

"Let y equal Z," I said with more confidence.

"Again," Gay said.

"Let y equal Z," I said, matter-of-factly.

"X, the unknown, equals your mother. And y, the unknown, equals Z?"

"Yes," I said.

"Our Z.?"

"Z," I said. "A letter like y and x, known and unknown."

"Oh, come on, girl, come clean."

"Z.," I said. "Z."

"Z, the letter, and Z., Elizabeth?"

"Yes," I said. Suddenly I thought of Z.'s lost shoes. Let the shoe drop, I decided.

Then I read the rest of the poem line by line, and the poem again in its entirety.

After, Gay said, "So clever, so true. It's a poem about letters and belles lettres."

I said, "I just this very moment wrote it."

"I can see you boldly setting forth in all directions there. Into mathematics, into motherhood, and into matters of the heart. Z.'s heart being one of those matters."

"Actually, that wasn't my—"

Gay said, "If not in this poem, perhaps the next?"

"I would never want to hurt her or Claire."

"You must give yourself permission to write anything you need to write," Gay said. "The only way out is through; I tell that to all of my students . . ."

"This is the second poem I've written about the alphabet. What I really want to write is a poem about virginity. But I can't seem to get it down on paper."

She sipped her tea. "Maybe the virginity piece is not meant to be a poem. Maybe it's an essay or a novel. And maybe it's not about virginity at all but about a loss of innocence."

I wrote in my notebook:

VIRGINITY AS LOST INNOCENCE.

"Right now you're writing alphabet poems. You must nurture them, shape them, be patient with them."

"Miss Farinette, what was she like in college?"

She had put her tea on the side table and was rearranging the cushions, making herself comfortable. For a moment, I had a feeling she was going to bed down.

"Z. She was your student, wasn't she?"

"It was a very long time ago."

"Do you remember what she was like, your first impression of her?"

"Elizabeth was an earnest girl, very bright . . . I remember her particular quality of sadness; the sorrow of being alone in the world, of being abandoned by someone very dear—"

"Did she write about flowers back then?"

"No, she wrote about horses, even though we were all writing about our mothers in those days."

"Did you see something in her then, some spark that told you what she would become?"

"No, not really. I looked at Elizabeth and I saw somebody very fragile."

Gay and I drank our tea in silence for a while. Then Gay stood up and said, "You know, I'm getting a little tired. Thank you, Annabelle, for sharing that poem. Knock on the door of an old lady with a cup of tea any time."

Then, when the house was quiet again, and it seemed like Gay Farinette was tucked in for the night, I took out my new credit card and made a long-distance call to Harry. I didn't know exactly what I would say, but it didn't matter. I missed him.

I let the phone ring for a long time, but there was no answer. Then, thinking I might have dialed wrong, I called again, and still, no one answered.

The Poet's Heart

The schedule was breakfast at 8:30, immediately followed by a mission statement by Gay Farinette, writing time, a catch-as-catch-can chili lunch, and Braun's Joni Mitchell, the Troubadour Poet lecture. Then we were to read our own poems; then break for a two-hour rest.

Braun came down to breakfast in a brightly colored silk kimono. An ancient Japanese cartoon face was plastered on her back. It was a cold morning to be making such a fashion statement, but here was Braun in her own home throwing caution to the wind.

Since this was a weekend of confessional poetry, I wanted to tell Braun that she should not even consider an affair with Z.'s husband.

"For Lars, with love from His Mistress," she had written in his book.

But then I thought, What if Braun simply signs books this way? What if the inscription was standard for her?

Yes, but what was Braun doing with Ben in that hotel room?

I wanted to tell her she had bad judgment.

As for my own judgment, I wished I hadn't gone to Lars for money. I wished I hadn't agreed to research the Villa of Mysteries.

I must have look preoccupied, because Braun asked me if anything was wrong. She had been extra careful around me since the afternoon she found me banging my head against her door.

I told her I was tired. I had had a late-night visitation from the muse.

Across the table, Claire was drinking black coffee. She looked bleary-eyed, hungover. Her hair was flat and greasy. She was in desperate need of one of her Gitanes, but Braun had declared her home and the property around it a no-smoking zone.

We cleared our places, then met in the living room for our assignment.

Braun said, "Of course, you all know the goal is to write poetry. But since Gay is here, I'd like to ask her: How do we grow as poets? How do we learn? I'm thinking of a poem by Theodore Roethke where he says—"

Gay winced.

"—we 'learn by going where we have to go.' So go." She held out her hands, giving the floor over to Gay.

Gay said, "Thank you, Miss Brown. I'm not going to speak long. My job here is simply to serve as agent provocateur. Today you will write from your heart. Remember, your poems are as individual as your fingerprints. There was Roethke, a man of his time, writing the poem Braun just quoted—but that poem is his story; what is yours?

"Poets, do not be fooled by friendly poetry! Yes, Roethke wrote good verse, but do you know that he had this to say about women writers: that they refuse to face up to what existence is and run 'between the boudoir and the altar, stamping a tiny foot against God'?"

Braun said, "Wasn't that 'shaking a tiny fist against God'?"

"Yes, yes. Foot, fist. What I have to say to all that is 'Fuck you, Theodore Roethke.' "

Claire threw me a look.

Gay said, "If you're going to be a confessional poet, you're going to have to start talking like one. Repeat after me: 'Fuck you, Theodore Roethke.' "

So we said, "Fuck you, Theodore Roethke."

Gay continued, "Now, Mimi had a lot to say about confessional poetry."

Mrs. Van Elder with her shelf of pink books.

"She hated the body. Whitman celebrated the body, but not our critic, no. We put our trust in Mimi Van Elder, but she turned out to be just one of the boys. Was it Mimi who said, 'Real life does not belong in poetry'? Was it Mimi who called generations of women writing about their lives, their children, their menstrual blood, 'pornographers'? Was it Mimi sitting on those award committees giving money to her right-wing disciples? . . . Yes, it was. And it was Mimi, the former poetry editor of that hallowed magazine—you know the one I mean—launching some of the blandest poets of our time . . ."

Mimi, the critic-cockroach, impervious to social change.

"Now, what is confessional poetry, anyway? I guess we need to start with confession, which is the disclosing of one's sin in the sacrament of reconciliation. It's the act of unburdening oneself. And did you know that in the Middle Ages torture was the means to exact a confession?

"I suppose what I mean to say is that when you set out to unburden yourselves this morning, understand that pain is sometimes necessary for a poem to be born. Human beings are born into great pain. Women give birth in great pain. Birth is about blood and pain. And that's a curse, and it's also a gift. Now go and enjoy the process."

That weekend I stood at a crossroads: whether to write a poem about my own lost innocence or to expose my feelings about the Bovardine family in a poem called "The Secret for Solving Poetry."

Let a = Z.
Let Claire = b.
And Lars, let him = c.
The formula for family is the formula for spherical geometry:
Sin a = *Sin b* = *Sin c*

It was the word *sin* that scared me. The sins of the Bovardine family were adultery, incest, drug addiction, blackmail, and a single-minded determination to ruin Braun Brown's career. If I ever published such a poem—if I dared say these things—surely there would be retribution.

I wrote in my notebook:

If a poet writes a great poem and nobody hears it—
If a poet writes a great poem and nobody reads it—
If a poet never writes—
no trees fall, no sound.

Let Braun Brown = sin.

I closed my notebook and sat there very content with myself. Finally, I had written a poem I respected. It was my signature, something nobody else could ever have written.

Then I sat in the circle and tried to be appreciative of everything that was written.

Meg Cross was ecstatic because she had written two poems: "Cross Dressing," and "Cross Fertilization."

The poems were a real departure for Meg, who had never tackled such subject matter before. Braun praised Meg for her bravery, and then Meg, overcome with feeling, said the workshop had been a true healing experience. Looking in my direction, she said how restorative it was to be in an environment where nobody felt compelled to rewrite your poem.

Then Claire read a very long, garbled account of what it was like to dress like a nurse and read poetry on your father's reading tour. The ending of her poem made reference to something she had seen on the news, a story about a nurse poisoning her patients through an intravenous drip.

Yes, I am a nurse,
and I'm now on TV—
They say I put Clorox in my patients' IV . . .

Gay asked if this was comedy or tragedy. Did the poem's joking manner obfuscate the important work it was trying to do? Was there a place for humor in poetry?

Then Braun told Claire that it might be interesting to try to write even more openly about her parents. She said not to be afraid of confession, not to retreat from difficult subject matter. The most credible poem, Braun said, would reveal Z. and Lars as fallible human beings, and tell us something about all parents and children. Could Claire find a way to humanize her parents for the reader? Then Braun gave Claire an exercise: Write a poem where a daughter tells her parents that she is gay. What would that poem be like? she asked.

Claire said she didn't know, but she'd give it a try.

Then it was my turn. I cleared my throat and without apology read "The Secret for Solving Poetry."

"Let *a* equal Z.

"Let Claire equal *b,*" I said.

"And Lars, let him equal *c*.

"The formula for family is the formula for spherical geometry:

"Sin a equals Sin b equals Sin c."

Braun looked at Claire. Claire shook her head. Then no one said anything for a very long time.

Gay finally broke the silence by saying, "Okay, girls, now tell me verbatim what Annabelle has said. Let's re-create that poem."

Claire said, "I'll re-create it. Fuck you, Annabelle."

Braun said, "Claire, let's show some respect here."

Claire said, "Respect?"

Braun said, "We're all trying something new this weekend. Even if it crosses a boundary and makes us uncomfortable, we have to be able to say what we need to say." She looked around the circle. "Is this clear, everyone?"

Gay said, "Let's re-create the poem before we forget it. . . . Jane?"

"Let a equal Z. And then b equals Claire; then c is her father."

Braun said, "That's one interpretation."

Meg said, "The formula for family is a mathematical formula."

"What kind of math?"

"Spherical geometry. It's circular."

Then someone added, "Yes, and it's related to sine. It's a sign that reads 'sin.' Sin a equals b equals c."

Gay said, "So, tell me, girls, what does it mean that we could re-create this poem in its entirety?"

Various ideas were presented.

"It means that the poem is its own complete world," Gay said. "A world in a bowl of soup. And, ladies, what is this poem about?"

"Math," someone said. And someone else said, "The family romance."

Then they said what they liked about the poem: They liked the fact that there was a problem and a solution. They liked the fact that each word had so many meanings. That every word was important.

But then they said they didn't like the style at all. There was too much style. In fact, someone said, "the poem is all style and no substance." Then someone said, "What is spherical geometry and do I, as a reader, even care?"

And Braun asked, "Do we need to know about spherical geometry to appreciate this poem?" The room was divided. People were getting edgy. They wanted to move on.

Finally Braun said, "I feel the poet has retreated from the real work of this poem. This is a very intimate voice; it wants to say more. It leads us to the edge of intimacy and pulls away. I wonder if it is written from the poet's heart. I wonder if the poet is too scared to say what is in her heart."

Gay said, "Yes, I agree, the poet has pulled a punch and run away. She lays down her formula, but she hasn't yet applied it. Unless this is the first poem of a series and there are more poems like this to come."

Then Braun said, "Annabelle, what do you think of everything we've just said?"

"Well," I said, "there was another line, but I didn't have the courage to say it, so I threw it out."

Braun said, "Just say it, Annabelle."

And so I said, "Let Braun Brown equal sin."

Gay was playing with a thread on her silk jacket. "Well, isn't that interesting," she said.

Braun said, "I assume the speaker is talking about me, but I realize the reader can't assume anything."

Silence. Inside that silence, the ticking of a clock. Braun said, "This is a cruel poem."

I said nothing. It was possible I had missed the lesson on cruelty.

Then Braun said, leaning in, "We don't choose our subjects; they choose us. But in this case, Annabelle, I think you had some choice. I think it's unwise to use poetry as a vehicle for unleashing your hostility and your aggression at Z. and her family. I'm going to overlook the fact, here, that you also chose to slander me. What could you be thinking?"

But hadn't she told me to write about Z.? Hadn't she taught me to push my poems to the edge of the abyss and beyond?

Then Gay stood up and said, "I'm going to get some tea. You, Annabelle, need to write about your own mother."

A Formal Feeling

When I returned from Boston, Maurita Collins let me know that I would no longer be working for Z. She had chosen a new assistant for the spring semester. I stared at her in disbelief. I knew Z. had a history of firing her assistants, but somehow I thought my status as apprentice meant job security.

As for my new assignment: No, Maurita said, I would not be assisting Professor Holmes in his big survey course, An Introduction to Modern Poetry but, rather, I would be working right here with Maurita, cataloging the Marshall Greene papers. She took me to a seminar room, where stacks of Marshall Greene's books were piled on steel gray bookshelves, waiting to be put in alphabetical order. I began to scan for a thick black paperback: Harry's beat-up copy of James Joyce's *Selected Letters*.

And, here—Maurita opened the door of an abandoned office—was the Marshall Greene ephemera collection.

Apparently he was a man who emptied the contents of his coat pockets into his desk every day, and what had survived him were thousands of crumpled pieces of paper. (Remember, he had been at the university twenty-five years!) There were Juicy Fruit wrappers, receipts with indecipherable words written on them, restaurant bills with names scrawled across. I would learn to read his handwriting, Maurita said. And later, there would be phone calls to make. I would interview every person whose name appeared on a check stub, and ask them to remember what they could about that long-ago meeting with Marshall Greene. In time there would be a biography. The history of Marshall's pockets would be essential to that study.

Did I know Harry Banks? Maurita asked. He had been the last to work on the ephemera collection and had not been as thorough as she would have liked.

That happened on a Tuesday, a day Z. had office hours, so I knocked on her door. She was sitting behind her huge desk, looking down at some papers. She was probably expecting someone else, because when I opened the door she startled.

"Maurita tells me I am no longer your assistant."

"Well," Z. said, clearing her throat, "Maurita makes these assignments, and in the interest of fairness, there are other students waiting for a chance to apprentice with me."

"Did I do something wrong?"

Z. pushed her papers to one side of her desk and folded her hands.

"Annabelle, sit down please."

"Because I would like to know. Just last week you told me how pleased you were with my proofreading, how expertly I had read your galleys."

"Annabelle," Z. said, "I'm going to be perfectly frank. You're not going to like what I have to say, but hopefully you will learn and grow from our conversation today."

I was looking down at my sneakers, now beat up and torn. I would need to get another job, find a way to compensate for my lost income so I could keep my apartment.

"Annabelle, there are some things you do very well. You're a good proofreader, a talented researcher, and are skilled at simple tasks like filing papers and organizing books."

I nodded in acknowledgment.

"But you really were not a very good assistant, Annabelle. You lost things; remember my shoes? You didn't listen well, and you forgot to follow up on important details."

I said, "I think there has been a series of misunderstandings."

Z. said, "Not to mention that you have no concept of a deadline. I had planned on having a draft of that Emily Dickinson book by now."

"I wish you had told me that."

Z. said, "A good assistant would have created a deadline for herself. It was your responsibility to move that project along."

I wondered if Claire had shown Z. the poem I'd written at Braun's retreat.

I bit my lip, said softly, "I wish you had told me, I could have tried to fix things."

Then Z. got up from her desk, and I got up too.

"Annabelle, it was beyond that."

One tear rolled down my cheek, and Z. saw it. She shook her head.

I wanted to tell her how painful it was to be losing her, but suddenly I thought of the mistake Harry had made with Marshall Greene. Loyal to the point of invisibility, he'd never even asked Marshall for a letter of reference.

"Professor Z.," I said, before turning to leave, "would it still be possible to get a letter of recommendation for my file?"

"Of course. Just leave the form in my mailbox."

And then I told Maurita I had a personal emergency and needed to go home. By that time, I'd been crying for quite a while in the stall in the women's room and my eyes were pretty bloodshot. Maurita gave me a perfunctory nod. I imagined she had been through this before.

Harry would understand, I thought. So I called him, and instead of the ringing phone, I got a message that his number was no longer in service.

I went over to his apartment building. I waited in the vestibule until someone let me in, and then I knocked on his door. A pretty young woman in a denim shirt answered.

Was she the new me?

I checked to see if her breasts were "swung."

"I'm looking for Harry Banks," I said.

"Oh yes," she said. "We're subletting. He's gone."

"Gone?" I said. "Do you know his number?"

"No," she said, stepping back inside. "Actually, yes." The room was light and airy. She had rearranged Harry's things. She peeled a note off the refrigerator. "Here's his address," she said.

He was in Trieste, Italy. I could write to him in care of the local post office.

I must have looked confused, because she said, "Oh, I think he said his fellowship ran out. So he said he was going to Europe to get in touch with his 'inner Joyce.' "

The woman laughed.

Harry could be so strange.

The Dead, I thought. I've got to read *The Dead*.

Then I glanced over at the bookshelf where Marshall Greene's Rolodex once stood. Beside it was Harry's IBM Selectric, and suddenly I longed for the sound of his typing.

A few days later, when Maurita had gone out to a meeting, I found Harry's copy of Joyce's *Selected Letters* on the shelf of the Marshall Greene library, buried it in my backpack, and walked home.

I sat cross-legged on my futon, looking through the book, thinking of James Joyce, so overwrought with his love for Nora that it spilled onto every page.

I remembered the beautiful color stipple engraved flower book. I didn't know when I gave it to Z. that I would ever want it back, that I would consider it a gift from Harry to be cherished.

I had wanted to fall deeply and passionately in love. I had wanted an affair that would change my life, one that would inspire me to plumb the depths of my soul. I had wanted to have emotions so strong that no metaphor could contain them.

I had not counted on grief, regret, sorrow, and rage.

In truth, I did not enjoy having such strong emotions.

Perhaps I was not cut out to be a poet after all.

I put Harry's Joyce book in a padded envelope with a pair of woolen socks.

I pictured him in the middle of nowhere, bundled in his big fisherman sweater, finding my inscription.

FOR HARRY,

WITH LOVE FROM HIS NORA—

ANNABELLE

A month later, signs went up around the English Department inviting us to Z.'s induction into the Society for the Preservation of American Poetry. Maurita had free tickets for everyone.

At first I thought I would not go. But in the end I went because in the beginning I was simply her reader, a young woman alone in her suburban bedroom asking herself "What is poetry?" and answering: "This book that you are holding in your hands."

Besides, I wanted to give Lars back his money.

I had a seat in the orchestra section with a clear view of the stage. Jason Spence brought the event to order.

He said, "Our celebration tonight is twofold. We celebrate the publication of *The Selected Poems of Z.,* and name Z. chancellor of the Society for the Preservation of American Poetry."

He was wearing the black cashmere turtleneck I'd bought at Bloomingdale's and a new tweed sport jacket. It was a simple, understated look, one that honored his attachment to his threadbare past.

"I'd like to open this evening with a quote from the Society's esteemed late poet-librarian, whose generosity will endow our reading series in perpetuity. In the words of Mr. Frances Fowler, 'I lift a golden chalice to celebrate the word—' "

Spence's voice reverberated throughout the auditorium. It was an elegant hall of red velvet and brass. Above the stage, these names were carved into the wood paneling: Plato, Milton, Shakespeare, Tennyson. And on the stage sat the seven somber chancellors of the Society for the Preservation of American Poetry.

Claire was sitting next to Lars in the reserved section. She turned around, and when we made eye contact, she looked away. Whatever she was going through was no longer evident on her person. She now had a lovely short haircut, which put the accent on her eyes, which were big and blue. She wore one pair of earrings, simple gold hoops. I had been hoping to ask her how she liked Harvard, but such a conversation now seemed unlikely.

"This fall there will be a full investiture in Washington, D.C., when she assumes office. At that time Z. will deliver the keynote address on the state of American poetry."

"Now, about our esteemed colleague, the poet Z. . . . The author of thirteen volumes of poetry, her work has been translated into more than twenty languages. Z. holds honorary doctorates from three universities and has an endowed chair at the University of New York City.

"*Poetry Journal* has called Z.'s work 'sultry, and evocative.' One scholar said this of her early masterpiece, 'The Garden Outside My Window':

> Z. is a gardener who is sensitive to what she plants; she knows what poems take root. And, like any gardener, she is sometimes forced to use a pickax to break the rock-hard soil. The hands of the poet are callused and dirty, but she perseveres. She scatters her words like tiny seeds. What blooms in the end is the garden outside our window, a glorious island of beauty.

"That you are here tonight for this sold-out event is a testament to Z. and a tribute to the strength of her poetry. Z. has shaped generations of young writers and—I believe—has shaped American letters through her elegant, evocative dialogues with the natural world. We can no longer think of sex without thinking, Flower. Now, forgive me if I say this prematurely—I think we all want to say this: Welcome, Madam Chancellor—"

Z. walked onstage. She wore a long, tight black dress, which flared out a bit in the back, forming a train that never touched the floor.

Spence shook her hand, then kissed her cheek. She said she was honored to be there.

Then Spence introduced Daniel Scott, outgoing president of the Society and editor of *Poetry: America!,* who would be interviewing Z. at tonight's event.

Scott came onstage with a young woman who was holding a plaque. She handed it to Spence, who read:

"Founded in 1912 in an effort to keep the American word alive, the Society for the Preservation of American Poetry is pleased to name Elizabeth Bovardine chancellor on this night, the second of April, nineteen hundred and . . ."

His voice was drowned out by applause.

Spence continued, "I'd like to read the words at the bottom of the plaque." He paused, adjusted his reading glasses. "Actually, it's our new motto. Here it is: 'A poetry by the people and for the people shall not perish from the earth.' "

The three put their hands on the plaque and posed for the photographer. Spence shook Z.'s hand again and said, "Congratulations." Scott kissed her on both cheeks. Then the poet and the Society's president moved to Windsor chairs at the center of the stage. Here she was, the poet Z., stunning in her black dress, bathed in the adulation of a thousand fans. Someone attached a microphone to her collar.

The interviewer said, "What an honor it is to be here with you."

INTERVIEWER: The book you just finished is called *The Flower Dream Diaries.* Can you talk a little about your new flower poems? I am especially interested in the Wisteria series. Let me quote the first lines of the title poem:

Little hysteria, you cling to a building—
I should have jumped, disguised the thought,
written about my father years ago . . .

z.: Wisteria grew out of my interest in hysteria. I'd been reading a lot about Freud and Dora. Started thinking about the vines, the bushy flowers, et cetera, you know. Cough, cough. I was trying to grapple with sexual and intellectual history.

INTERVIEWER: (Laughing) In "Maiden Pink," you go back in time to the sixth century B.C., appropriating the voice of Sappho, or what we surmise to have been Sappho.

z.:   MAIDEN PINK
       A simple flower, like a button
       braided through a young girl's hair.
       Each star, a button
       braided through my daughter's hair.

I remembered the exact bench I was sitting on when that description came to me.

INTERVIEWER: Talk about your writing process.

z.: I write all the time. When I'm not writing, I'm gathering references, researching my work. I wrote my last book in a white heat. I'd been collecting notes for quite some time and then it all suddenly came together and I literally did not stop until I was finished. I wrote from early morning until late evening, leaving my desk only for meals and, now and then, to sleep.

INTERVIEWER: Tell us about those masculine flowers. As you know, we're quite pleased to be publishing your new cycle of poems, *Consider the Orchid,* in the summer issue of *Poetry: America!* Would you read something for us?

z.: This is a two-line poem. Listen closely, because it will go by in a flash.

SONG
Your large buds your long leaves
Your soft hairy stem, flower!

Laughter. I felt a rush of blood to my ears. For a second I thought my head might explode.

INTERVIEWER: I admire your use of punctuation in that poem.

Z.: Yes, for some reason I find myself moving away from the traditional rules of grammar in the interest of creating a greater sense of urgency.

INTERVIEWER: Recently, you showed me your work in progress "A Weed Away." How are we to interpret the transition from flowers into the realm of weeds?

Z.: The title is an allusion to Miss Jane Elliot, an eighteenth-century writer, who is survived by only one poem 'A Lament for Flodden.' Here, I am imagining myself Miss Jane Elliot writing a book of flower poems.

INTERVIEWER: That you can call up the voice of a poet we know almost nothing about is a real feat of imagination. The way you managed to weave in *King Lear* is startling. Let me quote:

Someone has pulled out my lashes
and left me with weeds
and planted a garden bereft of flowers.
Oh, sacred flower, you have no luster now—

And then something seized up in me. The reason these poems were unlike anything Z. had written before was that she had not written them. *I,* her former assistant, Annabelle Goldsmith, of Huntington Station, Long Island, had written them.

I was trying to stay calm, to convince myself that I should be flattered. Had Emily Dickinson minded that the world thought Ralph

Waldo Emerson the author of "Success is counted sweetest" when her poem appeared nameless in that anthology?

I tried to think of one memorable poem written by Ralph Waldo Emerson, and I couldn't.

Z. was a thief, a shameless thief. She stole.

"After great pain, a formal feeling comes," Dickinson had written. Here was my formal feeling.

As the crowd rose to its feet, I walked toward the back of the auditorium and, when the doors opened, got on line at the signing table. A half hour later Z. arrived with Jason Spence and his assistant, a young woman who looked a lot like Z. Spence whispered something in Z.'s ear as she sat down, and she smiled up at him. Then he touched her arm.

There were so many fans ahead of me, so many multiple copies to be signed, I thought my turn would never come.

Finally, I was face-to-face with the flower poet.

"Annabelle," Z. said, holding out her hand. "So pleased you could make it." She opened to the title page and started signing the first book. She was writing something personal.

I stooped down so I was at eye level with her trademark black glasses. I was so close, it must have looked as if I was about to kiss her.

I said, "Professor Z., you read beautifully tonight."

She stopped signing and looked up at me.

Her hair was jet black.

"Why, thank you, Annabelle," and then, with that touch of false modesty I recognized as the real Z., said, "You really thought so?"

"Yes. You read *my words* beautifully tonight."

She was wearing that uncomfortable smile I knew too well. It said, I haven't got time for this.

Then I said, "I want to say I was really taken aback that you would use my lines, my exact words . . ."

She cocked her head to the right.

Spence was now at the periphery holding a wineglass.

I said, "You know as well as I do, Professor Z., that I wrote those words."

"There's that grandiosity of yours again, Annabelle. I had so wanted to help you master it."

"I have the notebook to prove what I'm saying, Professor Z."

The woman behind me was getting impatient. She was telling the person next to her that this was what it felt like to be behind someone at a tollbooth who throws all their change into the net, misses, and gets out of the car to go scrambling for it.

"Your name?" Z. said, craning her head to make eye contact with the woman behind me.

The woman stepped in front of me, so I was displaced to the side of the signing table.

"Sarah, with an *h*."

I was standing there waiting for my chance to cut back into the line when I saw Arthur Feld.

"Annabelle! Annabelle!" he said. He was with his wife and daughter. I had met them only a few months earlier at his reading.

That was when I noticed Lars Bovardine walking straight toward me.

"Annabelle." Lars held out his hand to shake mine, and then drew me into his body. "It's so nice to see you. You don't come around anymore."

"Lars, this is for you. I wanted to pay you back."

It was a check for nine hundred dollars from my mother.

He threw his hand down in a gesture of disgust. "Really."

Then Arthur Feld cut in and I said, "Lars Bovardine, this is my poetry teacher from Long Island Community College, Arthur Feld."

"Glad to meet you," he said, pumping Lars's hand.

Around the periphery of the room, people were sitting in ladder-back chairs, drinking wine. I opened my backpack and took out the books I had brought for Z. to sign. My time with her at the table had been so upsetting that I hadn't even looked over to see what she was writing.

FOR ANNABELLE,

WITH AFFECTION AND GRATITUDE,

Z.

For a moment, in spite of all that had transpired, I was really touched. Here was a thank-you from the heart that acknowledged all I had meant to her. I remembered the afternoon I fell asleep at my desk, how Z. brought me tea, let me nap on her sofa. She had admired my talent, called me a "writer with promise." She had given me the gift of key money and a studio apartment.

She had led me to a room of my own.

But all that quickly evaporated when I opened my copy of *Flowers of Fate* and read the identical inscription:

FOR ANNABELLE,

WITH AFFECTION AND GRATITUDE,

Z.

That night, I stood in the back of the room for a long time and watched her greet her readers. Everyone had a story to tell her: when they had first discovered her poetry, how much her books had meant to them. Some offered greetings from a former student or a long-lost friend. Z. listened to each vignette and said something kind in return.

She had taught me artifice and art; I would miss her.

My Letter

———

A few days later, I got a letter:

> Dear Annabelle—
>   I have enclosed a draft of your letter of recommendation and the form. Please type this letter and forward to Career Services.
>
> Z.

I opened the envelope, and there was nothing but the blank form with Z.'s signature at the bottom. I wondered if this was Z. placating me, offering me the opportunity to write my own ticket in return for silence on my plagiarism charge.

Or perhaps this was simply Z. thanking me for all that I was to her.

Most likely, I thought, this was the real Z., a woman incapable of putting a letter in an envelope.

My dilemma lasted about a minute. I imagined myself a great writer writing the story of her life. I typed:

To Whom It May Concern:

I write this letter in support of Annabelle Goldsmith. During her tenure as my apprentice, Annabelle proved herself to be self-less, dedicated, and invaluable. She is a superb line editor who knows the difference between *affect* and *effect; whorled* and *whored.* She is well read and erudite, has an intuitive sense of timing, and can be relied upon to perform any task, no matter how trivial or grand.

Annabelle is also a gifted poet. Her poems are quiet and affect-ing. They open out to the true darkness of a woman's soul. Her po-etry: a rare distilled flower that grows through a crack in the sidewalk or a lush tropical bird-of-paradise that blooms in a glass-house in the city. Her voice is original and bold. "What is poetry?" I ask, and Annabelle's poems cry out in answer.

Annabelle is, and will always be, a credit to her sponsors, and, furthermore, I believe she will make a unique contribution to the poetry of our time. I wholeheartedly give her my highest recom-mendation.

I would like to report that the money, the teaching offers, the solicitations from magazines came pouring in, but I couldn't lick the envelope.

I told myself that the world recognizes great poetry, and that even-tually it would recognize me too.

I put my letter of recommendation in the far reaches of my desk drawer, in the place where I had once hidden a pamphlet called *Your Blossoming Womanhood.*

So I was repressed, regressed, self-defeating, but at least I was true to myself. I sat down to write the poem of my liberation, and this is what I wrote:

APPRENTICE TO THE FLOWER POET Z.

A NOVEL.

Acknowledgments

I wish to thank the New York State Foundation for the Arts for a generous creative writing fellowship.

Thanks also to Robin Rolewicz, Carolyn Kim, Veronica Windholz, and the friends and family members who endured me during the many years I wrote this book.

I am deeply grateful to my editor, Ileene Smith, and my agent, Charlotte Sheedy. This book is also for them.

APPRENTICE TO THE FLOWER POET Z.

A Reader's Guide

Debra Weinstein

A Conversation with Debra Weinstein

Jennifer Morgan Gray *is an editor and writer who lives in Washington, D.C.*

JENNIFER MORGAN GRAY: Was there a particular image or idea that inspired you to write *Apprentice to the Flower Poet Z.*? Did you begin with a character, a certain plotline, or perhaps a poem?

DEBRA WEINSTEIN: The idea for the book came from a sentence I found in my notebook: "Such was the nature of my relationships with Professors T., X., and Ms. Z." Who was Ms. Z.?, I wondered. She seemed to be set off and quite distinct from the other letters. The narrative voice from this passage seemed self-assured and funny, and so I continued to write in this vein. So I would say inspiration came by way of language and voice.

JMG: Annabelle's love for poets and the process of writing poetry is evident on every page. How does her writing style and process compare

re there any writers—poets, novelists, memoirists—
for inspiration?

love Emily Brontë's *Wuthering Heights* because it is strange and
mysterious, a wholly original novel which breaks from tradition and
form. In the 1850 preface, Emily's sister, the novelist Charlotte Brontë,
apologized for the perverse nature of the book, saying that it "was
hewn in a wild workshop" and that the writer who possesses the creative gift owns something of which [she] is not always master. I have always been interested in the mystery of writers' lives and the act of
transgression that allows them to make use of that creative gift.

When I sat down to write *Apprentice to the Flower Poet Z.,* I wasn't
really reading anything. It was my hope to be free of influence. Ini-
tially, I had imagined Annabelle to be a doctoral student writing her
dissertation on the Flower Poet Z., and her writing goes terribly awry
when she starts focusing less on the poetry and more on the poet.
Annabelle's creative process is a lot like mine. Before I write, I go
around absorbing information and gathering words and phrases.
Annabelle also edits poetry as I do—ruthlessly.

JMG: The poems and written words of many characters—among
them Annabelle, Z., Arthur Feld, Ben, Meg Cross, and Harry—figure
prominently in the novel. How did you get into the mind-set of these
different characters in order to write in their distinct literary voices?

DW: Sometimes it was simply a word that I associated with a character when creating a poem. With Ben it was "downtown." Naturally, I
thought of the Beats, and so then I found myself creating a beat and
four words to accompany it. For Meg Cross, the word "cross" would
define her oeuvre.

Annabelle's poems needed to reflect her struggle in the world, and
so I had to understand her psychology very well to create them. Aside
from that, I felt her poems needed to be written in an original voice—
one that would reflect her as quirky, sardonic, irreverent, and utterly
her own person. When I was in college, I had written a very technical,

funny poem called "The Mathematician's Daughter Elopes." It was, in a sense, a young woman's formula for separating from her family. I used that poem—and the concept of alphabet as identity—as a blueprint for Annabelle's work.

JMG: "Writing poetry is its own reward," says Z. at the very beginning of the novel (p. 9). Does Annabelle agree with her? In what ways does Z. adhere to this philosophy, and how has she fallen away from it? How does Z.'s statement mirror your own attitude about poetry?

DW: When Z. says this to Annabelle—and later, when she recites Dylan Thomas's "In My Craft of Sullen Art"—she is saying that the act of creation is its own a reward. Poetry is one of those what-I-did-for-love fields. You go into it because you can't imagine a life without it. Of course, for some poets, there are rewards beyond the act of writing. But in this passage, Z. is letting Annabelle know that there's not much to be had in the poetry field (awards, publication, honors), and furthermore, Annabelle should not come looking to the Flower Poet for help in acquiring anything. I think that in this passage, too, we begin to see Professor Z. as a hypocrite. (She is, after all, a celebrated award-winning poet with a university position, so it's not exactly true that poetry is a thankless profession.). But I do think that Z. still yearns for poetry's intangible rewards. More than anything, she would like to be in the thick of the creative act, writing a great poem. We meet her at an incredibly busy phase in her life, when she is short of inspiration. Part of Annabelle's job is to write flower descriptions to help jumpstart her creative process.

JMG: The delineation between the words "apprentice" and "assistant" is very important to Annabelle. How would you define the two terms? In what ways can the mentor-apprentice relationship benefit both parties, and how can it be detrimental?

DW: I think of an apprentice as an artisan who is learning from the master. An assistant is a helper, a secretary, one who does menial tasks.

Annabelle is both apprentice and assistant to Z. I wrote this book as a way of trying to figure out how these relationships work, but I can't say I fully understand them. I think what we have here is two people using each other in subtle and overt ways. Z. is using Annabelle to get her laundry done; Annabelle is using Z. as a model of how she should be in the world as a woman and a writer. For Annabelle, the greatest benefit the job has is getting to spend time with the writer she admires.

JMG: *Apprentice to the Flower Poet Z.* is your first novel. How does the process of writing poetry compare to that of fiction writing? Were you able to write the two forms simultaneously, or does each require an entirely different mind-set? Along those lines, how does the experience of having a book of poetry published compare to publishing a novel?

DW: For me, poetry is all about compression and fiction is all about expansion. I've never been able to write a long poem, so my ability to write a novel surprised me. What I love about the novel is the accumulation of detail that ultimately reveals character. And I love dialogue. Being able to write both fiction and poetry is a little like being ambidextrous and bisexual. You move easily between two seemingly unrelated experiences, and it happens without too much thinking. However, I will say that the occasion that moves me to write a poem is different from the one that will move me to write a novel. The urge to write a novel is about having questions I want to puzzle out, people I want to know more deeply, conflicts and relationships I want to explore. Poetry is about wanting to capture a moment in time through language, lyric, exaltation, despair.

When my poetry book came out, it was reviewed in five journals, including *The Nation,* and that was very exciting—I remember the thrill of reading the very first review from *Publishers Weekly;* it was like walking on air. My poetry book had a print run of about a thousand copies, and of course, I understood I would never reach a large audience. So when my novel went out into the world, I felt a sense of overwhelming gratitude each time I got a review. I suppose what was so touching was that people were actually reading my book.

JMG: Reviewers have praised the spot-on satirical nature of *Apprentice to the Flower Poet Z.* How was your depiction of this rather cutthroat poetry world based on reality? Did your own experiences as a published poet come into play while you were writing about this sometimes vicious environment?

DW: My depiction of the "rather cutthroat poetry world" was based on some articles that I'd read in the newspaper. As a graduate student, I did type the poems of the visiting professors and sadly learned that I was remembered more for my typing than for my poetry. After publishing my first book of poetry, I suffered a crisis of faith. I realized that the opportunities to earn a living as a poet were limited, and so I turned to fiction writing.

I have always been interested in the phenomenon of the celebrity poet. In her day, the poet Edna St. Vincent Millay was like a rock star. Elizabeth Hardwick, musing on Millay, wrote that she was an "unconventional person who wrote conventional poems." Why do certain poets capture the public's attention? Louise Bogan said, "It is a dangerous lot, that of the charming, romantic public poet, especially if it falls to a woman."

Part of my goal in writing this book was also to educate the public about poetry. What is poetry? I'm not sure that we know yet, but perhaps we are a little closer to the answer. People do tell me that after reading this book they start writing again or go to the bookstore and browse the poetry aisle. They're not as afraid of poetry.

JMG: How does Annabelle's difficulty with writer's block mirror Z.'s struggles as a poet? How does each woman attempt to unlock her creativity? What techniques do you employ when you face writer's block?

DW: Annabelle is blocked because she feels diminished when she compares her poems with the poems of the Flower Poet Z. Z. struggles because she is tired of writing about flowers but hasn't the courage to try writing about something different. Z. works through her writer's block by hiring assistants to do her research. Annabelle works through hers by asking established writers for advice. Writing is hell, but not writing is hell, too. When I'm blocked, what works for me is forcing myself to write with the understanding that this forced writing will most likely be terrible. I usually feel better writing badly than not at all.

JMG: Annabelle's relationship with Harry is unconventional, to say the least. Can you talk a little bit about it?

DW: "I'm not perfect, but I'm perfect for you" was the concept I used to think about the romance of Harry and Annabelle. Knowing Annabelle, I imagined that even in love she would find herself in a mentor-student relationship. And she might also find herself giving voice to the erotic side of her masochism.

Something I took away from a college literature course was the idea that people like to seduce people with stories about seduction—and so James Joyce's steamy letters to his wife, Nora Barnicle Joyce, became the vehicle for Annabelle's seduction. But creating a sex life for these characters wasn't easy. Sex is hard to write well, and what we desire is highly individual and specific to each of us. If I could do it over again, I might lose the gloves and heels, but then again I might not.

JMG: Z. has a fascinating relationship with Mrs. Van Elder. Is the character of Mrs. Van Elder based on anyone in the real poetry world? How did you arrive at the name for her character?

DW: Some people have assumed that Mrs. Van Elder is a famous literary critic. But in fact, Mrs. Van Elder's name comes from something W. H. Auden said about Adrienne Rich's first book of poems when he awarded it the Yale Younger Poets Prize. Auden praised the poems for their formal qualities, saying they "are neatly and modestly dressed, speak quietly but do not mumble, [and] respect their elders. . . ." Z. is a writer whose work is conventional and seeks to preserve the "old-world" order, the status quo. For this she is rewarded.

JMG: The theme of Annabelle's search for a connection with a mother, and a family, seems central to the novel. Does Annabelle view Z. as a maternal figure? How do Annabelle's feelings compare to those of Z.'s own daughter, Claire? Are there any other figures that Annabelle looks to as role models, both inside and outside her immediate family circle?

DW: Annabelle has a poetry father, her former teacher Arthur Feld, so it makes sense that she would go looking for her poetry mother. Ironically, in choosing Z., Annabelle picks a woman very much like her own mother. Like Mrs. Goldsmith, Z. is distracted, disconnected, and usually not too interested. Observing Z. and her daughter, Claire, Annabelle notes that Z. doesn't even hug Claire when she returns from her reading tour. Of course, for Annabelle, there is still much to envy in this relationship. Z. finds Claire a publisher, gives her entrée to important poets and editors, and takes her clothes shopping.

Early in her life, Annabelle has looked to her therapist as a role model, but Dr. Sanger pales in comparison to the urban academic women she meets in this story. Annabelle's refusal to return to therapy is about not wanting to examine what is painfully obvious—that she has gone to Z. looking for something that she most likely never will get.

JMG: I really enjoyed the character of Braun, who inspires both devotion and ire from other characters in the book. Why does Z. feel such antipathy toward her? Is Claire's attitude toward Braun a rebellion against her mother? How does Braun both help and hinder Annabelle's development as a writer and as a person?

DW: Z. feels that Braun has succeeded in the poetry world because of her connections, and this galls her, since Z. believes she had to struggle to achieve her station in the field. Z. also thinks that Braun has set the women's movement back by writing a book called *His Mistress*. But Z. isn't exactly a gift to feminism, either. Claire develops a crush on Braun after interviewing her for Z.'s Emily Dickinson book. But it's probably time for Claire—who has just written *The Needlepoint Poems* in honor of her mother—to rebel against her. (Sex with her mother's rival could serve as such a rebellion.)

Braun's message is to take risks, and she teaches Annabelle not to be intimidated by Z., to use her as the subject of her writing—which ultimately backfires when Annabelle takes the advice and writes about Braun. But Braun isn't the best role model for Annabelle, because she has her own anger toward Z., who is trying to get her fired for sexually harassing a student. Anyway, it's complicated, triangulated, and what we have here is a futile attempt to unseat the queen, which will never happen—not in this novel, anyway.

JMG: Z. commits the ultimate writer's betrayal by appropriating Annabelle's words as her own. What compels Z. to do so? Did you ever envision a dramatic confrontation between Annabelle and Z. at the end of the book? Have you ever had anyone steal your ideas?

DW: Of course, Z. had paid Annabelle money for these lines, but I honestly don't think she remembers that these are Annabelle's words. After all, Annabelle has really learned to write like Z., and she can sound exactly like her. But perhaps, because I love my characters unconditionally, I am too forgiving. There was a dramatic confrontation in one version of the book—Annabelle was hauled out of Barnes and Noble by a security guard—but it really didn't seem to be in keeping with the tone of the story.

When I was a young writer, a very famous teacher appropriated a line from a poem I had written and used it as a refrain in a poem dedicated to our writing workshop. When she presented the poem to the class, I was speechless. Later, by phone, I confronted the teacher, who told me that she didn't consider what she did an act of plagiarism. But that question—What constitutes imitation and what thievery?—has stayed with me.

JMG: What has Annabelle learned from her "apprenticeship" to the Flower Poet Z.? How has it changed both her attitude about writing and her worldview in general?

DW: I think that Annabelle has learned that the adult world is far more complex than she imagined, and that to succeed as a writer, she will have to be aggressive. Z. may be a terrible teacher in some respects, but through her example she has shown Annabelle how to be powerful and self-sufficient, and to take from the world.

JMG: When Annabelle sits down to write her "poem of liberation," she begins to write a novel instead—called *Apprentice to the Flower Poet Z.* Why didn't she write a poem instead, or call it a memoir instead of a work of fiction?

DW: For Annabelle, writing fiction is the best revenge.

JMG: Do you feel at all compelled to continue Annabelle's story? Would you consider writing a sequel, or do you feel that the arc of her experience is complete?

DW: I would love to see Annabelle publish her novel, get married, and try to live a "normal" life. I would also like to see her get into analysis and work through some of the more troubling issues we saw emerge in this novel. But I have no plans to write a sequel.

Reading Group Questions and Topics for Discussion

1. *Apprentice to the Flower Poet Z.* is told through the eyes of Annabelle, a college student in her junior year. How is this time a turning point for Annabelle? In what ways does she seem like a young child, and how is she wise beyond her years? Describe how Annabelle grows as the book unfolds.

2. Trace the various apprenticeships throughout the story and evaluate the difference between "apprentice" and "assistant." How does Weinstein play with the shifting roles of mentor and apprentice throughout the book?

3. Discuss the novel as a satire of the world of academics and poetry. Given the fact that the author, Debra Weinstein, is a published poet and writer, do you think this depiction is accurate? What aspects of the literary world are criticized and what attributes are celebrated?

4. From the outset, Annabelle is consumed by poetry. Consider how poetry forms her identity and also how Annabelle retreats behind it.

Compare the attitude of the non-poets around Annabelle (including her parents and therapist) with the attitude of her literary mentors about her devotion to poetry.

5. Discuss the novel"s literary erudition; how do well-known writers, like Dickinson and Joyce, figure in the story? Describe how Annabelle takes cues for living her life from their writing.

6. Why do you think Z. chooses Annabelle as her assistant? What does this designation represent to Annabelle? How does she imbue her tasks, even the most mundane, with importance?

7. "I need an assistant who will be wallpaper," says Z. (p. 28). What does she mean by this? How does Z. both cultivate Annabelle as an apprentice and treat her as a personal assistant? In which ways is Annabelle well suited to staying in the background? Does she want to be brought to the forefront?

8. Discuss Annabelle's disillusionment with her own family and how it propels her more strongly into Z.'s clan. Do the Goldsmiths support and defend Annabelle, or do they impede her development? Consider alternative mother and father figures in Annabelle's life; what does each lend to her evolution into womanhood?

9. In what ways are Z. and her daughter, Claire, alike? How are they different? Describe how each admires and resents the other. How does Annabelle fit into their relationship?

10. "Are you a lost person?" Claire asks Annabelle (p. 190). In what ways is Annabelle out of place, both in this poetry world and in the larger world? Who else is grappling to find his or her way, and who do you think will be successful?

11. What does the support of Arthur Feld mean to Annabelle? How does she attempt to stay loyal to him and his teachings, both to her

advantage and to her detriment? Does Feld attempt to live vicariously through Annabelle? What other mentors does Annabelle seek out as the story unfolds?

12. Describe what about Harry Banks is alluring to Annabelle. Do you think that she is looking for a conventional romance, and is that something that Harry can provide? How does Annabelle's sexual awakening influence other aspects of her life, including her writing?

13. What are Annabelle's feelings about New York City? How does her hometown on Long Island seem provincial and backwater in comparison? Discuss how Annabelle's upbringing has enabled her to flourish both as a poet and as a person and, alternatively, how it has constrained her.

14. In which ways is Z. a chameleon, both as a writer and as a person? How does she reinvent herself? Based on Lars's memories, how is the Elizabeth that came before different from the Z. of the present? What do you think Z. and Lars had in common when they met and fell in love?

15. Consider how Z. embraces her identity as the Flower Poet, and how she chafes under it. If you could sum up Annabelle's identity in a similarly pithy moniker, what would it be?

16. Why does Z.'s family come to depend so much upon Annabelle? Do they take advantage of her? Do you consider Annabelle and Claire's friendship a real bond or merely one of convenience?

17. "I wonder if I will ever write with such ease," wonders Annabelle (p. 210). Ironically, much of the book that Z. has just completed is composed of Annabelle's own work. How does Annabelle's attitude about writing differ from that of Z., in terms of both their process and their devotion to the craft? Before and after the plagiarism, does Annabelle's perception of Z. as a poet and a person change?

18. At the retreat, why does Gay tell Annabelle to "write about her own mother" (p. 228)? What has compelled Annabelle to compose "The Secret for Solving Poetry"? Why do the assembled poets view Annabelle's poem about Z. and her family with such contempt and disdain? How does this confuse Annabelle and belie her notion of honesty in poetry?

19. "She had taught me artifice and art; I would miss her," says Annabelle of Z. (p. 240). Why do you think Z. fires Annabelle? What are the lessons that Annabelle has learned from Z.? Discuss why Annabelle doesn't have a dramatic public confrontation with Z. at the end of the book.

20. Do you think that Annabelle believes the words she writes about herself in Z.'s recommendation letter? Do you believe that Z. forgot to write the letter or that she left it for Annabelle to do as a peace offering? Why doesn't Annabelle send the letter to Career Services?

21. At the conclusion, Annabelle decides to write a novel about her experiences with Z. What compels her to do so? Why doesn't she write a memoir or a poem instead?

Poems Cited

"As I Walked Out One Evening," "Tonight at Seven Thirty," W. H. Auden (1907–1973)

"A Virgin Life," "Fidelia arguing with her self on the difficulty of finding her true Religion," Jane Barker (1652–1732)

"To the fair Clarinda, Who made love to me, Imagin'd more than woman," Aphra Behn (1640–1689)

"Upon the Burning of Our House," Anne Bradstreet (1612–1672)

"To Damon," Jane Brereton (1685–1740)

"Pastoral," Lady Jane Cavendish (1621–1669) and Lady Elizabeth Brackley (1626–1663)

"After great pain a formal feeling comes," "Hope is the thing with feathers," "Success is counted sweetest," "We play at paste," "Wild Nights!," Emily Dickinson (1830–1886)

"Love's Alchemy," John Donne (1572–1631)

"A Lament for Flodden," Jane Elliot (1727–1805)

"To Earthward," "The Oven Bird," "The Road Not Taken," Robert Frost (1874–1963)

"To the Virgins, to Make Much of Time," "Upon Julia's Clothes," Robert Herrick (1591–1674)

"Harlem," "The Negro Speaks of Rivers," Langston Hughes (1902–1967)

"Song: To Celia (I)," Ben Jonson (1572–1637)

"Ode on Melancholy," John Keats (1795–1821)

"Trees," Joyce Kilmer (1886–1918)

"Gloire de Dijon," D. H. Lawrence (1885–1930)

"Daddy," "Lady Lazarus," Sylvia Plath (1932–1963)

"The River-Merchant's Wife: a Letter," Ezra Pound (1885–1972)

"Elegy for Jane," "My Papa's Waltz," "The Waking," Theodore Roethke (1908–1963)

"Despisals," "Käthe Kollwitz," "The Poem as Mask," Muriel Rukeyser (1913–1980)

"Can it be that I still long for my virginity?" Sappho (circa 610–580 B.C.)

"Consorting with Angels," "In Celebration of My Uterus," Anne Sexton (1928–1974)

"The Snow Man," Wallace Stevens (1879–1955)

"In My Craft or Sullen Art," Dylan Thomas (1914–1953)

"Perfect Woman," William Wordsworth (1770–1850)

"They flee from me that sometimes did me seek," Thomas Wyatt (1503–1542)

"The Circus Animals' Desertion," William Butler Yeats (1865–1939)

© Philip Friedman

DEBRA WEINSTEIN received NYU's Bobst Literary Award for Emerging Writers upon publication of her volume of poetry, *Rodent Angel*. She is a recipient of a National Endowment for the Arts Creative Writing Fellowship for poetry and a New York Foundation for the Arts Artists' Writing Fellowship for fiction. She has been in residence at both the MacDowell Colony and Yaddo. Her poems have appeared in *The American Poetry Review, Tikkun,* and *The Portable Lower East Side.* She lives in New York City.